About the author

Hedley Harrison graduated from London University and joined a major oil company progressing to senior management and seeing service in the UK, Nigeria, Australia and the North Sea. He has published two novels with Book Guild Publishing: *Coup* in 2011 and *Disunited States* in 2013.

By the same author

Coup, Book Guild Publishing 2011
Disunited States, Book Guild Publishing 2013

CHINA WIFE

Hedley Harrison

Book Guild Publishing
Sussex, England

First published in Great Britain in 2015 by
The Book Guild Ltd
The Werks
45 Church Road
Hove, BN3 2BE

Typesetting in Sabon by
Norman Tilley Graphics Ltd, Northampton

Printed and bound in Great Britain by
CPI Group (UK) Ltd, Croydon, CR0 4YY

A catalogue record for this book is available from
The British Library

ISBN 978 1 909984 73 8

The practice of slavery is as old as civilisation but the format has moved with the times.

1

'Linda Shen?'

'You're resident in Shanghai?'

The young woman made no response. It was obvious that the immigration officer had the facts in front of him.

Used to seeing all of the world and his wife, the immigration officer noted the finely drawn features and slight figure of the well-dressed and confident young Chinese woman in front of him without any obvious sign that he had registered her existence. But he was well aware of her.

'You're married – recently?'

Again the documents and her ring provided the answer for her.

'Say as little as possible,' had been her husband Shi Xiulu's instruction. 'Don't give them the chance to ask follow-up questions.'

She hadn't contradicted Mr Shi despite her better under-standing of how the UK immigration system worked. In her short time as a married woman in China she had learned that husbands, particularly ones like hers, were not to be challenged openly.

So she had said as little as possible. It did not put the immi-gration officer off.

'Is your husband a British citizen?'

That opened up a different line of questioning.

'Tell the truth wherever possible,' was also a part of her instructions.

'No, he's a Chinese citizen.'

'Yet you are travelling on a British passport?'

'I'm British – British born.'

'But I thought that the Chinese authorities didn't allow dual nationality?'

Even if this were true, the immigration officer wasn't really interested in the answer. His questions were only to give time for Linda Shen's credentials to be checked against the database. The highlight on his computer screen told him that this was the woman whom they were expecting and to let her through into the UK. The Border Agency and various UK police forces were informed of her arrival. A short message of confirmation and appreciation was received in Beijing.

'They only queried my British passport.'

Linda didn't tell her husband that she had been concerned about the length of the hold-up at Immigration and about the undemanding questions that she had been asked; there didn't seem to be any point. It was a small piece of rebellion; the thoughts of her new baby gurgling its day away in the care of her mother-in-law ensured that such rebellions were always going to be small. At least she was in Britain, even if she wouldn't be meeting any of her relatives while in the Manchester area, and even if she wouldn't be able to make contact with her former colleagues at the Border Agency.

The immigration officer had asked where she would be staying. To Linda's surprise, he didn't seem interested in why she was visiting.

They must know something, she thought to herself.

The sense of freedom that she had felt on the aircraft, overlaid by her longing for her baby son, evaporated the moment she had emerged with her designer suitcase from the customs hall. The dozen or so hours on the Qantas flight from Hong Kong quickly became a cherished and regretted memory. Her promised personal assistant – her 'minder' in her eyes – was there waiting for her. The placard bearing the scrawled 'Linda

Shen', held awkwardly by a squat, tough-looking Chinese man in his forties, was in her face before any thoughts about contacting her former friends at Heathrow could surface. She was instantly trapped. Her minder/assistant turned out to be deferential in a contemptuous, disdainful masculine way but quick and efficient in all that he did. Only at night would she be free of him.

Over the satellite telephone line Mr Shi had given his wife further instructions: blend into the background, behave as any British young wife would. Except that a stunningly attractive young Chinese woman with as much Gucci and Prada about her as she had was never going to blend into the background in cosmopolitan London, let alone in the Manchester suburbs – even if the Border Agency and the Greater Manchester Police hadn't been looking on.

'She's made contact.'

The smilingly obsequious manager of the Twin Dragons showed Linda Shen to a seat where she was quickly joined by a party of young Chinese people of her own sort of age. A free night out at a restaurant that they would never be able to afford for themselves, no questions asked, was hard to resist at the going rate for university tuition fees. The smooth-talking Chinese man who recruited and accompanied them offered no names and asked for none. What he and the gorgeous young woman, who seemed to be the main guest, talked about the four Liverpool undergraduates couldn't really have cared less about. They were the rent-a-crowd employed to cover for their two unnamed companions; that was fine with them.

The attempt to mask the meeting between Linda Shen and the principal fixer for the main Chinese organisation in the Manchester area did not fool the police surveillance team. For them, the fact that the meeting had taken place was as important as what it was about.

Cambridge Evening Spectator
Late Edition – Friday, 23 May 2003
BIZARRE CORNER-SHOP ROBBERY
Around 3 p.m. on Wednesday, 21 May, two supposedly Muslim women wearing traditional black burkas and sunglasses that rendered them completely unrecognisable, entered the corner shop of Mr Malik Hussein only a few hundred yards from Addenbrooke's Hospital. Having presented Mr Hussein's seventeen-year-old daughter, who was alone serving in the shop, with a computer-produced note and a small leather bag, they forced the terrified girl to empty the till.

'They had these things pointing at me under their clothes,' the poor girl said, who was convinced that the objects aimed at her were weapons.

According to Detective Constable Karen Cater, not a word was spoken and the two women quickly left with just under £260.

'On further questioning,' DC Cater said, 'Miss Hussein, having recovered her composure, volunteered that she thought that the women were definitely not Muslim and that in fact one of them could have been a man.'

It seems that, after snatching the cash, as they approached the shop door, one of the 'women' hesitated to allow the other to leave first. This, Miss Hussein said, showed both a deference and a courtesy that was not normally shown to Muslim women or between Muslim women except in a mother–daughter situation, which this was obviously not. But it was not untypical of the behaviour of Westernised men.

The police declined to comment on Miss Hussein's remarks about Muslim culture but acknowledged the possibility of the Muslim dress being a disguise.

At approximately 4.15 p.m., as a group of students dressed in a variety of costumes began a noisy procession through the centre of Cambridge as part of Rag Week, a heavily made-up

4

young woman dressed as a Harlequin handed in a leather bag containing just under £260, in denominations that appeared to match the money stolen from Mr Hussein, to the Rag office.

A member of the Rag Committee contacted the police when they saw the reports of the robbery in the morning daily paper.

The police and the university authorities ascribed the incident to an ill-conceived Rag prank and condemned it totally. The whereabouts of both the two Muslim women and the woman dressed as a Harlequin are still unknown.

2

It was a cold, well, cool, crisp morning. The Australian version of winter is never really challenging, although snow does fall in Melbourne occasionally. It had in June 2009, Julie had heard. She hadn't actually been in the country then. At that time she had been enjoying the almost non-existent warmth of a Scottish summer, during a posting to Edinburgh that had been the envy of her colleagues.

Even now, in June 2010, Julie really wasn't acclimatised to the day-to-day weather of Melbourne. Arriving in April, she had been told, was a good time. The temperature difference with the UK wouldn't be that significant. There was no doubt that her body clock had adjusted to Australian time but her temperature control hadn't yet adjusted to the cyclical nature of the weather. It wasn't the temperature in itself; it was the rapidity of the changes that she struggled with. She never seemed to choose the right clothes. As she had discovered during all that hurried packing, she had a rather more extensive stock of clothes than perhaps was typical of a young woman in her late twenties. Clothes were her passion, but a large choice wasn't much help when you could never judge how the weather would evolve during the day.

It was the same with her hair. She'd had her cherished near-shoulder-length black locks cut off in the panic of moving to Australia and in the anticipation of long hot days and swarms of flies. But the days had yet to be hot. Having short and manageable hair, she acknowledged, however, was not a bad thing.

Nonetheless, she had noticed that, although she was probably in the middle range in height, weight and age of the women that she was seeing hurrying on and off the trams and the underground trains of Melbourne's transport system, she was sartorially inferior. In Melbourne's business district, the young Australian women didn't seem to do casual.

All of this indecision and confusion rather depressed Julie. In Edinburgh while working in the UK Border Agency enforcement section, despite her relative youth, she had been recognised as a sharp and dynamic decision-maker, able to analyse and react swiftly to situations and to push through the necessary solutions. In her department, the turnover of illegal immigrants deported – on whose fate it had been Julie's job to make adjudication decisions – was higher than it had ever been. Her quick no-nonsense approach was much appreciated by her bosses.

But then suddenly it had all gone wrong.

Questions had been raised over certain of her past decisions and she had found herself passed over when a new division in Aberdeen was formed. Discussions with Lothian and Borders Police had been stressful, even if they hadn't led to anything. Worse, from Julie's point of view, was the fact that the nature of the concerns expressed about her had never been fully spelled out, and what had been said had seemed to her to be insincere and contrived.

She had had a strong sense of being set up. But she couldn't conceive of any reason why this should have been so.

But the painful realisation that her career in its present form was almost certainly over produced the strong suspicion that it was Tariq who was responsible for her woes. She had spent nearly six years of her life, starting with her original university infatuation with him, in a relationship that had for all of those years been, it transpired, entirely one-sided. From the initial excitement of what she supposed to be first love, it had always been Tariq who had led.

What Tariq had wanted she had willingly given to him or done for him. As she came to realise, it was he who had steered her into the Border Agency, he who had urged her into the enforcement work. And now it seemed that the manipulations that she had been an unwitting partner to had been anything but innocent. And even if the Scottish police couldn't make the link between the increase in the number of Chinese women seemingly disappearing into the British countryside and her favourable decisions on their immigration status, Julie knew that such a link existed. She was mortified at her own gullibility and at her blindness to Tariq's role in manipulating the system through her. But still she didn't know why he had done it.

So mortified was she in fact that it never occurred to her that Tariq's judgement of her capabilities had been amazingly prescient. Neither did it occur to her until very much later in Australia that others among British officialdom also appreciated her capabilities and that Tariq's manipulations were trivial compared to those that these people were capable of. Her sense of being set up, and not by him, strengthened every time she went around the mental loop of her relationship with Tariq al Hussaini.

She had resigned.

Abandoning her entire future in Britain and picking up on a suggestion from her erstwhile boss, she had set off for Australia. Again, it was only very much later that Julie recognised that her decision to resign had been seeded and that the suggestion that she emigrate hadn't been a casual effort to assuage her hurt at her seeming career failure; it had been more purposeful than that. Tariq had pleaded with her to stay, but as she now knew that it wasn't their relationship that was driving his pleading, she was resistant to the pressure he attempted to put her under.

But in the short term her confidence had been all but destroyed by the recriminations and the subterfuges necessary to extract herself and her worldly goods from Edinburgh and to get herself settled in the Victorian capital. 'Settled', though, was a term that Julie herself would have been unlikely to have used: after six weeks in Melbourne she was realising that, despite its extensive similarities to Britain, Australia could still seem like an alien society. And it wasn't just the uncertainties of the variable weather.

However, somewhere under what she hoped to be her temporary disillusionment, the old Julie wasn't quite dead and she sleepwalked her way through renting an apartment and registering with an employment agency and establishing the beginnings of a stable lifestyle. It was the employment agency, under gentle official coercion, that had set her up for an interview bright and early on Tuesday, 8 June 2010, though they had not been very clear what the job was about. The fact that her life was being carefully stage-managed still didn't occur to Julie.

Suspicious, but mindful that her finances were in need of serious replenishment, something of her old spark returned as she attempted to tease out the job description from the agency. She failed, but curiosity as well as financial expediency eventually prevailed – rejecting the interview was never really an option.

But that was Tuesday and still over twenty-four hours away. Monday nonetheless was already under way.

Julie had rather hurriedly drawn on her stock of clothes as she belatedly prised herself out of bed and out into the crisp morning to still the rumblings of her empty stomach. The bootleg jeans were fine; the boots were less so, imprisoning her legs and making her ankles ache. But this she decided was more about the height of the heels and the time lag since she had last worn them than anything else. But she didn't care. With a job in prospect, she had at last felt positive again and free from the demons of her recent past. The rest of her was warm and comfortable, and for the moment her time was her own.

The double-glazing-deadened clanking of the trams down Spring Street as she sat in what was becoming her favourite corner coffee shop brought her back to the reality of Australia. Even if she wasn't a part of the frenetic early-morning hustle around her, it had a familiarity about it. There was no snow but the wind was blowing rather viciously up the street and she was glad that she had succumbed to an urge to be warm and had stopped off for breakfast here, rather than following her original intention of breaking her fast in Melbourne Central. The window shopping could easily wait until later. Not that she needed much urging. She was too fond of the exquisite scrambled egg for which this place was famous. Getting colder and colder as she had walked, and with the prospect of some anonymous glutinous mess of eggs at the end of her journey, rather than the real thing, it was a decision that essentially made itself.

It was obvious that many of the clientele of the coffee shop were regular and looked-for daily visitors. Julie wouldn't have counted herself as one of these but she was slowly becoming one. Her welcome was assured and the slow recognition of her as one entitled to a favourite seat on the padded bench at the back of the eating area was apparent. Tables were mostly for two but generally rarely occupied by more than one at this time of the morning. The service was slick and Julie was impressed by the facility with which some of the long-standing customers were served with their first caffeine fix almost before they had even got themselves seated. And, with the mixed hopefulness and trepidation that was Monday morning, the sense of being in a somehow alien world diminished some-what.

The noise level was low and dominated by the hissing and spluttering of the shining Gaggia coffee machine as if the early-morning privacy of the customers was not to be disturbed by unnecessary chatter nor their concentration on the sporting or financial pages of *The Age* broken by needless courtesy greetings. And being Australia it was usually the sporting pages that demanded first attention. Very few financial crises would have outweighed the need to know whether the Ashes series was going to go to the wire again. And, again, being Australia it was probably unnecessary to read the actual printed word to be in the know. The faces of those seeking their coffee fix after a Metro or car journey would readily have been able to tell you how things had gone.

All of which being said, the coffee shop was rather more crowded this day than Julie had ever yet observed it. She put this down to the total absence of customers sitting outside. The diehard smokers had been forced into abstinence and inside by the arctic blast whistling between the canyons of the office buildings that verged on Spring Street and filled the space behind it.

It was this unusual intensity of people, still discreet in their noise and movement, that attracted Julie's attention to the figure temporarily blocking the shop doorway rather than his Greek-god good looks. Like the diehard smokers, he was obviously trying to escape the wind, or so Julie imagined, but unlike them it was equally obvious that this was the first time that he had set foot in the coffee shop. This gave her a fellow feeling.

Always alert to the needs of her customers and to the proximity of competing establishments, the waitress steered the man towards Julie's table. Single occupancy, of necessity, was going to have to be foregone.

'Do you mind?'

Julie was hardly going to say no!

The silence between them wasn't going to last either.

'You don't like scrambled eggs, then?'

Julie took in the obvious humour in the man's remark; the

11

relish with which she was consuming her breakfast was clearly all too apparent. The sparkle in the clear blue eyes that met her more complex, almond-shaped brown ones lingered as she considered her reply. The muffled but persistent opening bars of Tchaikovsky's 1812 Overture emitting from her shoulder bag somewhere under the table cut off her half-formed response to be replaced by a distinctly unladylike curse under her breath. The blue eyes opposite sparkled even more.

The speed with which Julie untangled her mobile phone from her belongings impressed the man. Starting to lever himself to his feet in a question of whether she needed privacy, she flashed a negative in a quick, friendly smile. The displayed mobile phone number wasn't immediately familiar to her; not that many numbers were after so short a sojourn in Melbourne, but that meant that she didn't know whether she would mind being overheard or not.

'Julie Kershawe.'

To the man sitting opposite Julie, the ensuing conversation must have seemed bizarre in the extreme. From time to time she glanced across at him, half embarrassed, all the time rather irrelevantly thinking that no man had the right to be quite that gorgeous.

'Tariq, I don't want to talk to you!'

'I don't care if you've been up half the night waiting to talk to me!'

'I don't care if you bought a new mobile phone especially to call me!'

She stabbed at the button to cut the call off.

Her companion focused on her more obviously as her silence seemed to demand filling.

But whatever he might have deduced from the one side of the conversation that he had heard, and despite the steady rumble of background noise he had heard, his face gave no sign that he was about to make conversation about it.

Nonetheless, he produced a knowing smile that seemed to

invite a confidence from Julie. But, despite being very aware of the silence, she was not inclined to offer one. She was happy to wait for him to take the initiative.

The intrusion of Tariq into her new life was most unwelcome and something that she needed to think about; it wouldn't just be about buying another mobile phone.

'So what's a Pom doing here in the winter then?'

It was so crass a question that they both laughed. Their amusement attracted the waitress and coffee top-ups. The atmosphere became almost light-hearted.

'Have you really got time to hear my life story?'

Well, yes, he certainly had; but he was only actually going to be interested in the more recent part of it.

3

Tolpuddle. TUC Martyrs Museum.

Mid-afternoon, mid-May, the A35 Puddletown bypass was largely undisturbed by any significant traffic flows. The brown information signposts seemed to be the only things of interest to take notice of.

'A Trades Union Museum devoted to the Tolpuddle Martyrs. Never knew that.'

Susie Peveral's cut-glass accent suggested a background that might support such ignorance.

David Hutchinson, a well-known freelance journalist/ photographer, was currently acting as guide and driver to Susie to a part of Britain that he particularly enjoyed being in.

'They weren't martyrs in the burned-at-the-stake sense,' Hutchinson said. 'That's just a bit of Trades Union mythology. They were farm workers who were transported for forming a union. They were soon pardoned and shipped back, but they made convenient heroes to glamorise the rather dreary face of trades unionism.'

David Hutchinson completed the tale.

'OK, so you're not a union man, then?'

Susie's question, a mixture of laughing mockery and sarcasm, went unanswered.

The mention of unions triggered other thoughts from their Oxford days.

Susie Peveral was the Student Union representative, and later President, touting for members at the Freshers' Day gathering at their Oxford college. Barely eighteen and sensitive about both his age and his presence at such an illustrious seat of learning on a bursary and scholarship, David wasn't at first very responsive to young Susie approaching him as a union representative. The son of a miner whose childhood had been blighted by the sort of suicidal industrial action that eventually brought the ire of Mrs Thatcher down on the trades unions, he could never really relate to his father because David senior was immune to normal social and economic logic. Perhaps presaging his future intellectual capabilities, his rather damning rejoinder to his father as he approached his tenth birthday that 'you couldn't eat industrial solidarity' set the tone for a fractured relationship that was never quite repaired.

He emerged from his reminiscences.

'Thought we might stop off at Dorchester and get a bite to eat. If we head for Poundbury, you can see what the daydreams of our illustrious heir to the throne can look like in hard concrete and brick.

'OK, so you're not a monarchist either then!'

The mockery was there again.

'Susie! Lunch!'

'OK,' she said. 'Lunch, if Poundbury can boast a decent restaurant.'

It could and did, and they were back on the A35 heading on towards Honiton and Exeter after a lunch that satisfied Susie's delicate vegetarian tastes as well as David's appetite for red meat.

Being an alpha male, and having the added attraction of a colourful and exciting professional life, made David Hutchinson attractive to women generally. But taking up with the erstwhile Student Union President was as much a surprise to him as it was to her. She simply wasn't his type. But as the relationship grew, it became as much gastronomic and alcoholic as sexual, and seemed to give Susie a vicarious satisfaction that David found hard to understand. But then his uncle wasn't an earl.

It was after they had had that session in London in 2003. David had met her in the street, literally. In Whitehall. She was a high-flying Foreign Office Assistant Secretary. With only his university experience to draw on at that point, she had still seemed the arrogant upper-class tart he had always characterised her as. She, in her turn, obviously still thought that he was somehow beneath her but was happy to know that he was off to the O2 Arena for a photo-shoot with her favourite pop star.

'We'll take the coast road rather than the main road. Burton Bradstock. You can see the famous "Jurassic Coastline". More to the point, we can stretch our legs and walk along the cliffs.'

'OK. You're the boss of this expedition.'

The mockery was replaced by affection. Despite her inability to express the thought, Susie was clearly enjoying herself.

Parking at the National Trust car park at Burton Bradstock and making their way along and up the more tortuous first part of the cliff-top walk stalled any conversation. Not that that bothered either of them. One of the deeper attractions between them was their relaxed tolerance of each other's silence.

The grandeur of the scenery put any thoughts of the show that Susie had put on at the O2 Arena out of his mind. Her sudden and unexpected grab at him, in a storeroom backstage, took David so much by surprise that it almost inhibited his ability to give satisfaction. But satisfied Susie was, and to his further amazement anxious to have more at a later date.

'Jesus, David!'

They were now very much back in the present.

As freelance journalist-photographer, in a whole variety of locations around the world, David Hutchinson had seen plenty of dead bodies.

From the moment that he realised that what Susie was

16

pointing at was a body floating in the sea about a hundred metres offshore, they both dropped instinctively into professional mode. Hutchinson immediately unshipped his BlackBerry and began to make notes in the Notebook application but soon stopped. They were on holiday and it had been a clear decision to leave the tools of their trade at home; if you don't count the multi-capabilities of a BlackBerry mobile phone as a tool of trade. Susie used hers to call the emergency services.

'Stay where you are – we'll get someone over to you.'

The instruction from the police was clear, and, in any event, neither of them was very keen to make their way back down to the shingle beach since all they would be able to do was stand and stare while others did the work. And standing and staring wasn't something that either of them was very good at.

'Ms Peveral?'

The conversation with the police officer was brief and confirmatory. She could see for herself what they could see and knew as well as they did that the next actions would involve neither them nor her. They both very readily dropped out of professional mode again.

An inshore lifeboat was quickly launched from the beach. With two police divers in lieu of the normal crew, it didn't take them long to recover the body and to do an extensive, if futile, search of the surrounding waters. The massive cliff overhang ensured that the action on the beach, when the lifeboat returned, was invisible to the two friends, and soon the police officer cleared them to leave if they so wished.

They did so wish. This was an unlooked-for intrusion into the calm relaxation of their holiday.

Later ensconced in a small hotel at Seaton and in pursuance of their plans to leave the real world to one side, neither Susie nor David wanted to watch the early TV reports of the events on the Dorset beach. It wasn't until two days later that either of them read anything about the incident in the papers.

What David Hutchinson then saw caused him some surprise. The dead man had a face that he recognised. He'd taken the photos from which the newspapers had culled the one that they had printed. He'd also been given a list of the names of the people who had been wanted to be included in the pictures; and in his business you had to have a good memory for names and faces.

The photograph wasn't the best he had ever produced. Blown up from the group photograph, however, the man's features were clear enough. And the photo-shoot was definitely of the sort that would have stuck in his memory.

4

Tariq's telephone call unsettled and depressed Julie Kershawe. All her angst, wretchedness and sense of violation at the collapse of her relationship and the deception that it represented instantly resurfaced in her mind. She could still offer herself no explanation for why he had behaved as he had done; nor could she understand the Muslim mind-set to which everybody else attributed his contemptuous treatment of her.

Her companion watched her face as it mirrored her thoughts and her struggle to repress her hurt and allow her anger to predominate. Isolated in the frenetic morning activity of the coffee shop, Julie and her Greek god presented two totally different pictures of humanity. She was suddenly agitated. He had a calm about him that Julie would have seen as entirely in keeping with his celestial presence had she been in the mood to analyse the situation. She wasn't.

Julie wanted to hate Tariq but she couldn't. At least, as she sat there she couldn't. Nonetheless, she was sure that another feeling was struggling for life. Revenge is said to be a feminine feeling; Julie wouldn't have believed that but she would have acknowledged a growing desire to pay Tariq back for his treachery and for her loss of years of life.

The desire for revenge was a reading of her character that would not have surprised those of her early schoolgirl friends who had kept in touch with her. As a teenager, if Julie was considered to have had any fault, it was her unforgiving attitude to anyone whom she felt had slighted her. It was a trait

19

that lost her friends but it was one that was recognised by those who valued her other inherent characteristics.

It was these other inherent characteristics that were the topic of interest that chilly, steamy coffee-bar morning. Not that Julie would have supposed that the man sitting opposite her was there as a result of anything more than a chance encounter.

And as if he had nothing else in the world to interest him her companion watched her body language change as her face settled. From slumping slightly forward she straightened up, her breasts pressing out against her well-fitting deep-mauve sweater, her barely made-up face returning to animation and her carefully manicured hands returning from her lap to rest on the table. She wore no rings. Not given to too much intro-spection, Julie simply looked across the table at the man and appraised him without much consideration of him beyond his obvious good looks.

A positive, if neutral grin, signalled that she was ready to resume the more light-hearted interaction of earlier. In response, he seemed to come more alive himself and to be more ready to engage in conversation.

'OK, Julie?'

His accompanying grin was infectious and openly question-ing.

'OK, Julie, so what *is* a Pom doing here in Melbourne in the winter then?'

The question had been lodged in her mind even before he asked it for the second time. She had come to recognise it as a fairly regular conversational opener. Her subconscious had already been working on a response, or, at least, the tone of a response.

Bred to a rigid set of parental morals, Julie had been dis-appointed in herself at the weakness that she had shown in her teenage and early adult life. If her tendency to be unforgiving was regretted by her friends, her tendency to be weak when

20

confronted with an attractive and powerful male was undoubtedly a matter of regret to her. That the regret at her weakness was inevitably linked with her late partner, Tariq al Hussaini, she was ready to admit. That that same weakness had allowed rather more young women of Chinese origin to take up British citizenship, when certainly not entitled to do so, was something that she found hard to admit.

Not that it mattered: her superiors, without too much evidence, appeared to have also felt that she had behaved badly, which was why she had been eased out of her post and was now a free agent in Australia. And eased out her subconscious told her she had been. But it was always a feeling coupled with a sense that her removal was somehow contrived.

'Shit,' she told herself, 'that's all behind me.'

Preoccupied with the immediate and short-term, Julie had no way of knowing whether this optimistic assessment was going to be true or not.

What was in front of her was a tall suntanned young man, whose age she was having problems fixing. Age accompanied with good looks that no ordinary mortal ought to have been entitled to was a combination that had now fully got her attention. The man was clearly expecting an answer to his twice-posed question.

Come on, girl, be truthful; it really is all behind you.

'I'm on the run,' she said, with a delighted grin that challenged him to ask from what.

He asked.

'I used to be a sort of policewoman…'

She paused; she wasn't sure whether the amused raised eyebrow signalled disbelief or not.

'UK Border Agency,' she said. 'Stopping undesirables getting into Britain, or at least trying to.'

He didn't challenge her statement. He seemed to know what the UK Border Agency was and accepted what she had said.

'And did you stop all the undesirables?'

What she had jokingly said she was running away from never got an airing. The tone of seriousness in his question didn't register with Julie. She just picked up on the emphasis on 'all'.

'No... No, that's never possible.'

The next pause came where a name would normally have come into the conversation, but she didn't have a name for him.

'Alan,' he said.

She was impressed by his speed of perception.

'No, Alan, you never can stop all of the undesirables, even from entering an island. Not if they want to get in, or...'

'Or if someone else wants them to.'

The pause this time was precautionary. Flirtatious young men didn't usually get stuck into the details of immigration policy and prevention tactics. And, of course, it was a sore point with Julie.

The renewal of her angst must have shown on her face.

'Can you cope with yet more coffee? Or is there something else you have to do?'

Julie was grateful for Alan's prompt move to change the subject and relieve her angry self-reproach. Taking the conversation as a part of a casual and friendly early-morning encounter she didn't see the fleeting look of satisfaction that appeared and disappeared from his eyes.

'Jones, Myers and Melbourne Central,' she said. 'Mainly looking. No money. I don't have a job yet, although I'm working on it.'

He didn't seem surprised.

'I've only been here a few weeks. I've been settling in, finding my feet. Still, my first job interview's tomorrow.'

Julie recognised that she was suddenly nervous. Why was he making her nervous?

'Best of luck. That's what Poms say, isn't it?'

She nodded. But alarm bells were now ringing strongly in

her head. Alan had given absolutely nothing of himself, yet he now knew everything about her current life. Suddenly, there seemed to be something unreal about him.

Artificial? she thought to herself.

If she had known more about Alan she would have realised that, although the situation was contrived, it was brilliantly done; she had told all before she had suspected anything.

She knew that she had to end the encounter.

She gathered her things and slipped her arms smoothly and sinuously into her padded anorak. Alan stood up with her. He held out his hand.

'Please to have met you.'

Why was he? As she mechanically paid for her meal and moved into the icy blast of Spring Street, he didn't follow her. He seemed to have paid in advance and slipped away into the side street before she had got her bearings among the tide of the still-hurrying office workers.

What was that all about?

Since she wasn't going to be able to find any evidence that her flat had been entered and her belongs exhaustively searched, the idea that Alan had been set up to distract her attention was never going to enter her head.

Her aching ankles and her tight jeans might be going to limit her day's window shopping, but she set off for Melbourne Central, and an array of shops that rivalled any that she had seen in Britain, in good spirits. She successfully replaced her mobile phone, happily passing her old one on for charity once the SIM card had been destroyed. She was now, electronically speaking, a new person.

5

Alice Hou never knew why she had been singled out for kidnap.

Her life in Brazil had been hardly ideal and she knew that girls like her could have a better life in North America. But she was equally aware of the horror stories of abuse and violence at the hands of people traffickers. However, confident in her ability to look after herself, such stories hadn't put her off.

Ending up wet and uncomfortable after a remote river crossing into Canada, somewhere on the border of Michigan and Ontario, the horrors that she had endured weren't those that she had been led to expect. How she got to such an isolated place within the generally crowded confines of the border area she had no clear memory of. Having arrived at her final destination after a journey up the length of America from Mexico, all she felt was relief and optimism.

But she soon found that the original stories of abuse and violence were true.

Settled in a low-paid job, she was forced to part with most of her earnings and live under the close supervision of the Chinese man who had in effect bought her from the traffickers. Unusually she was not subject to sexual violence, but was groomed both to improve her employment status and to fast-track for citizenship. The Chinese man who ruled her life knew all about value added and the returns that could accrue to himself if Alice could earn more. And her value as a Canadian citizen was even greater.

But in the specific world of women trafficking there were levels of sophistication and villainy that Alice was unaware of but which came to dominate her life. The modest returns and ongoing income that Alice's gangmaster was earning from her were easily outbid. After only a few short months in her new life in Calgary she was sold on to a commodity supplier far more ruthless and internationally connected than the men who had got her into Canada.

Alice Hou wasn't her given name; the belief of her earlier traffickers was that she would be less conspicuous and more easily assimilated with a Westernised name. The commodity supplier was unconcerned about any such subtleties. The clients he worked for were Chinese Chinese; they were equally uninterested in what anybody outside their peer group in China thought.

The Canadian immigration authorities knew full well that Chinese girls were being smuggled into the country, often from South America, but as fast as they closed down one entry route another was opened up. The US authorities stretched beyond limits by the human flow from Mexico were much too inter-ested in the Hispanic horde descending on them to worry about the odd Chinese woman. It was this lack of attention to detail that first the ordinary trafficker and then the commodity supplier were able to take full advantage of.

And then, unwillingly, Alice was on the move again.

The packaging tape over Alice's eyes and lower face was pulled tight and allowed her little facial movement. As she returned to consciousness she could taste the vomit in her mouth. She panicked. Struggling for breath and unable to do anything but keep swallowing back the burning bile that kept surging up, her whole body seemed to be on fire. She knew that, if the reflux got into her nose, she would die.

As she attempted to writhe into a more comfortable position, she began to understand that she was naked and the same tape that covered her face bound her wrists behind her back and her ankles. With something stuffed into her ears she could only feel through her skin as all her other senses had been neutralised.

Jesus, she thought, something of her lost Catholic upbringing beginning to emerge. *Help me, save me!*

Her writhing and the crawling feeling on her skin continued. Forcing herself to be still, she realised that the crawling feeling was something moving beside her.

Then everything settled down and the only sensation that she was aware of was a swaying motion that suggested that she was in something that was moving.

In common with many immigrants, both legal and otherwise, Alice was better educated and much more intelligent than her short career as a Canadian waitress would have suggested. Had she known, it was these particular characteristics that had attracted the commodity supplier and led to her present situation. The fact that she had a rarity value as a virgin wasn't something in the coming days and weeks that occurred to her.

What the hell's happening to me?

She would have said it out loud had she been able.

Having at last mastered her breathing and her stomach, she cautiously moved the only part of her body that she could. As she probed sideways with her bound legs, her heel touched upon something hard but with a textured surface.

God, that feels like hair, she thought.

Whatever she was touching moved away and the calf of her leg in its turn touched upon something warm, firm but soft. She felt it move against her.

It's someone else!

It was another thought that would have been articulated had her mouth been fully available to her.

What hit her on the back of the head she had no idea. Stunned, she instinctively straightened herself up and drifted into semi-consciousness. The same warm, firm but soft feeling of something moving against her was lost to her as her senses momentarily switched off. The back-heeled kick that had rattled her brain was equally instinctive.

It was only when the Canadian authorities became aware of the disappearance of four Chinese women, all of whom were overqualified waitresses, that more than the usual alarm bells began to ring and the various sections of officialdom began to wind themselves into action. Investigation of the immigration status of the women, Alice Hou, Janice Liang, April Cheng and Patience Zhang, rapidly revealed both the unlikely synthetic nature of their names but also the apparent replication in exact detail of their entry into Canada. At least, that was true of three of them. How Janice Liang got into the country was shrouded in more than the usual mystery. But since she had disappeared any consideration of this was deferred until she had been located.

As the police probed more deeply the shape of the people trafficking organisation that had apparently brought them to Alberta at last began to emerge, along with the apparent dissimilarity of the four women from the generality of single Chinese women who sought a new life in Canada. It also emerged that these dissimilarities had made it much easier for the four women to acquire citizenship. That the four were Canadian citizens made the search for them more intense, if increasingly fruitless, and led the police and senior immigration officials to postulate that the citizenship issue was somehow significant.

'I think I'd put money on it that they've been kidnapped for a very specific purpose.'

The senior investigating officer from the Alberta Royal Canadian Mounted Police had been around long enough to see the obvious patterns in the information that he was receiving and the behaviour that it was characterising.

'I'd also put money on our never finding out!'

It wasn't that he was naturally pessimistic; it was more that, as they trawled more and more into the depths of Chinese female immigration, they found that such disappearances, although extremely rare and one-off, had occurred before. Bodies were never found and there was never anything to suggest that the women had been spirited away into the wilder areas of Canada where bodies had a better chance of never being found. The senior officer's instinct was not challenged. But Interpol was informed.

It was an unusually warm late-May Sunday afternoon. For the inhabitants of Victoria Island and for the streams of visitors attracted from the oppressive atmosphere of Vancouver, seeing how the other half lived was a regular pastime.

Big houses, private jetties and sometimes very big ocean-going cruisers were very much the grist to this sightseeing group's mill. But only the adventurous or the insatiably curious would have taken the trouble to get close to the jetty where the biggest of all the cruisers was moored.

'So what d'you reckon that's worth?'

The two minimally clad students were adventurous. They had chosen the spot overlooking the boathouse and jetty more for is seclusion and its suntrap potential than to be able to gape at hardware that they would never in their wildest dreams be able to afford. The two girls watched the luxury vessel glide alongside the jetty. It was obviously too big to get into the boathouse.

'My dad says seagoing cruisers belonging to Russian oligarchs can cost hundreds of millions of dollars.'

Since neither girl really had much of a clue about such things the conversation lapsed.

'I wonder what they've got in there?'

A large flat crate was being carefully manoeuvred along the jetty and then was lifted by a small mobile crane on to the afterdeck of the cruiser. What happened once it had been taken on board the girls couldn't at first see, but as the vessel immediately put to sea they saw that it had been moved inside the superstructure.

'Must be valuable. They wouldn't be that careful if were just a load of provisions for the voyage.'

Dozing in the warmth of the sun, the two girls had soon forgotten both the cruiser and its seemingly precious cargo. The idea that they had just acquired some information that would be valuable to the police, not only in Canada but also in Australia and China, needless to say, never occurred to them.

European Times
UK Edition – Thursday, 27 May 2010
SUSPICIOUS BODY IN THE SEA
Dorset Police confirms that the body found in the sea off the Jurassic Coast near Bridport was that of an East European man with connections with organised crime, in particular with people trafficking. The identity of the man was known but has not been released by the police.

The exact cause of death has yet to be determined. A post-mortem is being carried out in Dorchester but the police confirm that they are instigating a murder enquiry.

Dorset Police declined to confirm or deny speculation that the man was connected with a series of increasingly violent clashes between rival gangs of suppliers of illegal farm labour. East European and Chinese gangs have been involved in a number of incidents reported to the Lincolnshire and West Midlands police forces.

The UK Human Trafficking Centre, in a report to the Home Office leaked to the press, have identified an increasing trend for the trafficking gangs to be controlled not only from East Europe but also now from mainland China. Greater Manchester Police in a separate report to the Home Office has also reported an increase in inter-gang violence between the traditional Chinese gangs most usually centred on Liverpool and a loose confederation of much better organised and resourced groups. The new gangs were beginning to not only expand into protection and the sex trade but were targeting the trafficking of both legal and illegal immigrant labour. The Manchester conclusion confirmed the Trafficking Centre's analysis.

'The thing that distinguishes these new gangs,' said the Chief Constable of Greater Manchester, 'is their active opposition to drug trafficking in the areas that they are seeking to dominate.'

None of the police forces involved in the people trafficking

30

or drugs trade were prepared to comment on the significance of this unusual feature.

The body in the sea in Dorset was said to be of a powerfully built man showing no signs of drug or any other abuse.

'Definitely not one to meet in a dark alleyway,' was the comment of the police sergeant who first secured the body from the sea.

The discovery of the body has been reported to Interpol and Dorset Police say that it will be forwarding details of the man to its colleagues in Eastern Europe directly, as a part of the established cooperation on people trafficking.

6

Melbourne trams were one of Julie's delights. The sleek, articulated modernity of the trams appealed to her as more European than British and different from anything that she was familiar with.

Than Australian! Julie corrected herself.

It was one of many things that Julie found that she was admonishing herself for. But as hard as she tried she found it very difficult to distinguish an Australian persona for herself from a British one. It was a common problem for newcomers and soluble only with time.

Trundling down St Kilda Road sedately and unhurriedly, she took time to rehearse her story for the interview. Her confidence in herself renewed, she knew that her reasons for upping sticks and coming to Australia made sense to her but she acknowledged that to a potential employer her behaviour might have seemed ill considered, even fickle.

The tram stopped and Julie scurried across in front of the halted traffic to the pavement. Since she had never had a car in Britain and her resources didn't stretch to one in Australia, she found, as a non-driver, the multi-streams of traffic down streets like St Kilda Road a little intimidating. With the trams running down the middles of the streets she could understand why the traffic needed to stop, but there was nonetheless something counter-intuitive to her way of thinking for the arrangement of traffic to be as it was.

Her watch told her that she didn't have too much time to

dwell on the vagaries and benefits of trams versus traffic and the other oddities of driving in Melbourne.

She could see where she was heading. The curved glass-fronted face of the building where her interview was to take place towered above the other buildings in its immediate vicinity. All she needed to do was negotiate a couple more road crossings and she would be there. This she quickly did.

Used to wearing the characterless black business suit uniform of a woman civil servant, Julie was determined as a part of her new Australian personality to be more adventurous in what she wore. The light seemed to her to be brighter and the women that she had seen seemed to wear more colourful, if still restrained, clothing that combined fashion with comfort. Within her reasonably extensive wardrobe she decided to follow their lead.

They'll have to take me as they find me! she had thought to herself as she had appraised herself in the mirror before setting out.

Julie wasn't unaware that there was a serious risk in her attitude, but she was instinctively adopting her father's 'start as you mean to go on' approach that had usually worked for her. And, if she didn't get this job, she could read beyond the employment agency's professional optimism to know that there were other opportunities out there.

At least my ankles don't hurt any more. All that walking seems to have cured the problem.

It was only when she got back to her apartment the previous day that she had made this discovery, and now on the Tuesday she happily pulled on the same boots but now with the only miniskirt that she possessed. She had scarcely ever worn it before – since Tariq had always let his Muslim upbringing show through and criticised her for its immodesty. It was another conscious decision to be more true to herself. Never a feminine, girly girl she nonetheless was fashion conscious in her own way and felt good about what she was wearing even

33

before she drew some admiring looks on the tram. Her black leather jacket, that signalled the tight figure underneath it, did nothing to discourage the looks of approval either. Her short black hair was blown askew by the gusting wind, but with her usual understated make-up it gave her a confident enough look that reflected how she both felt about herself now and about her prospects at the interview.

In the sterile glass splendour of the office building that she was entering she was quick to notice that the same purposeful activity in terms of comings and goings was apparent that she had noticed in Spring Street and the surrounding area. She liked the sense of urgency about getting on with life and getting things done that was usually well hidden in Britain. Melbourne, she knew, was the thriving business capital of Australia, but she hadn't expected to see its manifestations so obviously displayed.

Still, if I've learned anything in the last few weeks, it's that Aussies are nothing if not up-front.

As Julie approached the reception desk in the building foyer, the ebb and flow of people had left a void. There was only her and the receptionist. At least, so she first thought.

'Miss Kershawe?'

The broadly smiling Chinese girl clearly knew that she could only be Julie Kershawe because she directed her around the reception area to the bank of lifts behind it in an elegant but very clear movement of her right hand. With a major Chinese population in Melbourne, it wasn't her racial origins that set Julie into alert mode. Later, when she thought through her day, she acknowledged that it was the unlikely circumstances of one of the applicants for a middling administrative job in an organisation being met and whisked through the formalities of arrival in such a slick and professional manner. What limited experience she had told her that generally you were left to flounder in this situation, despite your potential employer's pious protestations that it was a good test of character to see how you overcame the vagaries of organisational indifference to get to your interview.

As they entered the lift, the Chinese girl handed Julie an already prepared visitor's identity badge. Used as she had been to looking for and seeking out anomalies in people's behaviour and presentation, Julie knew that somehow this particular middling administrative job on offer was going to be different. But she didn't have the time to generate this as more than an impression before she was in the interview room. And still there were no signs of the expected roomful of other nervous candidates; in fact there were no signs of any sort of anteroom. Julie's level of alert cranked up. This was not looking like a normal interview at all.

The room that she was shown into immediately gave her a feeling of unreality. Her perception that something very unusual was going on was heightened. The Chinese girl disappeared as mysteriously as she had appeared. It felt almost James Bond-esque, but she didn't really get time to consider whom and what she was being confronted with before the obvious dynamic of the situation forced her to concentrate.

The room was large and carpeted thickly, forcing her to pick her feet up to avoid catching her heels in its pile. The sense of unreality increased. The room was unlit. Whatever was decorating or furnishing the side walls and the rest of the room she didn't register. She was drawn, as she realised she was supposed to be, towards the end of the room. The floor-to-ceiling windows flooded the end of the space with light. The table backing the window and the three people sitting at it were formed into silhouettes. There was a single chair placed to face the table.

What on earth is going on? she thought.

Julie couldn't restrain an amused grin. In the full light, the grin was immediately apparent to what she instantly characterised as her 'interrogators'.

This sure as hell is going to be different! she told herself before focusing on the panel of people in front of her.

She walked up to the chair and sat down.

'Do sit down, Miss Kershawe,' the voice in the centre of the three people said equably, the boldness of her action not seeming to bother him. It was almost as if he had been expecting her to be as positive.

Julie tried to discern something of the man in front of her against the bright light behind him; she didn't get much of a chance.

'James Frederick Kershawe, father, banker, Hong Kong resident for seventeen years.'

The man on the right of the chairman, as she looked at them, started off on a monologue that instantly got Julie's attention.

'Li Chou Yu, aka Alicia, married to said James Kershawe in Hong Kong thirty years ago. The daughter of a local Hong Kong businessman and entrepreneur, a university lecturer and a well-known opponent of Chinese Communism.'

Julie's heart missed a beat; she had never heard her mother's origins identified in such a way before.

'Now resident in Ewell in Surrey, two daughters both born in Hong Kong but pre-Handover and British citizens.'

'Julie Alicia Kershawe, twenty-five, single, UK Border Agency enforcement section, now unemployed.'

It was the man to the left of the chairman who was now speaking.

Julie hadn't taken much interest in the body shapes in front of her. Now as the third man spoke she found herself concentrating very hard. It was the voice. She knew at once that she knew the voice. Where from? It was recent.

Everything was going at such a pace that she was momentarily seized with panic.

What is this all about?

And as the question formed itself in her mind she knew.

'Alan you already know,' the central voice said.

Alan she already knew!

The ocean-going cruiser that edged its way into the isolated inlet in the North Queensland coast had made its way across the Pacific in a series of careful stages calibrated to its needs for fuel and other supplies, but – having made the trip several times before – in an easy and trouble-free way.

That was a relief for the crew, although they well knew that the most difficult part of the long journey for their passenger cargo was still ahead of them. After their last trip they had received intelligence that the Queensland Police had been asking questions. A party of Brisbane students, partying in celebration, had seen their vessel, had been surprised by its size and luxury, and had shared their experience along with several very cold beers with the locals in a nearby pub. In a small community where everybody knew everything about everything, there was mild consternation that they had missed something interesting and unusual.

And what was interesting and unusual inevitably came to the notice of the local police. Equally in this case it also came to the notice of the owner of an out-of-town Chinese buffet restaurant in Cairns and thence a warning was sent to the operators of the mysterious ocean-going cruiser.

So, as the cruiser dropped anchor on its latest trip, precautions had been and were being taken, both onshore and on board, against any unexpected intrusion into their activities. The nervousness was understandable. The step-up from drugs, currency and other contraband to human cargo had been a first for the cruiser's Chinese crew, one which was highly paid, but with risks that were commensurate with the high fee.

Alice Hou and her three companions had been set free from their packing case once the cruiser was well out to sea off the US west coast and out of range of coastguard vessels. Sightings of other vessels were rare; their route was chosen not only to manage their supply situation but also to avoid recognised shipping routes. Their only moment of concern was when they had crossed the path of a US aircraft carrier group, but this was more about making sure that the much larger vessels saw them and avoided them rather than any fear of discovery of their business activities. The fouled and evil-smelling packing case that the girls had initially travelled in had been dumped overboard and girls clothed from stocks held on the boat. Their ankles had been manacled but they had otherwise been left free in order that they could be used as slave labour in the service of the crew of the vessel.

Speaking a mixture of Spanish and English, the girls sought to cut themselves off from the crew and avoided speaking Mandarin Chinese unless addressed. It was the fearful and instinctive reaction of strangers in a frightening and seemingly hopeless situation. They each showed their fear in various ways. April Chang was almost terrified into rigidity to start with while Janice Liang seemed to be able to cope with her fears much better than the others. Alice and Janice gravitated together because of their better command of English. None of the girls did more than cooperate minimally with the crew, and only then when they were driven to it. Discipline was in the hands of a man that Alice Hou equated to her Canadian gang-master. He was unforgiving but, to the girls' relief, rigid about the crew's behaviour as well.

Despite the fact that escape was impossible, unless they sought to drown themselves, they were watched continually and locked up whenever their cleaning and cooking duties were complete. They were separated at night. This was supposed to be as much for the girls' protection as anything.

'We don't want damaged goods arriving in Australia,' was the instruction.

And in the organisation that was moving the girls around the world such instructions were obeyed.

On approaching any of the ports of call, Alice Hou and her

companions were generally restrained again and stowed out of sight below decks and in the bowels of the vessel. Accommodation had been prepared for as many as six girls to be hidden in this way.

Mobile phone calls were made the instant the cruiser had anchored in Australian waters. A practised sequence of actions was then initiated.

By the time the Queensland Police got wind of the arrival of the vessel it had already discharged its cargo of Chinese women and gone. Not, of course, that the police had any bankable evidence that that was what it was doing. Their inevitable assumption was that, if the cruiser was doing anything illegal, it was more likely to be drugs than people. People trafficking to Australia tended to be a much cruder activity, utilising barely seaworthy vessels rather than million-dollar yachts.

That was not to say that there weren't people in Australia who knew much more about what was going on in the Queensland inlet than the people traffickers would have liked them to.

Of course, Julie already knew Alan. He was hardly someone whose physical attributes made him forgettable, although, as Julie realised later on, handsome as he was, his features were nonetheless surprisingly difficult to actually define beyond their Greek-god purity. It was something that mystified her.

And, of course, both the interrogators, and now Julie, knew that her having met Alan was not a coincidence.

Again, reaching into her past experience she also knew that she had somehow to gain leverage in the conversation that was to follow since they clearly knew a great deal about her.

'OK, so I know Alan. Perhaps you'd like to tell me why he was sent to spy on me before this interview?'

'Perhaps we wouldn't!'

Beyond the initial courtesies it was the central figure's first real entry into the interview. The response was curt but friendly enough to inhibit a protest from Julie.

'You left the UK Border Agency because you were suspected of facilitating the entry into the UK of a number of people whose background was not well established and proved to be false, and the people in question have now all disappeared from the radar in the UK.'

It was another demonstration of their knowledge.

She clearly wasn't going to get much time to wonder who these people were or how they knew what they knew. Except that the thought quickly surfaced with her that they had to be something official. There was no way that her brief conversation with Alan could have yielded the level of knowledge that they were displaying.

'OK, so you know all that. What are you asking me? The police were clear that they didn't have enough evidence to prove any case one way or another.'

'Indeed not.'

'What the hell does that mean?'

A dialogue developed with the man on the right. As the light changed marginally, Julie could see that he was about forty, dressed in the sort of tweed suit that her father used to wear and with the sort of face that you would probably have forgotten within half an hour of last seeing him. From her dealings with MI5 and on the odd occasion MI6, she knew this guy was Security Service.

But again, why he was there and why she was being interviewed by him, she had no time to think deeply about.

'Why did you rob the convenience store in Cambridge and then give the money to student charities?'

'Jesus,' Julie muttered, 'where did that come from?'

'Your friend Tariq set you up in that robbery. I guess it was a Rag Week prank to you, but he had your career and future in his hand nonetheless as a consequence.'

Julie had been here many times since had Tariq thrown her

over. Until now, her brain just hadn't let her accept that her relationship with him had been based on a simple piece of blackmail, simple and trivial, but she could see how Tariq had early on detected her sense of honour and loyalty to her father and mother and her desire not to let them down. In her straight-forward, schoolgirlish innocence, it had been a big deal and she had been easily manipulated. But now as the point was presented to her, dispassionately and openly, it all seemed rather silly; she suddenly had a sense of closure.

'Yes, and the little shit exploited it whenever he wanted something and usually after sex.'

Julie heard herself say this with amazement. Closure was one thing, now she had made herself vulnerable in front of strangers.

The right-hand man didn't seem to see it like that nor did he seem to want to exploit this perceived vulnerability.

'Tariq was double-crossing his masters as well as you.'

It was another quick-fire switch.

The man spoke the words in some distaste as if it were schoolboy language rather than a statement from a senior Security Service officer.

Julie was leaning forward in her chair towards the man.

Masters! What's he talking about? Julie couldn't grasp the concept of Tariq having anyone he was subservient to; he was too confident in himself and too pleased with himself.

'You let in a number of Arab men, said to be members of his family, and at least three Chinese girls. Am I right?'

'It was only *two* Arab men,' Julie said.

The interrogator didn't pursue the point. The man appeared to have a different line of enquiry in mind. The body language and atmosphere intensified again and Julie sensed that they were now on to a subject where they were genuinely looking for new information. But Julie felt constrained to add more detail.

'There were more than three Chinese women that I recall.

41

There were also four Chinese men. All of whom Tariq wanted me to reject for the effect.'

'Thank you, Julie. Despite your rejection, it seems that the men in question actually reapplied for entry elsewhere. They were key figures – your Border Agency colleagues believe there's a labour importation scam and are still investigating.'

This wasn't a surprise to Julie.

'And all of these Chinese people have disappeared?'

'Only the women. The men are gang bosses, gangmasters, or whatever you call them in the UK. They aren't really our interest.'

A slight clattering and a cold draught made Julie pause and look around. The Chinese girl was arranging coffee on a discreetly lit table in a corner behind her.

Hell, now they're on to the blow cold, blow hot bit, Julie thought.

Her past experience again made her familiar with interrogation techniques.

She was wrong.

As the three men questioning her emerged into the light, their whole attitude changed. It was if they'd decided to give her the job and she was now one of them. And as it transpired in the more informal conversation over coffee there really hadn't been any doubt about her being employed by the Australian Security Service on a short-term contract. Even if nobody had yet broached the subject of what she might be required to do.

'Mark Hallingford arranged for you to come to Australia. We have been working with him for some time.'

Julie was astonished. Almost every opening gambit in the conversation had come from nowhere. At least now perhaps an explanation was beginning to appear from the murk. Mark Hallingford had been her boss in Edinburgh; he had been very supportive when he had discovered Tariq's manipulation and had indeed pointed her at Melbourne as a place to restart her life, even encouraged the switch of location. Now Julie was being told that the whole thing had been arranged.

How long the Border Agency had known about Tariq al Hussaini and his activities Julie would never learn. This was of only passing interest to the Australians. That he was seen as a dangerous young man even back in Iraq, she would never be told. That he covered his activities by involvement with a number of entirely innocent organisations again was hidden from Julie. The corner-shop robbery had, however, eventually rung alarm bells in official circles in London when it was picked up from the police database and checked out and referred to Baghdad. A waiting game had been initiated. Again, she was never likely to be told, but much of what had happened to her once Tariq al Hussaini's activities had been identified had been engineered to keep him from suspecting that he was being watched. And as the authorities closed in on Tariq the situation had been ideal for inducing her to move to Australia. This was a piece of straight exploitation set up to meet an urgent need from the Australian Security Services. With her reputation and job prospects destroyed in the UK, her background and particular skills could then be used free of any official involvement.

Despite its limited interest to them, the three Australians, all of whom were privy to as much information as there was, acknowledged the cynical and cruel manipulation of Julie Kershawe, not only by Tariq al Hussaini, but also by the UK authorities. That was the business they were in, but it gave them just the operative that they needed.

'It's disappearing Chinese women that we need your help with,' the centre man and chairman of the interview panel said.

'People trafficking?'

Julie, of course, knew that this was happening; it was a major blight on modern society. One of her arguments of self-justification about letting the three Chinese women into Britain officially and openly had been that it would prevent them being sucked into the vice trade and other exploitative activities. But what had this to do with Australia? That she would find out when she met up with the people that she would be working with.

For the time being she couldn't avoid a feeling of anti-climax.

The offer that was made to Julie was at once attractive and frightening. Julie was attracted and frightened.

Alan accompanied her to the lift and out of the building. It had been the weirdest interview that she had ever experienced and yet she had still come out of it with a contract with the Australian Government.

'Maybe that's how things get done here!'

'Pardon me?'

As they waited for a tram, Alan was still with her. Julie found that she rather liked that and looked forward hopefully to the rest of the afternoon and onwards.

7

While Julie Kershawe could neither remember the names of the three young Chinese women that she had let into Britain, nor feel any contrition for her actions, Linda Shen was fully aware of the names of two of them, even if they were different from those Julie couldn't have recalled. That there was a third she had no knowledge of. Uncooperative, resentful, this young woman had been introduced to the brutal sex trade of Warsaw and was the only one of the three who had initially truly disappeared from Britain.

Equipped with their new names, ground through a harsh finishing school located in a remote Skye farmhouse, the two Hong Kong eighteen-year-olds were now accomplished and marriageable young women. Whether they were ready for a return to mainland China and their life there Linda neither knew nor particularly cared. Her job was to take them back and deliver them, and their recently acquired British passports, to the men who had been chosen for them.

The fact that she had had an experience almost similar to theirs, except that she had escaped from a Manchester backstreet and prospered by her own efforts, Linda kept stubbornly buried in her deep unconscious mind. Honest enough to recognise that, despite the deliberate cruelty of being separated from her child as an act of control, the life that she had been forced into, basically for access to her British passport and freedom of movement within the European Union, was infinitely preferable to that she had been snatched away from. With common sense as well as intelligence, she found that luxury and unlimited funds and an increasingly manageable relationship developing with Shi Xiulu, her enforced husband, were almost a fair exchange. Whether the two young women in her care would come to take a similar view, again, she neither knew nor cared.

'You know what to do?'

Linda's minder did.

Relations with the man had improved over the week that she had been in Britain. Forced into partnership and not too subtly reminded of his dependence on her husband she had come to a working arrangement with him. The minder accommodated his patroness with as much good grace as he could muster and she had used him to advantage. The trip to Skye was the only part of the week when the two of them had been thrown together so closely that she had had virtually no privacy. She had no quarrel with any of the arrangements that he made or the efficiency with which he had made them. She had become used to such service back home in China and, however much she disliked the man as an individual, she knew that she would be helpless and at risk without him. She also knew that her husband had no love for her; he merely wanted to secure an heir and the reach into the world outside China that was denied to him at the present time but not to her. That he had his heir pleased him; using the child to ensure his wife's loyalty was common sense to Mr Shi.

And all the time his wife's activities were being monitored, even facilitated, by the UK authorities.

The minder would remain in Britain. Another minder would meet her at Hong Kong, but this one she was familiar with and she knew his vulnerabilities. And on her own ground Linda had become very good at exploiting people's vulnerabilities.

The company of two young women on the way back to China would ease her journey but she still had to be on her guard with them.

While the official policy of the Chinese Government was to invest wisely and profitably in countries like Britain, the legion of corrupt businessmen and officials who were siphoning off much of the profits produced were making investments of their own. Getting illicit money out of China was by no means easy; the pervading state security controls were steadily making electronic management of funds too cumbersome for safe use, so many innovative ways of laundering money were being developed.

'Electronic means are suspect and must be used with care.'

Mr Shi was used to parroting this to his wife as he explained his latest scheme to her. His sideline of selling his expertise in cheating the authorities to his associates and fellow corrupt businessmen had the prospect of being a huge earner even after expenses had been deducted. Based on a reversion to human rather than electronic activities, his schemes were labour intensive but generally reliant on wives with more freedom of movement than the Chinese Government was prepared to allow to the businessmen themselves. Wives were traditionally obedient and generally subservient to their husband's interests, although Mr Shi was well aware that his own wife had a streak of independence in her that he was sensible enough to try to harness rather than suppress.

Linda Shen's role as a courier was becoming increasingly complex and her trips to Britain and the US more convoluted, as electronic means of money movement were augmented and partially replaced by this human activity.

Linda hated the trips. They took her away from her son, the only thing in her life that mattered to her, but the rewards were beginning to build up. Her husband had hardly expected that the expertise that she was developing on his behalf wouldn't be put to use on her own account. What he didn't realise was that his pretty and, to him, seemingly scatty wife had as good a financial brain as he had, if not better. Untutored, she was taking time to understand what was possible for her and she

47

was building funds in various locations in Britain. Neither greedy nor impatient, as was her husband, she knew that keeping below his radar was the key to success.

As she shepherded the two young women on to the Qantas flight to Hong Kong and said a relieved farewell to her minder, what Linda didn't know was that events in Canada and Australia were being shared around the world and the interest being taken by a range of police, immigration and intelligence services in the movement of intelligent and displaced Chinese women was intensifying.

Storing the two new cherished British passports alongside her own in her copious designer handbag, she felt satisfied that she had fulfilled her husband's plans, advanced her own and taken another small step towards safeguarding her child's independent future.

8

'Good heavens!'

David Hutchinson's surprise was almost comic. The email on his BlackBerry was totally unexpected.

'What?'

Susie Peveral and David Hutchinson had settled like a couple of companionable old-age pensioners on a seafront bench at Seaton in Devon. It was an idyllic setting. The gentle swell hissed and swished only a few feet away from them; excited small children and dogs formed the backdrop. A peace so different from their normal lives re-established itself after the traumas of seeing the body in the sea off the Dorset coast.

Neither Susie nor David was prone to too much self-analysis but both were struggling to understand why the sight of what, for David at least, was sadly just one more body was having such a depressing effect.

Seeing the report in the paper had also been a bit of a shock to David – partly because he hadn't expected to see someone he had known, however fleetingly, and he had photographed, in the media as a murder victim, and partly because the photo commission that he had undertaken, which included the dead man, had not been one that he had relished and he had done only as a favour to someone whom he now regarded as rather less than a friend.

He knew he was jaded and he guessed from the various comments and hints from Susie that she also felt herself to be, too. Their decision to take off into the West Country without their usual working paraphernalia was something of a recognition of this.

'Ever been on a tram?'

'Only in San Francisco.'

The double-decked trams of Seaton were a novelty to Susie. With a burst of schoolgirl enthusiasm she scurried up to the top deck and to the front of the tram and subsided into a seat with a sigh both of depth and of contentment.

'Well,' said Hutchinson as they rattled away into the countryside, 'we did plan to get away from it all and do something different.'

'I'm not sure that spotting a body in the sea was exactly getting away from it all!'

'No.'

'You knew the dead guy, though?' Susie asked.

Now that the conversation had got started, she was keen to know more of David's involvement with the dead man.

'Hardly knew him; I was asked to take a photo of this bunch of businessmen at a lunch. For some Middle East trade magazine, I was told. The dead man was one of the guests. The *Chronicle* must have got access to the magazine.'

'Copyright fee?' Susie grinned.

'No chance.'

'So why were you so surprised when you saw the guy's face in the paper?'

Hutchinson pondered on how much to tell Susie or whether in fact to just close the conversation down and not tell her anything at all. Killing off the conversation didn't seem too friendly, and talking about it, he thought, might perhaps exorcise his discomfort over the assignment.

'They were a mixed bunch, Chinese certainly; one at least could have been Middle Eastern; but the rest, it was hard to tell. They were all very wary of each other. No sort of social context to the gathering. The point is, some underling took down the names as I organised them for the shot. The name that the underling gave this bloke was not Middle Eastern; I'm sure it was Russian, East European – I don't know, it was very different.'

'The police said he was identified by documents in his pockets.'

'OK,' said David, 'so that's incontrovertible proof?'

'Why are you so edgy about this?'

'The bloke who asked me to take the photos got me into an East European night club – don't ask where – and I got some shots of under-age girls being groomed for prostitution and made a lot of money. It was a bit dodgy … no, no, it was hellishly dodgy. But I owed this bloke. So I took his group photo. It was a clunking good payday, too, but the sod was using the whole thing as a lever in the internecine warfare that seems to be endemic among these East European criminals. Not my finest hour and something that has made me think a lot about what the hell I'm doing with my life.'

The underlying thought at the back of David Hutchinson's mind surfaced at last.

'OK, David' – she was thoughtful – 'so you're not happy with what you do any more; what are you going to do about it?'

'I just wonder whether there was something … some injustice … I could right some wrong, do a book … I don't know. All I know is I don't want to write about and photograph dead bodies, sick children, ravaged villages any more.'

The tram was passing through the sort of countryside that was familiar to David from childhood. For Susie, who had spent her whole life within the broad confines of Greater London, the lushness was unfamiliar and very welcome.

After the burst of intense conversation they lapsed into silence once more and took in the further views around them. But it wasn't quite the same relaxed, untroubled silence as before.

David Hutchinson felt disturbed. Susie's reaction passed him by but she seemed almost pleased that he was apparently ready for some new and different challenge.

The rest of the day passed.

The mood was better in the evening. David had made enquiries at the guesthouse about the whereabouts of a good country pub. For someone with a vast wealth of experience in living and eating in a staggering range of countries and places, the English country pub had become something of a Holy Grail for him. A major part of their trip was about sampling traditional English pubs.

'Great idea' was Susie's response to David's suggestion for their evening.

Branscombe had been suggested.

The meal was every bit as good as the guesthouse owner had predicted. The conversation drifted, as neither wanted to revert to the discussions about the dead body in the sea. And inevitably, as they drifted, they took in childhood, school, university and their upbringing in general. Both were cautious, even coy, at first until they realised that the lessons of their childhood were the same for both of them, despite their vastly differing backgrounds.

'Overbearing fathers with no more ambition than our following in their footsteps come what may.'

Susie's summary seemed to David to exactly fit his situation.

It was a warm evening and the food had been good. The strictly limited amount of wine drunk had also been good. The single malt was for later back at the guesthouse. Both were now fully relaxed again and savouring the sort of peacefulness that they had hoped for.

'I reckon,' Susie finally said, 'there's a story somewhere in both our backgrounds. Maybe more so in yours since a poor little rich girl in token revolt isn't as good a tale as a poor little poor guy totally breaking free of his background.'

David's chuckle said that he agreed and that he was in no way put out by the characterisation.

Back at the guesthouse David produced the bottle of single malt whisky. The guesthouse terrace overlooked the sea; it was an obvious place for a nightcap.

It was then that the insistent vibration of David's BlackBerry in his jacket pocket caught his attention.

'What?' Susie repeated as David read the email.

Later, David realised that she knew what the email was going to say.

'Susie, your secretary is inviting me to a meeting with you!'

9

Hong Kong Airport was new, vast and luxurious and its shops and services were definitely beyond the means of all but a few Chinese, although in the new China this number was increasing rapidly. The international terminal was the last word in spaciousness, in layout and facilities, and in its scope for people-watching.

Everything was clean, even excessively so, well tended and customer-friendly in a way that virtually no other airport terminal in the world seemed to be. It seemed that all the lessons from around the world had been learned. The air conditioning was arctic cold; movement along its great thoroughfares was easy via a travolator or for those with time and curiosity by walking. The travolator, the moving walkway so beloved of European airport designers, was a novelty that attracted interest among even the most seasoned travellers as it made its arrow-straight way along the whole length of the upper gallery of the terminal. Brightly lit with an arched ceiling, the moving walkway seemed to define the pace of the terminal in sedate contrast to the usual frenetic activity in such places. Even the politely tooting passenger buggies seemed to move more slowly than at Heathrow or Schiphol.

Passengers of the small variety found the travolator an instant source of entertainment. Very few people among the Chinese passengers actually walked; it was if they were determined to get their money's worth.

Transiting flights to London and Australia didn't spend

54

much time in Hong Kong. It was often little more that a refuelling stop, but passengers were disgorged into the terminal and gravitated almost automatically to the merchandising area. The plaza of shops seemed to encircle and enclose the idling passengers; those who had seen it all before gravitated further into the coffee lounge area. Whether this was less luxurious by design, in order to focus passengers' attention on the high-end shops, it would have been hard to say. A snapshot of the whole area on any day would probably have demonstrated that the luxury goods shops won out every time.

'You know what?'

The strident female American voice commanded attention even from those not within her general orbit.

'You know what? Nothing seems to have a price tag. How are we supposed to know what things cost?'

There was agreement, disdain and amusement at the woman's ignorance about the culture of the top end of the luxury goods market among the more knowledgeable listeners. The likes of Gucci and Prada didn't as a matter of course attach gaudy labels to their sales items; a discreet enquiry was the norm. The oft-quoted dictum 'If you need to know the price, you can't afford it' generally prevailed.

In any case, it was clear, even to the casual observer, that everybody was looking and nobody buying. So a more relevant question might have been, 'Who buys this stuff anyway?'

It was a question that might have occurred to a pair of idling suited men who seemed to be interested more in who went into the Gucci shop rather than who might be buying something there. It was an interest that began to sharpen after a flight from London had arrived and discharged its payload while the Qantas staff refuelled it.

A Chinese man in a suit that could probably have bought the two watching men a whole wardrobe of clothes each arrived briskly at the Gucci shop, and the men went visibly on to the alert.

The muttered exchange between them accompanied by some brief but sage nodding of heads clearly indicated that the man was expected. More discreet muttering into lapel microphones ensued.

The sauntering transit passengers and the scurrying crew-change staff seemed oblivious both to the well-dressed man and his watchers and, as they spilled over into the aisles leading into and out of the plaza area, to the uniformed police officers as well. Police officers were rather more in evidence in many parts of China than was common in the UK or Australia, so people, locals and visitors, largely took no notice of them.

And as the watchers watched, in the coffee lounge above, they themselves were being watched.

The two plain-clothes police officers stiffened as an obviously holidaying couple of either American or Antipodean origins, their loud and colourful shirts and baggy shorts not only inappropriate in the chill of the terminal building but also at odds with even the increasingly relaxed norms of Chinese society, seemed to get into a tangle of gyrating bodies. The two officers then relaxed. The pantomime of the cold contemptuous look of the expensively sartorial Chinese man and the looks of near outrage from the visitors signalled very clearly the 'get out of my way' message that had been transmitted.

The man looked at his watch. Another gaggle of people went by; an incoming flight from Melbourne had disembarked its load, temporarily adding to the throng in the terminal building.

A loudly chattering Qantas crew surged into the plaza area intent on taking over one of the parked aircraft. A chauffeur joined the man outside the Gucci shop. And in the opposite direction a pair of women in cabin attendant uniforms approached assisting a young woman who appeared to be ill. A medical bag was slung over the shoulder of one of the cabin attendants.

Another pantomime started as the Chinese man and his

chauffeur greeted the trio, play-acting anxiety over the ailing young woman. It was clearly a pre-arranged meeting and unrelated to any desire to spend money on goods in the Gucci shop.

'Jesus!'

There was now no doubt where the casually dressed couple, whose exclamation caught the attention of the bulk of the time-filling passengers in the plaza area, came from. Americans, nervous about being in China anyway. The woman's voice was at once strident and anxious.

A cloud of dark green descended on the group of five people. The two cabin attendants, more alert than the man they were meeting, immediately turned and set off back along an access way heading for the exit.

The sharp cry in Chinese was followed by an explosive roar as the police opened fire at the running figures. Both women were hit and collapsed and slithered in their momentum along the access way until they cannoned into the wall. Neither moved once their motion had been arrested.

'Go, go!'

The Chinese police didn't really need to speak to indicate what the shocked passengers should do. They were shepherded quickly from the plaza area, the shops were closed and a security blanket came firmly down.

The observer from the coffee lounge above was nowhere to be seen.

HEDLEY HARRISON

People's National Daily
English-language Hong Kong Edition – Tuesday, 22 June 2010
INCIDENT AT HONG KONG INTERNATIONAL
AIRPORT
The police arrested a Hong Kong banker yesterday afternoon at the airport on suspicion of importing an illegal immigrant following a brief incident in which two women suspects were killed.

In an operation in coordination with the police forces of Australia, Great Britain and Canada, the People's Police made the arrest based on information received in this instance from the Australian Federal Police that a young woman would be on a flight from Melbourne yesterday and that this young woman was being brought to the People's Republic against her will and against the immigration protocols agreed between the People's Republic of China and the Commonwealth of Australia.

The names being used by the two women accompanying the enforced illegal immigrant had been passed to the People's Police, and surveillance established at the airport to intercept them if and when they arrived from Australia. Until the trio arrived, the police had no idea that the immigrant would be met by the banker.

The young woman taken into custody was in a distressed state having been both drugged and restrained during the flight from Melbourne. The police wouldn't elaborate on what exactly had occurred on the flight.

The People's Police is being unusually forthcoming about the incident, in the hope that the people of Hong Kong will be vigilant against a possible rise in the illegal traffic of young women into China.

The police made no comment on the role of the banker in the incident other than to confirm that he was there to meet the women. All that is known about him is that he is wealthy, has several houses in PRC and abroad, and he is single. The

58

police are currently investigating his contacts and associates, particularly in the three countries with whom the PRC is cooperating.

10

Teasingly, Susie refused to disclose the purpose of the meeting that she had invited David Hutchinson to.

With more than half the whisky gone, both she and David were sufficiently relaxed and psyched up for him to take this refusal as a challenge, and as they headed to their bedroom it was obvious that Susie was going to enjoy the process of resisting him further.

'It's holiday; it's holiday!' she chided him playfully.

Visions of the O2 Arena and their first encounter were at the forefront of both of their minds. Their trip to the Arena had been characterised by studied indifference from David and a patronising aloofness by Susie. Yet inside she was seething with a confusion of emotions that she had struggled to understand ever since. Aristocratic and privileged as she was, her only contact with people of David's working-class background had been with family servants, yet this man, against all of her perceived stereotypes, had thrived at university in a way that she could only envy. Yet it had only been when she saw him in the street and impulsively forced him into conversation that she had realised that David had got inside her head at Oxford and had never been out of it.

The pop star that David had been going to interview and photograph had been totally unknown to Susie. Her claimed passion for him had provided the excuse she needed to force herself on David, impulsive and irrational though it might be. Infatuated in the moment she gave no thought to what might happen when they got to the O2 Arena. The pop star's no-show had solved the problem and provided Susie with an unexpected opportunity to be alone in private with David.

Backstage she had simply grabbed at him and began kissing him with a passion that he later admitted both took him by surprise and released his own pent-up feelings at being in the company of someone he saw as spoiled, toffee-nosed and arrogant.

Scrabbling at his trousers and sinuously dropping her skin-tight jeans, she forced David inside her before he could draw breath. After that it was pure passion. It was the first of many snatched moments of meals and sex in unlikely places until David suggested that they put the relationship on a more stable basis by taking a holiday together. Susie, a very different Susie from their university days, had been very positively enthusiastic about the idea.

Now well into the holiday, despite unforeseen distractions, well fed and well watered with expensive whisky, Susie was out of her miniskirt and pants before he had got more than a couple of buttons undone.

'Come on then!'

As they were both finally naked, Susie moved away from him but beckoned him on to her.

'Jesus, Susie, talk about high-class tart!'

But he was ready for her now and as they entangled on the bed he could smell her expensive perfume and she the stale soapy smell of him that had driven her wild at the O2 Arena. She relaxed against him and went with his motion. As usual, David was surprised and delighted by the vigour of her response.

After Seaton, they skipped the rest of Devon, neither Exeter nor Plymouth holding any potential interest for them. A big city was a big city and they had both seen plenty of those. In line with the 'country pub' philosophy, they weren't interested in the corporate or big time, but much more in the simpler things of life.

The humid warmth of the Tropical Dome at the Eden Project seemed oppressive against the drier warmth of a Cornish afternoon, but neither Susie nor David took much notice.

'A bit like Port Harcourt when I was last there,' said David.

His piece on the Nigerian Government's efforts to defeat the Ogoni rebels in the Niger Delta had been much praised. At least, by everybody but the local Rivers Province administration, which were less than impressed by the evidence of the combination of collusion and bribery that kept the rebels quiescent during an expansion of the Shell oil company's pipeline system. The subsequent sanctions imposed by the federal government on the Rivers Province Government ensured that David was never likely to travel in that part of Africa again.

The meeting room at the Millbank Tower was windowless and featureless. David was surprised by the large cast that had gathered. He had no idea why the meeting would require twelve people present and he never found out who all of the twelve people were.

'There's always the note-takers,' Susie said afterwards.

'Four?'

'That just says that there were four departments present.'

'Shit, Susie, why don't they just share the meeting notes?'

'No, no, you don't understand,' she said with a grin. 'The notes aren't just recording what was said and agreed at the meeting. That's too simple a view. They're about the people who will read the notes and assuring them that the department's view point was accurately portrayed.'

'You're joking!'

The light-hearted jocular tone of the conversation reflected David's relief that the meeting was over and that it hadn't proved anything like as demanding as he had expected. Nonetheless, a meeting chaired by a woman that he regularly had sex with was always going to have an element of challenge in it.

'So,' he said, 'I got myself a job.'

'And, you can be sure that you'll get paid for it!'

But it had taken two hours for them to get to this point of satisfaction.

Susie had started the meeting off by introducing only some of the people present. Of those she did introduce David learned that there were representatives from the Foreign and Commonwealth Office, the Department of Work and Pensions, and the Home Office.

It soon became clear that the various attendees didn't sit together by department. Whether this was by design or simply a reflection of the arrival times of the participants of the meeting David never had any idea. But it did make following the flow of the meeting more difficult and at times confusing. It didn't, however, take long for the various departmental agendas to become apparent.

The most difficult part for David was that those present had either been well briefed or were so actively involved in the issues under discussion that no background was ever offered. But it was very clear what the underlying topic for the meeting was.

'The illegal immigrant routings are getting more sophisticated. From contacts in Canada and Australia we've learned that the source of immigrants has been expanded, to South America – to Brazil, to be precise. A large-scale operation has been discovered by the Canadians that has allowed a whole stream of migrants to get under the American radar. The US is so fixated on Mexico and stopping both the illegals and the violence crossing the border that it has become much easier for people-trafficking routes from further south to be built up and to bypass the US control system. They aren't looking for them so they don't find them. The key point is that they don't stay in the States; they move on to Canada and into the labour force there. From what we are discovering, the movement is very specific and very well resourced.'

David wasn't clear whether the speaker was Work and Pensions or from the Security Service.

'Two other trends are emerging. One, many of the illegals are Asian, mainly Chinese, with the odd Japanese. Two, among the general run of illegals of all social categories simply out to make a better life there is evidence of a small number of middle-class/professional class women being trafficked. They are thought to be second-generation immigrants to Brazil, maybe Argentina, facing prejudice, hoping to move out and on to a better life in Canada and beyond.'

'Beyond,' said David without thinking.

'There's evidence that some high-value illegals are being seized in Canada and moved on – we suspect, to Australia.'

It was a switch of departmental spokesperson. It was obvious that this aspect of what was being described was either new or unusual, but David got a sense that many of those present didn't rate it as important as the larger-scale activities. The term 'high-value illegals' grated with David.

'Identities are being established in Canada, even if the jobs that the illegals are doing don't live up to their homeland qualifications, and then they are being selectively snatched and they are disappearing from Canada.'

The Home Office speaker didn't provide any more details. But, since the number of these women was tiny, the interest wasn't actually in them; it was more the men who were getting past the system. These men formed two categories: IT and computer specialists, and general and semi-skilled workers. The belief was that the specialists moved on to Britain and Europe – Russia too – while the others were dispersed in a fairly obvious fashion around Canada. Easily picked up and deported, the Canadian authorities saw these men as a smoke-screen or cover for the more valuable workers.

The problem of the trafficked educated women formed no further part of the meeting. David thought this surprising; Susie, for whom this was a major issue, was furious, but the agenda that she was having to work to was not hers but came from on high.

There was detail here. There was reference to documents held, and court cases pending, but the consensus was that these were only scratching the surface.

It was also apparent that much of what needed to be done to shut down the trafficking operations, which were undoubtedly continuing, was outside the borders of the UK and outside of the control of the British Government. The suspicion was clearly there, however, that at least some major areas of the activities, even if they were worldwide, were being managed from inside the UK. This made it a British responsibility, even if the overall controlling function might not be in the UK. Such intelligence that was emerging about this controlling function always seemed to point to mainland China.

But the meeting was drifting and Susie reasserted her control.

'Everybody knows what's going on,' she said. 'Our people in Brazil tell us that it appears to be mainly the Chinese who are leaving, both legally where they can and illegally when they can't. The Government doesn't want them to go. Too many of them are educated and professional and so represent a significant drain of resources.

'But – and there's always a "but" – they are not indigenous. Indigenous being descendants of the early Portuguese and Spanish settlers. According to the Government, they are not discriminated against but nonetheless they seem to be resented by the increasingly vocal and active indigenous people. And, as Brazil gets more prosperous, which it is doing at a pretty smart pace, the resentment is increasing as these incomers are perceived to be taking an unfair share of the growing wealth.

'That said, our sources in Brazil also suggest that this perception is far from universal. But there is a degree of mainland Chinese interference going on both in resource exportation and in other less official areas of activity. It is also increasingly this that is causing the resentment and the backlash against the local and settled Chinese.'

David began to think he could see where this was going.

The UK was building strong commercial links with Brazil and there was no way that anything was going to be allowed to interfere with that. Yet haemorrhaging professionals and the like was a problem. Britain could not be seen to be in any way involved in this, however remotely. Whatever needed to be done was going to have to been done very carefully and initially probably outside of the formal inter-country links.

'Our problem,' Susie continued, 'is that we don't really know enough about what is going on beyond half stories and vague suppositions. The linkages to the UK, and within the UK, are convoluted, and are seemingly mixed up in the rivalries between the long-standing trafficking groups and intruding Chinese gangs. One thing is clear; to protect our Brazilian interests we have to unravel what is going on in the UK before we can move on to the international ramifications.'

David knew exactly where the meeting was going!

'And an independent investigation would both give credibility to the problem but also avoid any suggestion of British Government interference.'

It was the first significant thing that David had said, but it justified his being there, and even if it sounded like he was writing his own terms of reference Susie gave him an amused but grateful look. Being the good Foreign Office girl that she was she was always looking for the win-win situation, and getting David to make the investigation, something that he was well capable of doing, was in her view the way to achieve that end.

And, much to David's amusement, Susie installed herself as the link to the investigation.

11

David Hutchinson had had no idea about Susie Peveral's role in coordinating diplomatic and intelligence services. Their relationship hadn't developed sufficiently for her to share government secrets with him.

People trafficking was as old as time and, despite its evolution from the traditional slave trade to its modern variations developed by the sex industry, there was still a huge base load of people movements that were fundamentally economic.

People had always wanted to move to a better life and there were always people ready and willing to help them and to exploit them; this, too, was as old as time. The only things that had changed with the evolution of modern society were the ever-increasing range of countries from where the desperate economic migrants originated and the sophistication, reach, and commercial and technical knowhow of the organisations that trafficked them. Basically people trafficking was big business and it was Susie's firm conviction that its control was in the hands of large criminal syndicates that operated as much out of the importing nations as the exporting ones.

Susie knew all of this and more in great depth. Combating the traffickers was also big business and it was Ms Peveral's role in life to see that British knowledge and expertise were shared and used to maximum effect. Her seniority allowed her considerable freedom of action; this, coupled with a flexibility of mind that David readily recognised, also allowed her to step outside the more traditional Foreign Office modes of thinking. This wasn't always popular but it was the basis of her accelerated rise up the Civil Service ladder.

The combined use of both diplomatic and intelligence sources, something that it had been hard for Susie to get acknowledged and established outside of the normal historic run of the Cold War, the War on Terror and other such openly international challenges, had achieved some notable successes. These successes were not so much in the head count of illegal immigrants captured and returned to their source countries – that was a sad business that nobody took much pleasure in – it was more in the mapping of the traffickers' organisations and geographical activities. The complexities of the immigrant pathways and the complexities of the money-laundering routes that Susie Peveral and her cohorts had discovered forced a new awareness of the problems on to the world's political leaders.

The biggest shock to the British political consciousness was the scale of involvement, worldwide, of UK-based criminal groups. Prompted by such organisations as the Nigerian National Agency for the Prohibition of Trafficking of Persons, the United Nations had moved to the forefront of highlighting the problems, not just in Africa, where trafficking had been historically endemic, but also in the more so-called advanced countries.

'This UN Report makes interesting reading.' And if the Foreign Office Permanent Secretary thought something to be interesting reading, it was inevitably going to be.

'Modern Communications and Their Impact on the Illegal Movement of People around the World.'

It was the work of a new UN department whose inception owed much to Susie Peveral's endeavours.

People like Susie were used to the portentous and obscure titles of official documents. But what they were normally interested in, of course, was the content not the title. In this instance, it was the unexpected conclusion, buried in the detail of the report, that South America had emerged as the source of a new wave of migrants, who were being transported with surprising ease from Brazil, Argentina and even Chile to Canada and beyond – even, it seemed, to Australia. It was this document, along with Susie's and the Foreign Office's own intelligence, that had proved to be the genesis of the project that David Hutchison had agreed to undertake.

Back in the security of her own office after the briefing meeting with David, and after having successfully sold the idea of using external help from the media to force people trafficking up the public agenda as well as the Government's, Susie was almost exultant. Unlike an in-house report, at least David's work was guaranteed to be published, even if its circulation might end up being truncated.

And as she allowed herself a brief moment to daydream, a ping from her computer brought her back to reality. She was being copied the sort of document that both intrigued and irritated her. It said so much yet it still didn't say enough. But it did open up a new area of investigation with as yet unknown implications. The Australian brief suggested that the two strands of the overall trafficking endeavour that were emerging within their jurisdiction might well be totally separate.

'So,' she said addressing the computer screen, 'trafficking Chinese women to Australia may not be a part of the mainstream operation. But it's certainly riding on the back of it.'

The computer screen could offer no more elucidation than the words that she was reading.

The organised worldwide movements of illegal economic migrants, movements that were generally based on men, with women only as dependants, were still the politicians' principal focus and their nightmare. Trafficking women for the sex trade was always there as a basic operation, financially underpinning everything. But as the global activity had developed and become ever more organised and ever more commercialised, the sex trade part had moved into the background as it always attracted far more official attention than the trade in economic migrants. However, it was always seen as an inseparable part of the same illicit business activity. Now the Australians seemed to be saying something different; there was this presumption of a separate activity. At least there was for Australia; it was a potential complication that Susie knew had to be taken account of.

But was it as clear-cut as it seemed? Was it too simple a conclusion in such a complex environment? The bulk of the male and family immigrants, or potential immigrants, into Australia were certainly not trafficked by the big players emerging in the investigations around the world, as far as the Australians could tell. Whether that meant in their area that there were only local operations wasn't clear. Much of the Australian experience suggested small-scale activity, but they had no evidence that that was necessarily the whole story.

For women trafficking, particularly Chinese women, however, the evidence for a complex international operation was now beginning to emerge, even if the numbers that were being talked about were often single digit. Again, the picture was not clear.

'Maybe David will be able to throw light on it.'

Women trafficking, as a specific topic, wasn't strictly in David's brief but his known tendency to regard his brief as merely guidance was one of the reasons why Susie had wanted him.

The Australians were still not clear how the Chinese women were getting into the country, or more particularly why they were being brought in, but they had taken steps to be more proactive in this area. The inferences of British involvement in these steps meant nothing to Susie. The Australians had also established, in the half-dozen or so cases that they had become aware of, that the women were all educated professionals.

Nonetheless, there was also a rapidly growing but intuitive suspicion that the women trafficked into Australia were actually in transit. The country's ease of access to China appeared to be the key.

The Australians were learning fast.

12

Alice Hou knew that she was now in Australia and that Australia was the same sort of country as Canada. She also knew from the periods on the cruiser as it made its way across the Pacific Ocean, when conversation with the other three girls was possible, that they all had originally been trafficked to Canada from Brazil. At least two of them had said that they had. The fourth girl in the group appeared to be too traumatised to contribute to the conversations.

'How old are you?'

Scrubbing decks with Patience Zhang had been one of the opportunities to exchange stories.

'Twenty-five.'

Alice herself was twenty- six.

It soon transpired that Patience and the silent April Cheng had been forced to leave Brazil because, despite its burgeoning prosperity and their professional qualifications, non-indigenous people like them had difficulty in finding jobs. Both had faced prejudice and even violence when they tried to seek employment. They had left São Paulo of their own free will, aged twenty-five, but had used the services of a people trafficker who, as always, promised the earth, took their money and left them stranded in Canada. Like Alice and the fourth girl, Janice Liang, they had all qualified for Canadian passports as a result of residence, having an occupation that meant that they would be no burden on the Canadian taxpayer and were of good behaviour. How this had been managed with such ease in the normally rigorous Canadian system none of them knew but their identities had consequently been cast in stone by the authorities.

Patience and April, like Alice, had all still been paying off the costs of their journeys to Canada when they were kidnapped. Because of the so-called interest on their debts, they were getting no closer to settling them. Alice knew that this was the traditional trap of people in her position, especially as the interest rate had doubled once they were made Canadian citizens. As Patience had learned to her cost, the only means of enforcement that the traffickers then had was violence and the threat of putting them into prostitution. As distinct from Europe, where the illegal immigrant problem was massive, the traffickers were more relaxed about how they kept hold of their girls in Canada and understood the basic economics of the situation. The more the girls thrived, the more they thrived. That was until such time as they were confronted with a greater economic power, in which case, as with three of the girls, they were happy to sell their merchandise on no questions asked. Whether Janice Liang's experience in this respect was exactly the same as the others, Alice was never able to find out.

'They raped you!'

Alice's horror was matched by Patience's surprise that nothing similar had happened to her. It hadn't.

'We've all been raped and beaten up,' Patience said.

Again, Alice was unclear whether 'all' included Janice Liang.

Like Alice, Patience had been working as a waitress, despite being a qualified accountant. April and Janice had worked in the kitchens of a large hotel in Winnipeg. They both had similar middle-class qualifications.

Of the four girls brought together to Australia only Patience and Alice were living in the dormitory over the shops in Little

Bourke Street in Melbourne. Neither knew what had happened to April and Janice.

The uncertainty of what was going to happen to them was very stressful.

An explosion of crashes and screams shattered the sleep of the six occupants of the dormitory. The noise was rapidly approaching up the stairs.

Sleeping top to tail in three narrow beds there wasn't very much room to move around. As the women tumbled out of bed, they trampled over each other. Tempers flared.

'Alice!'

A rather plaintive Patience pushed her way towards her travelling companion. Knowing only each other, they tended to keep only each other's company.

The two men who smashed their way through the door were unknown to the women. They were followed after a few moments by a third man who hovered in the doorway initially. The original two Chinese men who forced their way into the tiny room were clearly thugs, the muscle in support of the third man, imposing his will before he deigned to enter the action.

Alice couldn't understand the harsh shrieks that the men were uttering but the hand gestures were obvious. They were being ordered to their knees. Partially brutalised by their recent treatment, all six did as they were bid.

The man who entered the room when all of the women were submissive and silence had returned was tall for a Chinese. He was followed painfully by the man who had in effect been their jailer.

Jo Li – a punning nickname that none of the girls understood, for he was surly and anything but jolly – was bleeding from a cut over his right eye. His battered state as much as the fierce determination of the two foot soldiers and cold disinterest of the tall man intimidated the six frightened women into a state of abject obedience.

'Alice Hou?'

The tall man addressed Jo Li but Alice knew that it was a demand for her to identify herself. The cold harsh tones of the man made Alice quail. She didn't have time to wonder what worse could happen to her but she somehow knew that whatever it was had started.

She stood up.

One of the foot soldiers backhanded her across the face and barked something at her, the words of which she didn't understand, but which clearly was an order for her to stay on her knees. She subsided, her cheek stinging from the force of the blow.

'My apologies, Miss Hou.'

If she had been in less of a panic, Alice might have interpreted the tall man's remark as the sarcasm that it was. He probably couldn't have cared less if she was in pain, only if she had been damaged. Again, if she had been in any sort of state to think about it, Alice would perhaps have realised that, despite the endless taping up of her face and her arms and legs, there was never any actual injury done either to her or to the other three girls. The four of them had been knowingly preserved, even if it wasn't apparent to any of them.

Jo Li was forced to the floor and under one of the beds. The five other girls were then forced to lie face down on the beds, leaving Alice still kneeling in front of the tall man, head down and senses numbed by what was happening. She was used to being regularly trussed up, but the only force that had ever been applied to her was that necessary to overcome her resistance to being bound.

This was different; that much she sensed, even if the same care to avoid permanent injury was being taken.

Alice was conscious that another person had come into the room. She was only aware that it was a woman and of her presence when she saw a pair of booted legs appear in her vision. That she could only see the woman's legs and feet said that she was very close to Alice.

Alice couldn't see what she was carrying but she soon found out.

Pulling her head up by her hair, the woman forced a wedge of material into Alice's mouth. The taste of the gag surprised Alice. In the past, all sorts of unpleasant things had been forced into her mouth. This time it was sterile like a medical bandage. The material bag that was then pulled over her head seemed to be equally clean and sterile. The woman moved quickly to bind the bag around Alice's neck with what she felt was more of the dreaded packaging tape.

Fighting to prevent herself being sick, Alice tossed herself from side to side. The woman grasped her head firmly but, as Alice later realised as she relived the day, gently, and told her very loudly in English to keep still.

'If you don't struggle, you won't get hurt.'

As Alice also again later realised, unlike the way that she had been spoken to before, it was said calmly and without menace.

In her terrified state Alice didn't think to wonder why the woman might have known that she would understand English more readily than Mandarin. Equally, since she was so stressed out, she didn't register that the accent of the woman was neither Canadian nor Australian, the only two English accents that she knew. Who the woman might have been wasn't something that exercised Alice at that point in her life.

'Hurry up!'

Alice heard the demand from the tall man. She knew it was the tall man; none of the foot soldiers ever spoke. In her current state of mind, the slight anxiety in the man's tone didn't register.

Her hands were roped behind her and her ankles roped together. Again, it was firmly done and not as painfully as in her previous experience. She had a limited movement within the ropes that had never been possible with the tape. Alice was lifted by one of the foot soldiers. From the hard pressure on her stomach and the pounding motion that went with it, it was obvious to her that she was being carried over the man's shoulder downstairs. The motion and the pounding in her stomach began to make her feel sick. Sweating, and with her pulse racing, she desperately struggled to control her breathing and to hold down the contents of her stomach.

The journey away from China Town was lost to Alice. The various motions that she was subject to completely confused her. The sounds of shouting, of blows and of what was clearly more violence, were beyond her ability to grasp as her brain's functions began to close down. Jo Li's colleagues and various assorted elements of the Melbourne Chinese underclass had rallied to prevent the removal of Alice from their protection. Well aware that Alice was a valuable trading commodity and well aware that the anger of their gang superiors could be unremitting and even fatal, the fighting was fierce if brief.

'Into the van!'

This was one piece of the action that did penetrate Alice's brain. But the grinding of the opening of the van's doors was for Alice overtaken by her being thrown on to the floor of the vehicle and all of the breath being knocked out of her. Forced to take in air only through her nose, she lost consciousness briefly as her oxygen intake was insufficient. She could feel the bitter vomit in her mouth as she came to. Frantically, she swallowed back the acid; it burned its way back down her gullet. Eventually, she managed to gulp in some air through her mouth as the convulsive movements that she was making forced the material plugging it partially out of it.

'Mother of God...'

She wasn't a very good Catholic so she could only recite parts of the liturgy that had otherwise failed to lodge in her brain as a child

The next problem for Alice after getting control of her breathing was that her brain began to take over again. But her brain was by no means as in command of her thoughts as her body was of her breathing.

She went into an immediate panic. She could feel her whole body stiffen. Even as her laboured breathing settled down, her head seemed to get hotter and hotter. Again, she struggled not to be sick. The material in her mouth was soggy and now bitter-tasting, but the tightness of the bag over her head made ejecting it completely impossible.

Then she lost consciousness again and for a period knew nothing more of the journey that she was being forced to undertake.

Julie Li was concerned about the captive.

'I need to check that she's OK. She might have settled down, but we have to be sure she hasn't quietly choked herself to death.'

The tall man didn't seem very interested. He'd done his bit – he had removed this Alice Hou from the custody of the rival group; it wasn't his job to keep her alive.

'We've gone to all this trouble to procure this woman because she's supposed to be a virgin and twice as valuable as the rest. And we've started a war to do it. The last thing we need is for her to die on us!'

She was angry at the callousness of the man sitting lazily beside the driver.

But Kim Lee Sung knew she was right. Which bit of his half-Korean, half-Chinese self inhibited him from accepting and agreeing with what a woman said to him, he wouldn't have known. He was suspicious of this Julie Li, he didn't know where she had come from, he didn't like the Europeanised name she used and he didn't like the aura of self-confidence that she generated. She wasn't deferential enough for him.

'She's too Australian, too European,' he had said to the elderly Chinese man who had told him that she was joining his team.

Of course, he knew what he meant; she did have something

ın-Chinese about her face and about her manner, and she did
wear her skirts too short for the blood pressure of the younger
members of the organisation. Nonetheless, she was good at
what she did; she knew a lot of people in and around the
Australian Police, and enough manufactured dirt about them
to ensure at least their inaction in the face of the activities that
they engaged in.

Julie knew just about enough about Mr Kim to know that
the half grunt, half shrug was all that she was going to get by
way of agreement to check out the young woman prone on the
floor of the vehicle.

In the back of the camper van, she eased the bag from
Alice's head. It was very dark since they had long since left
Melbourne and its surrounding conurbations. She knew that
they were heading for Echuca but she neither knew exactly
where that was nor how long it would take to get there. Julie
knew very little about Australia outside of the confines of
Melbourne. In her new situation, this was something of a
worry to her.

Directed by feel and by smell, Julie removed the head bag
and caught the surge of foul-smelling liquid that it had held
back in another length of sterile material. She wiped Alice's
face both of accumulated sweat and vomit.

'Ahrr!'

The exclamation indicated that the foul smell had wafted its
way into the front cabin of the vehicle.

Unable to see Julie because of the darkness and her eyes
having been covered for several hours, Alice could get no sense
of the woman who was working on her. Her body ached from
lying on the hard metal floor of the camper van and from the
restraint of the ropes around her wrists and ankles; the quick
and vigorous way in which she was being wiped down told her
nothing.

'You'd better try and sit up.'

Still dressed in her scanty nightwear, Alice was freezing cold, numb in her extremities and still fighting the desire to be sick. She struggled to force herself upright; Julie didn't offer to help her.

As her eyes became accustomed to the gloom of the sleeping compartment of the camper van, Alice began to discern the outline of the woman who was wiping her face and neck again. But she still couldn't sense whether this woman was as hostile to her as the tall man whom she remembered from the dormitory. Where the man was she had no idea, but as she became more aware of her situation she had no doubt that he would be in the vehicle that they were travelling in.

Alice wore only a rather tattered T-shirt to cover her upper body, and Julie could see that she was both pretty and possessed of a very well-proportioned figure. And as she completed her task of tidying up Alice's face and inserted another wedge of material into her mouth, she became aware that her legs and the floor of the van were covered with yet more evil-smelling detritus.

'Jesus,' she muttered, 'she's shit herself!'

There wasn't much that Julie could do. Grabbing a towel from the camper van's tiny shower compartment, she mopped up as much of the faeces that she could and pitched the towel out of the van window.

'What are you doing?'

Alerted by the cold draught, Kim was out of his seat and turning to come back to where Julie was crouching beside the seated Alice.

'Ahrr!'

'I was getting rid of a load of her shit out of the window.'

Turning on the van light, something that Julie had tried to avoid, it was obvious what the problem was. Kim retreated.

'Get her sorted again!'

Once he was back in his seat beside the driver, Julie reached for her shoulder bag. When Alice saw the silver roll of packaging tape she let out a strangled cry of terror.

'I'm sorry,' whispered Julie, 'the hood is too foul to put back on. I have to do this to you.'

She tore off a length of tape and placed it loosely over Alice's mouth and pressed it down. She did the same with her eyes. As she watched, she saw Alice flex her face muscles and realise that the strapping was not as painfully tight as she had expected.

Julie pulled a blanket off one of the camper van beds and wrapped it around Alice.

Alice settled again after Julie withdrew. The sense she now got of the woman working on her was one of careful and caring treatment of her. As her primitive instincts began to reassert themselves and the desire to escape entered her head, she began to find the other woman's behaviour very confusing.

As the camper van passed through a small settlement and mobile phone coverage resumed, Mr Kim's BlackBerry bleeped.

The email was short and precise.

'Take the woman to the agreed address. Miss Li can get her some decent clothes and start tutoring her. She knows what's required. She will tell you when the woman is ready to move on. After the last cock-up in Hong Kong, we will need to plan the handover much more carefully. Our client is not only very wealthy but also very powerful, with a considerable reach. Send the camper van back to Melbourne, but, before you do, go to Swan Hill and hire a car for a month. You must try and leave no signature in Echuca. X.'

Mr Kim gave a wry smile. Mr Xu's signature initial always gave him a feeling of unreality. A parting kiss was just about the last thing that he could imagine his boss sending him. Requiring absolute obedience Mr Xu was just about the most intimidating person Kim Lee Sung had ever met; and he'd met a few people in his time.

It was almost midnight when the camper van pulled up at the water's edge near the river-boat landing jetty at Echuca. As they had envisaged, the area was almost deserted. The Murray

81

River was very low and the floating jetty was well down, creating quite a steep slope down to the water. The unequal height of the two men manhandling the large wicker hamper down to the skiff moored at the jetty caused some raucous amusement to the only observer of the scene. Satisfied that the man was probably too drunk to remember anything, the party set off upriver towards a group of moored river boats. Mingled in with the aging and picturesque paddle boats was a modern vessel with high, almost pyramidal, superstructure and a fore-deck sun lounge that allowed the hamper to be easily landed on the vessel.

Kim and the driver settled to watch a martial arts DVD that was among the stock that came with the home cinema equipment, leaving Julie to deal with Alice. She made her comfortable in the tiny dressing room that interconnected with the main bedroom, first un-taping her, and then withdrew to the galley kitchen. Julie had a lot of planning to do on how she would deal with Alice and Mr Kim.

A reheated Chinese meal bought on the journey that attracted only the contempt of Kim and the driver but seemed to satisfy Alice and Julie provided the only break in the two men's sustained binge-watching of violent DVDs. Allowing Alice to shower and then forcing her to sleep naked provided all of the security that Julie thought necessary. For Kim, it was as if Alice no longer existed; Julie existed only in so far as it was necessary to give her instructions. If Julie had had any fears of the two men taking advantage of Alice, they were dispelled by her limited but frightening knowledge of Mr Xu and his likely reaction to any despoiling of her prisoner. Alice was money, lots of it, and there was no way that she was going to be devalued.

Settled, with Alice imprisoned in the dressing room beside her, Julie lay awake and spent time considering her next moves. Improvisation was the only modus operandi possible. She still sensed Kim's distrust; she had work to do to overcome that, and she doubted whether she ever would completely. He, in his turn, she knew, was planning his actions for the next day. She had no idea what his instructions were but going to Swan Hill to hire a car and getting rid of the camper van and driver were a challenge because he trusted neither her nor the driver. Eventually, she slept.

Melbourne Gazette
Continental Edition – Thursday, 1 July 2010
POLICE RAID IN CHINA TOWN –
PEOPLE-TRAFFICKING OPERATION UNCOVERED
Police were called to a disturbance at premises in Little Bourke Street yesterday after there were claims of a fight between two groups of Chinese men and suspicions that someone had been taken away from one of the flats above the 'Golden Lion' buffet restaurant. The police were accompanied by Federal Police officers and Federal Immigration officers.

On arrival, the police were advised that it had been a domestic matter – a young woman was seeing a man that her parents considered unsuitable. The situation was now resolved. The injuries to at least one of the Chinese men however, seemed to be sufficiently severe for the police to insist on searching the premises and questioning all of the occupants.

None of the men remaining at the scene could give an explanation for why the vehicle, thought to be a cult VW Camper Van, had been seen speeding away from the alleyway adjoining the restaurant with little regard for the safety of the people in the vicinity. Opinions differed on how many other Chinese men had left the scene.

In a top-floor bedroom, which showed evidence of violent entry, the police found five Chinese women, four of whom were from Indonesia; the fifth was subsequently established to be a Canadian citizen. All five were taken into protective custody. Four Chinese men were arrested.

The Assistant Commissioner of Victorian Police later issued a statement saying that the discovery had added to evidence gathered in previous raids that had yielded a number of Chinese women apparently destined for the sex trade.

'We are hopeful that these young women will be able to add to our knowledge of the entry routes for these girls, some of whom are as young as fourteen.' At a later press conference the Assistant Commissioner commented on how a Canadian

woman, in her mid-twenties, had ended up in this situation.

'Her evidence has given us a number of leads on how she entered Australia but it has also raised questions about how she arrived in Canada and obtained a Canadian passport. The young woman was born in Brazil. Our Canadian colleagues have been informed of the detention of this woman and we are also keeping the Brazilian Embassy in Canberra in the picture.'

13

As she had left the offices in St Kilda Road with the gorgeous Alan, Julie Kershawe, now totally unexpectedly an operative of the Australian Security Service, was in a state of shock and awe. The shock related to the convoluted way she had been set up and induced into coming to Australia; the awe to how readily she had been accepted and co-opted into the secret workings of her new employers. Her new masters had clearly done an incredible amount of homework to satisfy themselves about her before so speedily welcoming her into their ranks. The fact that she was needed made her feel good, but in ignorance as yet of what she had been recruited to do her natural caution now began to surface. It was exciting, but she needed to know much more before she would be comfortable. The recognition that she had been so easily set up and manipulated by the Border Agency (through Tariq al Hussaini) hadn't done much for her self-confidence either.

And then, of course, there was Alan.

He was good-looking, enigmatic and largely unreadable and Julie was both attracted to him and somehow repelled by him as well. There was something so artificial about him that she found it difficult to be relaxed in his company. He seemed more like an incompletely sketched-out soap-opera character.

And as he shepherded her on to a tram, she was very conscious that, just as the situation at the office had been orchestrated, so had their careful departure.

'I thought I might show you some of the sights of Melbourne you may not have come across yet.'

Why this simple statement put Julie on her guard she wasn't sure. It sounded like a chat-up line but she wasn't sure that it was meant to be. Alan hadn't changed from the amiable, relaxed, unhurried and almost cardboard person that he had always been for her. But why would he now want to show her the sights on the company's time?

Maybe it was a chat-up; maybe it was a test?

Alan was impassive beside her; how would she ever know what he was thinking?

'Oh, shit, perhaps he just wants sex but isn't sure that he's going to get it!'

She laughed aloud at the thought and settled to see what would transpire. They were just getting off the tram near the Aquarium, so Alan only managed to give her a quizzical look before he headed off across the Yarra River, towards the tall buildings on the other side.

'The Eureka Tower.'

Julie had heard of it; she'd been impressed by its towering presence but she had never thought that she would ever have any need to go there.

Again Alan organised everything and they were rocketing up in a special lift to the eighty-eighth floor before she could grasp what was happening.

'I don't know about sights,' she said as they came out of the lift. 'I guess up here you get to see all of Melbourne.'

Alan grinned. It was a sort of mechanical schoolboy grin that was more an acknowledgement that she had spoken than an expression of pleasure. It didn't tell Julie anything.

'Come on then.'

Why the sudden hurry? thought Julie.

They funnelled into a roped-off area at one end of the viewing gallery and Alan spoke to the young man standing by a rather anonymous-looking door. And then, before she knew

87

it, Alan had led her into a glass-sided box – except that it was glass-bottomed and glass-topped as well, and it moved.

Julie stood beside Alan with her back to the outside wall of the glass box looking back at the door through which they had entered. Slowly, the glass cube moved away from the tower. Then everything was clear to her; she knew exactly where she was and why she was there.

Shit! she thought. *This is the Skydeck 88, the Edge. The bastard's testing me out.*

So he was but, as she turned to look at him, Julie realised that Alan was also testing himself out. For once, his eyes were readable and what she saw in them was anxiety. Alan was very uncomfortable about being suspended hundreds of metres above the Melbourne business area supported by nothing more than thick glass.

'Yes!' she said to herself in some satisfaction.

She moved into the middle of the cube. Below like a miniature moving picture Melbourne got on with its normal life. She didn't look down; she wasn't quite ready for that.

He's far more scared than I am, she told herself.

The experience didn't last long but the relationship between them had changed. Never since she had been at the height of her powers in her job in Edinburgh had she felt so much in command of herself and of her situation. Whether he had meant to or not, Alan had totally restored her feelings of self-worth and turned her into the capable and competent operative that his organisation needed.

When they left the glass cube, Alan reverted to his previous inscrutability. Julie tried to hide her exhilaration.

'That was clever,' she said to him.

She didn't explain what was and he didn't ask.

Lunch in a bustling Crown Plaza wine bar added nothing to her knowledge of Alan but clarified a few basics about the job in hand.

Alan's intentions towards Julie were clearly impersonal and

Julie found her thought processes almost in disarray. Something very physical in her was disappointed; she hadn't slept with a man since she had parted company with Tariq al Hussaini, and she found that she missed his exuberant lovemaking. She couldn't quite see Alan as an alternative, but she still had needs and his indifference did nothing to quell them.

Why were they so keen to reinforce the fact that the Chinese women that I let into the UK have disappeared? she wondered.

Feeling much more confident in herself now, Julie's brain had resumed normal service and was already questioning things that she remembered from her interview in St Kilda. Alan rather faded from her mind as she reconsidered the whole performance afresh. And it was definitely a performance, stage-managed with the outcome preordained. But why? The question kept coming back to her as she thought about her day.

After a long soak in the bath, a ready meal from her freezer and much cogitation, she decided that, although she had obviously been set up for the interview and the job over a long period, what she was needed for had to have something to do with the disappeared Chinese women. What, she still couldn't imagine.

As she questioned herself, her mirror provided her with a clue.

'I'm half Chinese but I could easily be taken for being fully Chinese.'

She could indeed!

Then it was next day.

Julie had been instructed to meet Alan at the Queen Victoria Market. She'd been there before. Someone of her limited financial means would inevitably gravitate to such a place.

Apart from the mass-produced Aboriginal trash artefacts, the market was much the same as markets that she had seen in

England and Scotland. Getting there by tram and foot was easy enough.

Idling at the tram stop as she set out, Julie wondered whether a stage-managed meeting at the market was another test. The arrangement was to meet at eleven o'clock with no location specified – was locating Alan the test? The delicately featured Chinese girl who was already at the tram stop gave her a friendly inclusive grin and looked as if she was about to open a conversation. The arrival of the tram forestalled the action, if she was. The girl did sit opposite Julie but, apart from the continuing ever-ready grin, there were no obvious signs now that conversation had been her intention.

Reminded of her own proposition that she looked much more Chinese than European, Julie studied the girl whenever she got the opportunity without actually staring. Black hair, high cheek bones and almond-shaped eyes; the defining features of the Mongoloid peoples were clearly there. The symmetry of the face and its delicate colouring were all of girl's own.

She's really beautiful: I'm not beautiful. … And she's a hell of a lot better dressed!

The jeans that the girl had been poured into Julie knew were expensive and Italian. The matching ankle boots and handbag owed more to Gucci than any Australian designer and the quilted jacket only attracted Julie's envy.

And she was getting off the tram at the market.

Letting her pass in front of her, Julie watched the girl – hardly really a girl; she guessed she was in her late-twenties – step neatly off the tram and head off towards the entrance to the market. Julie trailed after her, losing interest by the footstep.

Goodness!

Julie's interest returned sharply when the girl was met as she crossed into the open side of the market by a Chinese man of exceptional height. The man not only stood out above the various Chinese people that were near him but also above many of the white Australians as well.

'Kim Lee Sung. You will need to remember him.'

The visit to the Queen Victoria Market wasn't a test. From where Julie lived Alan knew exactly which tram she would get and when. He had quietly moved to her side.

'So why should I remember him?'

She got no answer. But Julie did get a surprise when she realised that she and Alan were unobtrusively following the said Kim Lee Sung and his girl companion.

It wasn't a hard task. The disparity between the heights of the two of them easily marked them out. Then they stopped walking and waited and, to her surprise yet again, Alan suddenly wasn't there. The diminutive girl walked back to where Julie was standing and took her by the arm. Julie allowed herself to be led up to Mr Kim.

'This her?'

The question was addressed to the girl, who nodded. Mr Kim gestured Julie towards a gap between the stalls. Feeling compelled to follow where he indicated, she moved off warily. As she glanced back, the young Chinese woman had dis-appeared as readily as Alan had. Julie was left with Kim who looked at her with some distaste, in much the way that many Chinese men did womenfolk. It was something that she was not used to but which from Alan's lunchtime briefing she knew she was going to have to learn to accept. Even in Australia among the Chinese community there were still plenty of men who saw women as lesser beings.

The rest of Alan's briefing had been much more interesting. And in retrospect she recognised that it had been predicated entirely on her being taken as fully Chinese. It wasn't clear which organisation she was going to have to infiltrate, but equally that was largely because the Security Service didn't really know. They only had whispers and rumours and a string of outcomes that they didn't much like. Her training as an investigative officer was key but, like her skill at karate, that was taken for granted.

This first meeting with Mr Kim provided nothing but another new mobile phone for Julie and an instruction to await a call. Whether the man remembered that Alan and the beautiful little Chinese girl had existed she had no way of telling; as yet, like Alan, she had found no way of reading him.

When she next saw Alan it was much more carefully arranged; she, he told her, was very much on probation with Mr Kim and his friends.

Their conversation was fractious.

'They call her Lucy Liu after the *Charlie's Angels* actress.'

'Shit, Alan, never mind that! Why did you just disappear like that?'

'I was only there to deliver you.'

'Deliver me. I'm not a parcel, for heaven's sake.'

'You are to Kim. Where he comes from women are treated as property. You're only as good as what you can do for him.'

'Which he obviously has yet to tell me.'

'Stay with him – he will.'

'So who is this Lucy Liu then, Alan?'

'She's a Singapore police lieutenant now on her way back home to resume her normal duties.'

'And if he asks?'

'He won't; he'll have forgotten her by the time you see him next.'

14

As an acknowledgement of, rather than as a thank you for, her successful delivery of the two Chinese ex-schoolgirls turned marriageable young women, Linda Shen was allowed to dally a couple of days in Hong Kong rather than continue on with them to Shanghai. It was the closest that her husband, Mr Shi, was ever likely to get to any sort of expression of appreciation towards his wife.

'Up there!'

Linda knew that the direction that she was giving to her minder was wrong. It was intended to be. The Hong Kong police's approach to traffic discipline was rather more derived from its British antecedents than from its Chinese. The minder's protest to Linda was cut short by the heavy intervention of a traffic police sergeant who regarded the man's efforts to overawe him with his employer's credentials as tantamount to bribery and arrested him. Linda's protests were token, and, as a woman's, ignored.

With the car impounded, Linda Shen was forced to walk.

'Yes!'

Her delight, seen by several passers-by, was expressed in a wholly un-Chinese display of punching the air. Her son and her married bondage forgotten for a few brief hours, she set off for Kowloon and the Miramar Hotel. Locating a mass-transit railway station and squeezing into the chaos of the late-morning commuter traffic stirred memories that normally she would have tried to suppress. Her life of luxury and personal transport had insulated her from such experiences in Shanghai, but she was as exhilarated by them now as she would have once have been in Glasgow or London. And, if nothing else, the air in Hong Kong was purer.

Born in Manchester, with a good tranche of A levels, she had been denied university by a cash-strapped father, who put all of his resources into educating his three sons. But her qualifications were enough for her to enter the only profession that her father would positively have opposed had she still been under his protection. Her quick passage through the Greater Manchester and Strathclyde police forces to the UK Border Agency had brought her maturity and independence. It had also brought her into contact with the seamier side of Chinese life in Britain and eventually to an uncomfortable journey that ended in Shanghai.

They didn't miss me.

The first time that she had been able to snatch an opportunity to trawl the Internet she had found that her disappearance had raised very little interest and was soon forgotten. In the private confines of the Border Agency, there was concern but this was more about their own loss than her well-being. She was aware that the computer wizards that her husband employed had similarly checked to see whether her tracks had been covered. A very private man for a variety of necessary business reasons, Mr Shi didn't want anything from his wife's past to cause him any problems in the future.

The old bastard knows full well where I came from and what I did.

Linda had confided in a couple of other trophy wives that she was allowed to socialise with. They, too, like maybe half a dozen other women in China, were also bought wives with backgrounds and valuable passports – and babies used to shackle them to their husband's interests.

For special guests, the Miramar had an exclusive internet café with protected and probably the most secure Internet access in China. It didn't take Linda long to check out her investments and to satisfy herself that they were both proving productive and were secure from the curious eyes of her husband and his hackers.

An hour's social browsing, lunch and then a more serious search for any references to the missing schoolgirls that she had chaperoned again led to dead ends. The Chinese and British police could find no trace of them after they were formally admitted to the UK. But it was only when they had disappeared that they had actually started looking. And it was now two years later.

At least, nothing will get back to him.

Linda never ever thought of her husband by his name; 'him' or the 'old bastard' were her normal forms of reference.

She probably cared no more about the two women than her husband did – she knew that they had not been physically harmed; that was enough. Her interest lay only with her son. She made it her business to know as much as possible about her husband's activities, not just to profit where she could, but to anticipate any threats to him that might affect her and her child. She knew that she could not escape for many years but she was equally sure that in the end she would be able to and was determined to be prepared. Nothing that she did for her husband during these years was going to cause any repercussions for her if she could avoid it.

Her flow of thoughts were suddenly interrupted.

'Julie Kershawe! Jesus, what happened to her?'

Her newspaper searching had exposed the story of Julie's precipitate departure from the Border Agency and the suspicions that surrounded it. Julie had been her superior briefly in Edinburgh and she had had great respect for her.

Linda couldn't believe what she was reading.

The reported story had been carefully edited. Since the newspaper was silent about the involvement of Tariq al Hussaini, both she and other readers of the articles had only a limited and sanitised view of events.

From her own dealings with Julie, Linda could not accept the idea that her boss had been involved in some kind of treachery as the media was implying. Used as she was becoming to the convoluted and devious machinations of her husband and his business partners, her instinct was to assume that there was much more to the story than was being published and it wouldn't necessarily reflect badly on Julie.

15

How the Singaporean police lieutenant had charmed her way into the confidence of the notoriously misogynistic Kim Lee Sung, Julie Kershawe – now Julie Li, using her mother's maiden name – never found out. Equally, how Alan became involved as a clandestine procurer of criminal Chinese women she also never found out. But what she was told was that she was now a fugitive from UK justice. An investigation into Tariq al Hussaini's activities in the UK had purported to implicate her as a participant in an immigration fraud. The Australian Federal Police were hunting for her, albeit in a rather sedate and unhurried way.

'Usual thing,' Alan had said, 'keep the cover story as close to reality as possible.'

Even if the reality was also invented, thought Julie, now totally convinced that her retreat to Australia was set up as much to provide her with a cover story as it was to expose Tariq.

'So now Mr Kim thinks that he has a hold over me?'

'He certainly does – we've made sure of that – and he will make that plain to you pretty damn quick, I don't doubt. Through his supposed corrupt contacts with the Federal Police we will be feeding enough information to him so that he knows that a police search is closing in on you. Lucy Liu sold him the idea that you were both tough physically but also very good at managing relations with the various authorities you used to have to deal with. She also fed him the thought that he needs someone like you around to help him handle the girls that he is trafficking. A bit of sophistication, she called it, but I doubt she said that to Kim! But be on your guard – he's a devious and sadistic bastard and a classic out-and-out bully.'

'And an out-and-out coward?' pondered Julie.

'I wouldn't count on it.'

It was their last set-up meeting. Alan simply faded into the background to watch. Mr Kim's true character wasn't the only thing that Julie couldn't now count on. She was on her own. Of course, she had been told all the usual spy stuff about the authorities denying her existence if she was caught – but this wasn't deepest Cold War Russia; it was suburban Australia. Not quite her own backyard but as near as. How substantial this denial would be she never had to find out.

Julie didn't feel that she was going to miss Alan – he might have a pretty face but he was far too cold a fish for her. Her instinct was to relish a new challenge, even if there were rather more unknowns than she had been used to dealing with.

Except I don't really know where this people trafficking thing is likely to take me.

Nor did she. Kim had set up another meeting with her in the Treasury Gardens, at a place that could be observed from all directions. Trust wasn't one of the man's strong points. She had a couple of days to prepare herself and to think out how she might develop her relationship with him. Lacking the beauty and allure of the Singapore police lieutenant but unaware as yet of what qualities she was supposed to have in the eyes of Mr Kim and his employers, there was little she could do beyond clearing her mind of her previous existence and rehearsing her Mandarin in front of her bedroom mirror.

But, if Julie Li (Kershawe) couldn't count on Kim Lee Sung's character, there were those like David Hutchinson who were beginning both to figure out and understand the character of the man that he came to know as Joe Kim.

Susie Peveral made it very clear to David that further briefing on the illegal immigration traffic would be given on a strictly personal and private basis.

David was more amused than alarmed.

How the shit had he got into this situation? The first time he'd seen this delectable woman in her true colours after university, she was up against some crappy stage furniture in that storeroom at the O2 Arena. Then it was her with her expensive designer jeans around her ankles and him with his cheap ones around his,

They had just arrived at the block of flats in Islington where Susie lived. Nothing was now further from David's mind than the ravenous young civil servant paying for her entry to a concert by her supposed favourite pop star by offering him gratuitous sex.

Things had very much moved on.

What David didn't know until very recently was that after the incident at the O2 Arena Susie had become about as obsessed as a woman of her self-contained character was ever likely to be with her former college acquaintance and had developed a yearning for the fierce straightforward sex that they had indulged in. She had wanted more. The work that she was doing on the international movements of illegal workers across and around the world and the opinion of her Permanent Secretary that a deniable independent investigation by a non-governmental resource might be the best approach gave her her opportunity.

Given her knowledge of David, it didn't take Susie long to devise a project that would be attractive to him. It was the knowledge of what she was planning that added to Susie's excitement and to the success of their ramble around the West Country. His holiday heart-searching only added to her anticipation of both a successful working relationship and a satisfying sexual one. The selling point she had made to herself was very much in terms of time spent in bed with him.

And success in her project wouldn't do her career prospects any harm either.

Everything went exactly as she had planned it; things usually did for Susie Peveral.

'Help yourself to a drink. I'll have a sweet Martini.'

Susie immediately disappeared into the nether regions of her flat.

Left to fend for himself, David renewed his acquaintance with Susie's apartment. It was tasteful, austere and minimalist. He rather liked that. But it seemed to offer no indication of Susie's personality. That didn't surprise him either.

'Jesus, it's so organised and sterile, it's hard to believe that she actually lives here.'

But he knew that that was Susie Peveral. Personal photographs would be hidden somewhere in a leather-bound album; her idea of decoration was enigmatic unframed oil paintings by obscure British artists and grotesque Japanese porcelain figures.

David shed his coat and hung it in the open-fronted hall cupboard. Her supply of drinks in the corner bar was expensive and extensive. Having helped himself to a generous portion of a single malt whisky that he knew to be rather rare and poured her an equally generous Martini, he sat down and waited. Familiar with the habits of a range of passing girlfriends of a variety of nationalities, he didn't bother to wonder where she had gone after she'd steered him into the light, bright and white lounge area. Women always wanted to attend to their make-up or change their shoes or something; it seemed like a virility point to David.

He hadn't really noticed what she was wearing at the briefing; only that, when she came to join him again, she'd changed. David took her slender, gym-honed body for granted and what she had changed into was expensive, simple and very effective.

'Thanks.'

Susie took the Martini from him and, with the guileless guile that he now knew to be typical of her, sat opposite him to display herself to maximum effect. Nothing was further from the image of a highly regarded and competent Assistant Secretary in the Foreign Office that he could imagine.

Susie was pretty but not beautiful. Her face had character and was always made up in an understated way. Her unremarkable middling-brown hair was always neat but natural looking.

'You're looking good!'

She smirked at the compliment; David hadn't offered her many.

By comparison with her managed looks, David's suntanned, open and friendly face immediately stirred Susie's emotions and brought colour to her cheeks. It was the admission of the final surrender to her more basic instincts over her usually controlled feelings that induced the blush. She wanted David and she wanted him with a steadily mounting urgency that she struggled to overcome. A keen observer by profession, he was used to seeing and translating emotions into words and actual pictures, so her obvious stimulation in his presence didn't go unnoticed.

She sat opposite him in a finishing-school pose, her slender elegant legs pulled together and turned half sideways. She sat back on the settee, her back straight; her ample firm beasts stood out but were not pushed out; in everything she did she moved easily and unhurriedly. She sipped her drink and pulled at her tartan miniskirt in an ineffectual effort to make it cover her knees. Both actions seemed to be instinctive rather than intentional.

God, does she never not *want sex? Damn her, she knows she's going to get it.*

The half-suppressed chuckle that went with this thought raised an eyebrow in Susie but nothing more.

'So, are you happy with what you're being asked to do?'

101

Susie wanted to get the business side of their relationship out of the way before the prospect of having David in her bed overwhelmed her.

'The study? Oh, yes!'

He had taken his jacket off and lounged back in the armchair that he had chosen to avoid being brought too quickly into body contact with her. Susie moistened her lips, aware of his equally well-honed figure as he relaxed his position. He wasn't quite six feet but his body was well proportioned and lean. Front on to her she tried hard not to stare at his lower body. She was beginning to feel warm.

Then it happened.

Susie stood up and in a quick movement dropped her miniskirt to her ankles and stepped out of it. When he realised that one of the things that Susie had been doing when she went to her bedroom to change out of her business clothes was remove her underwear, David's restraint broke down. Getting out of his trousers was a far less elegant exercise than her skirt dropping, but it soon got them on to equal terms.

The horny bitch must have planned the whole thing in advance!

Of course she had.

Susie backed towards the wall of the room. David knew that a repeat of the O2 Arena storeroom was required of him.

As she felt him thrust inside her, Susie lost complete control for the first time since that memorable day and mewed and moaned as she had at the Dome. The feeling of helplessness and surrender that came over her lasted until she felt David withdraw and then the feeling of power and control slowly crept back. But it was a feeling hedged around by a warm glow of satisfaction.

It was so different from the leisured times that they had spent in bed on holiday. It was as if they were two different people. Susie was fascinated by the way that they could fire up on such occasions as the O2 Arena and now, but mystified and

102

a little frightened that she could act with such abandon.

In the warmth of Susie's large and spacious bath, David's feelings were rather more mixed up than hers. The situation was simple to her. She had a job to do and had secured the help of the one man she most wanted in her bed. It was a perfect scenario. But Susie, as well as having the rapidly disappearing inhibitions of her background, also had its basic honesty. Self-gratification she knew full well was a part of what was going on.

David, on the other hand, had a vague sense of being used. But try as might he couldn't work up any real anger about it. Never one to stand on his dignity and for one whose only pride was in the excellence of his work, his irritation quickly turned to amusement. The idea of being paid in money and in sex seemed to him to be a great bargain. The idea of being tied down in a stable relationship was taking longer to assert itself in his mind.

She'd be absolute shit as a honey-trap spy, he thought.

And he almost said so. It wasn't that he realised such a comment would be very hurtful, it was more that he knew instinctively that Susie just wouldn't understand the inference; she took herself too seriously.

In any event, Susie had other thoughts to pursue.

'So what do you know about this bloke Igor Petrov?'

'Jesus! Susie. Where did that come from?'

As she laid back against him running her hand down the soapy wetness of his inside leg, the unexpectedness of the question made him almost forget the sensation that she was creating. Almost.

David arrested her hand before it encroached too far up and generated feelings that it might be too difficult to control. If she wanted to talk business, he was happy for that, too, but combining business and pleasure was more than he felt inclined to in their present situation. For once, Susie seemed to sense his hesitation. Gently, she eased his hand so that it came to rest around her right breast and gave a little sigh of contentment.

Pleasure seemed to win out with her, too; but only seemed to.

'Petrov?'

Strike that, he thought, *she's anything but shit!*

But she didn't wait for an answer.

'Have you ever heard of a Joe Kim?'

'Why do you want to know?'

'Do you know who he is?'

David was disappointed, even relaxed in a warm bath and after very satisfying sex, Susie, it seemed, still could never quite let go the business side of things. She was getting impatient. She wanted an answer. David answered her first question.

'I took Petrov's photo in circumstances that I regretted. That's it. That's all I know.'

'Petrov was an East European thug who for every fifty labourers and field workers he smuggled into the UK brought a young woman for purposes that we can only guess at. Latterly, these women have all been Chinese.'

'OK, OK.'

David reacted to the harder tone that Susie adopted as much because she was squeezing his hand harder around her breast as because she was challenging his reluctance to admit something that she thought he knew.

David had slept with many women, but he would have been the first to admit that Susie's combination of stimulation and inquisition was way beyond his experience.

Whatever he thought, or wanted, she was clearly going to mix business and pleasure!

'All I know,' he said, 'is that, yes, the dead man was an East European of pretty unsavoury character and behaviour. How he ended up in the sea off the Dorset coast I haven't a clue.'

David wasn't sure whether she believed him, or why she shouldn't have.

Out of the bath and in bed again, Susie at least seemed prepared to let the subject drop. But there was the second question she'd asked.

But who the shit is this Kim? David thought. *Why throw his name at me?*

He asked.

Susie pulled him on to her and found his mouth with hers. David pushed away.

'You're an irritating bitch,' he said as he settled her head more comfortably on his chest. 'So who is Joe Kim, then? Having started the conversation in your bath, we might as well finish it.'

Susie giggled. Her reversion to schoolgirl was one of the things that had delighted him on their holiday. Then she was serious again, almost.

'Last briefing,' she said with a twinkle.

'There's some sort of dog-eat-dog hassle going on among the people traffickers. Petrov could well have been a casualty of it. The police in Lincolnshire and West Midlands think that either someone is getting too greedy or someone is trying to take over the whole deal. We don't know.'

'Someone? Didn't you mention the Chinese? They seem to be into everything these days.'

Susie rolled around the bed so that she was kneeling over Hutchinson. As she sunk down again on to his erection, she shook her head to signify the conversation really was over.

Not quite.

She said, 'You need to look out for Joe Kim.'

David didn't have time to wonder what he was to look out for.

16

David Hutchinson's London flat was high up in a Barbican tower block. He loved the place; it had the ambience of the City of London, yet it also had a cosmopolitan atmosphere and was in proximity to everything that he enjoyed about London.

The telephone rang, interrupting his train of thought.

'David Hutchinson.'

It was a call that he had been expecting.

Susie Peveral had continued her mixture of business and pleasure into the next day. It was Saturday. Much to David's amusement and initial irritation, she both celebrated his commission to investigate the growing involvement of criminal gangs in illegal immigration and briefed him on it as well.

By the time they made it to a late lunch at Susie's favourite Thai restaurant there wasn't much that David didn't know about trafficked farm labour, the black market in professional immigrants, women forced into the sex trade, and Susie's concerns about the emerging trade in individual Chinese women that seemed to contradict the usual stereotypes and generalisations.

He was aware that this last was something of a hobbyhorse for Susie; his sense that his UK investigations were a precursor to something more challenging grew with every conversation with her.

Early rising was something that fitted very easily into David's lifestyle.

He was heading for Cambridge and towards Peterborough

and the A15 before he was fully switched on to what was happening.

The call from Susie's contact in the Home Office was an opening into the world of suspected illegal immigration that he had been looking for but it didn't come in the form that he was anticipating. He was about to be thrust in at the deep end in a way that he was used to but which he hadn't expected in the present instance. A flavour of the real world was what the Home Office mandarin called it in the usual understated way of the career public servant.

Once past Peterborough, he went into sat nav control until he came to the rendezvous point at a Lincolnshire country pub. It was a tortuous route that he had to take but that was not the fault of the sat nav; it was simply a tortuous road. The pub was well chosen for its remoteness but nonetheless accessibility to the farming area that was being focused on.

The slightly anxious-looking superintendent was the only one in uniform. No introductions were made but it was clear that he had been invited to join a group of police and Border Agency staff.

'OK,' said the superintendent, 'we're being joined by an investigative journalist contracted to the Foreign Office.'

Wariness was a feeling that David was used to sensing in those he dealt with – it was in the nature of his work. The tone of the superintendent's voice suggested that she would have rather that he hadn't been there; she had plenty enough to worry about without passengers.

The briefing seemed to be standard. Raids on farms with large numbers of seasonal and itinerant workers were commonplace and they very often yielded a crop of illegals. The day's events weren't expected to be anything but routine.

The flat open Lincolnshire countryside didn't make surprise very easy, but equally it was a fairly straightforward exercise to block off the various roads around the farm in question.

The briefing point that registered most clearly with David

was virtually the last thing that the superintendent said.

'Remember they're harvesting cauliflowers, so each one of them will have a very sharp knife!'

A veteran of Afghanistan, Iraq, Somalia and other such places, he was used to such warnings; but the need for the superintendent to make it was what he registered. Routine the raid might be, but the unexpected was still to be anticipated.

They moved off. The roadblocks had been quietly put in place while the briefing was being carried out.

A second warning was issued once the area had been sealed.

'There are three unidentified cars trapped in the area. We have to assume that they are there innocently in the first instance.'

Again, the tone of the warning from the man who appeared to be the senior plain-clothed officer suggested that, far from being innocent, the presence of the three cars was considered to be definitely suspicious.

He wondered what all that was about. He had no idea but he did have a sense that what he had heard at the briefing wasn't the whole story.

As they fanned out, David counted fifteen officers, although which were police and which were Border Agency staff he had no way of telling since to avoid alerting the farm workers they had abandoned their usual high-visibility jackets. None of the officers appeared to be armed. As they approached the working area, they could smell the damp sickly odour of the freshly cut cauliflowers as readily as they could see the array of machinery slowly advancing across the field. It was almost a scene out of science fiction. A phalanx of machinery moving forward slowly and steadily, accompanied by the heavy growling roar of multiple engines. There were three distinct sets of machinery and centres of activity. The nearest was only a hundred feet or so away as the officers approached; the other two were further back down the field.

David had never come across the equipment being used

before, nor could he at first identify the roles of the groups of men who were working around it. It was only when they got right close up that they saw that the bulk of the men were topping and tailing the cauliflowers after they had been mechanically harvested and were feeding them on to a conveyer belt and into the packaging system. The reason for the warning about the sharp knives was all too apparent.

As the group of officers surrounded the vehicle train, the harvester halted and the driver emerged from the cabin looking puzzled rather than apprehensive. He knew immediately what was going on.

Back down the field, the other two harvesting units also stopped, maintained their formation and waited.

'Everybody put down your knives!'

In gesture as well as words, the senior officer indicated what he wanted. The response was slow and tension rose. There were ten workers, not counting the tractor driver and the stacker who was loading the filled crates of cauliflower on to a flat-based trailer. The stacker turned out to be the only woman in the group, a Somali whose classic good looks seemed totally out of place in the muddy field.

Eventually, three workers thrust their long knives into the ground in front of them and stepped away from them. The others followed suit. It was a passage that instantly told the senior police officer that at least some of the workers spoke very little English.

An officer who had so far kept in the background stepped forward and spoke to the group of workers now gathered in front of the harvesting machine. The background of conversation among the workers had been enough for him to detect what language to speak. The question he asked was greeted with shaking heads.

None of the workers had any papers on them.

'That's how it usually is,' remarked one of the officers to David.

The tractor driver gestured to the Somali woman.

'She's the gangmaster,' the officer said.

It wasn't entirely unknown for the groups of labourers to be managed and found employment by a woman.

The Somali woman knew what was expected of her. Like most Somalis, she spoke reasonable English. Rummaging in a bag that she produced from the back of the part-loaded trailer, she handed the police officer a wedge of papers. Passed to a rather bored-looking middle-aged man who was clearly the senior officer from the UK Border Agency, everybody waited for the inspection to be carried out. Aided by a colleague the Border Agency officer went along the line of workers matching each up with a set of the papers from the package. He took his time.

Then, accompanied by one who was obviously a police officer, the Border Agency man repeated the exercise further down the field with the other two crews.

The driver of the first machinery chain began to show signs of impatience.

'He obviously knows everything's in order,' David muttered.

Everything was.

Returning the papers to the Somali woman, the police and their fellow officers gathered in preparation for withdrawing. From their point of view, it had been a wasted effort; at least, so far it had.

With a spluttering thunder of noise that settled into a throbbing mechanical clatter, the machinery restarted and cauliflowers began to flow into the crates again ready for transport.

The Somali woman didn't immediately resume her activities; her place was taken by one of the labourers. It was clear that, despite being legitimately contracted to supply labour to the farm and having all the necessary paperwork, she was not happy. As the harvester moved forward and away from her, the senior police officer followed her gaze to the edge of the field.

110

A group of four men stood together silently watching what had taken place. They were clearly the occupants of the cars that had got trapped by the police roadblocks. Three men, also Somalis, left the group preparing the cauliflowers. The other workers, East Europeans, continued their topping and tailing at an increased tempo, but the tension was palpable.

'It looks as if the cars certainly weren't there by chance then,' David said.

'Rival gang,' the officer who had spoken to him earlier said.

Again there was a weariness about the comment, an 'I've seen it all before' weariness that suggested that warfare between labour gangs and gangmasters was pretty routine also.

By common consent, the group of law officers coalesced and moved towards the four men, forcing them eventually back to their cars.

'Chinese,' said David.

'Why am I not surprised?' he then muttered to himself.

Nothing was said but it was obvious to the men that they were expected to leave and with an escort to ensure that they did so. Whatever their suspicions about what the men might have been doing there, the police were taking no chances – even if they didn't have any reason to detain them.

As the police and Border Agency staff dispersed, David was invited to a debriefing with the senior officers at the local pub where they had first met. It was lunchtime; the meeting was likely to be social as well as business and David immediately planned to use the time to explore the background to the day's events in more detail to help build up the picture of the activities that he had been commissioned to investigate.

As it turned out, he was to be more than satisfied with what he was told.

As the police escort separated from the three suspect cars at the Lincolnshire border, two headed into the Midlands and the third headed to Stansted Airport with a single passenger. As he

111

checked in for a connecting flight for Australia, the immi-gration officers noted that Mr Joe Kim, Australian citizen according to his passport, six feet two inches tall, had formally left the UK.

17

'I've never seen a Chinese man that big before,' David Hutchinson remarked to the police inspector whom he had sat next to at lunch.

The operation over, the police and Border Agency staff relaxed and introduced themselves. The superintendent had disappeared long since and the inspector in charge acted as host.

'Joe Kim,' the senior Border Agency man said, 'supposedly an Australian but with a tag on him both here and in Canada.'

'Ah!'

No names among the possible suspects had been mentioned at the meeting that David had attended with Susie Peveral, but they had slipped out during their consequent, less formal encounters.

'I've heard about a dirty big Chinese bloke.'

He didn't say that it was Susie who had mentioned Joe Kim.

'Well,' said Mike Ferguson, the Border Agency team leader, 'that one would sure as hell fit the description.'

They all laughed. But it wasn't funny. Joe Kim had a role in what was going on, as well as in, as they later found out, other trafficking activities, in Australia and possibly also Canada. He was known to the Australian authorities as a violent and unforgiving operator whom very few people seemed prepared to take issue with.

Inspector Dick Woodward, who was leading the police operation, had been pondering the presence of the man ever since he had appeared. Memories eventually clicked into place.

'Bloody hell!' he said. 'Not again?'

He also knew who Kim was. The man was on the police radar, and not because of his unusual height. Inspector Woodward's exasperation at the Chinese man was mostly based on the much lengthier report he was now going to have to make so that police forces particularly in the Birmingham and Manchester areas were aware that someone on their watch list had been to Britain and gone again. Mr Kim was suspected of being some sort of fixer for the mainland Chinese gangs who were steadily emerging as the new force in both people trafficking, in all its forms, and other more traditional and longer-established criminal activities.

Inspector Woodward filled David in. Knowing why the journalist was there, and despite his desire to avoid getting too embroiled with him, he was ready enough to share what he knew. As a good policeman he was quick to point out that what he was telling David was only half the story. For a variety of reasons, even after the passage of time, the events were still fresh in his memory.

The Lincolnshire Police, he told him, had been taken by surprise by the ferocity of the attacks on the Romanian farm workers. Smith's Co-operative had generally been regarded as one of the more enlightened employers of immigrant labour. It soon transpired that that was the most likely root of the problems that had unfolded in 2008. It was seen as an easy target by gangs of all persuasions.

At first, the police had thought the attacks had a racial connotation, as the workers most heavily involved were Roma.

'But we didn't hold that view for long,' said Inspector Woodward as he recognised that David's lunch-primed nods and grunts were encouragement. It was the sort of background that was very useful to David. 'Not that you would have been going to get much confirmation from the Chinese lot; they were

114

unlikely to be too cooperative even if we had known who to talk to.'

Back in 2008, it seemed, the tall Chinese man had been as enigmatic a figure then as he still was now.

'The common factor and key figure in all of this always does seem to be our Mr Kim, but he's about as elusive as the abominable snowman,' added an officer from the Border Agency. 'Based on past experience, after a fracas like this he'll be on his way to Australia or Canada, or somewhere else by now.'

Inspector Woodward sketched out the situation. Supplying seasonal labour, no questions asked, over the years had become big business even after the horrific events of Morecambe Bay. The regulation that followed that incident allowed the authorities to keep better track of where the largely itinerant immigrant communities were, gave them some hold on working conditions, but didn't prove very helpful in preventing abuses. It hadn't taken long for the criminal gangs already involved to refine their activities and to then use the regulation as a cover for the things that they had always done. Needless to say, the Chinese element in the supply of labour had remained, but the police and Border Agency sensed that they had upped their game. The whole activity had become much more sophisticated and was centred much less on isolated local gangs.

'Where there's a lucrative operation going on with very little hands-on oversight, there's always going to be competition for the rewards. And the poor powerless immigrants are the cannon fodder for the battles that develop, especially in large multi-crop areas like here in Lincolnshire.'

The inspector reminisced about a particularly bad incident in 2008. It was cauliflowers again which had been at the centre of the eruption, On one of the Smith's Co-operative's farms, like the one that they had just been investigating, the cauliflower fields were so large that they could accommodate four machinery trains. And, in line with their liberal policies, Smith's had recruited two labour gangs from two registered organisations. The one that employed the Roma workers they had used many times. The second crew were also East Europeans but the gangmaster worked for an organisation that had been registered only for a few months but which was offering very competitive rates.

'The Smith's people were cautious,' the inspector recalled. 'Experience told them that they should have established the group's track record before they did a deal. But money talks.

'Trouble started even before the gangs arrived at the farm, it seems. Working to the same start time, the mini-vans of the two groups arrived at the access road together. The van of the new group had a reinforced bumper and tried to shunt the other van carrying the Roma workers off the road. A third mini-van was idling about a hundred yards behind the first two.'

Eventually arriving at the farm's machinery area ready to start harvesting, the driver of the Roma vehicle had confronted the other driver. It was something of a mismatch to start with, because the Roma crew were supported by three large and tough-looking men who had arrived earlier at the farm and who turned out to be the minders for the Roma gangmaster.

'The long-standing gangmaster, it seems,' continued the inspector, 'was expecting trouble, as the other group had tried to muscle in on the work crews at another of Smith's Co-operative's farms a few miles away. Armed with baseball bats, the thugs quickly beat the driver of the second mini-van to his knees and left him bleeding heavily from a serious head wound. Deterred by the violence of the assault on their driver, the other East European workers, from Ukraine apparently, held back.

'They of course, knew about the third mini-van and a group of their own minders following behind.' The inspector shook his head in disbelief at the memory.

'The farm manager, seeing what was developing, had already called the police and I and my team of ten men in riot gear sped over there.'

The inspector continued his story, much of which he had gathered from witness statements from the farm managers given at the time. The odds were now decisively against the Roma gang's minders. Armed in their turn with baseball bats and iron bars, the Ukrainian thugs weighed in immediately the third mini-van had come to a halt. Again, none of the Roma or Ukrainian workers made any attempt to join the fight. By now one of the Roma minders lay in a crumpled heap beside the first damaged mini-van. He wasn't moving. One of the Ukrainian minders was on his knees a few feet away, his head almost unrecognisable behind the mess of blood and pulp that was his face. Elsewhere in the yard the other two Roma minders were being beaten down by their attackers.

Finally, the farm managers intervened. An explosion of noise overtook the shouts, groans and curses that were accompanying the fighting. The farm manager and his assistant cocked their shotguns ready to fire another volley into the air.

As the groups were forced to separate and an uneasy quiet took over, the wails of the emergency vehicle sirens began to fill the gap as the riot police and ambulances got closer.

The minders instinctively began to shuffle towards their gang's mini-vans.

'I wouldn't,' yelled the farm manager, uncertain of course whether the minders were carrying weapons in their vans.

Then, for a few brief moments, farce took over.

Suddenly a dark-blue 5-series BMW shot into the farmyard, braked furiously when confronted with a mass of bodies and vehicles, and then slithered to a screeching halt in one of the barns that opened on to the yard. The grinding clunk indicated that the BMW hadn't been unscathed by its unexpected and enforced trip into the Smith's Co-operative machinery yard.

The car reversed out of the barn and positioned itself ready to leave.

As the cacophony of official noise erupted into the farm yard in the form of two police vans, a police Land-Rover and two ambulances, it was clear that the BMW had been already in the farm lane and had been flushed into the yard by the following police vehicles. It was abundantly clear that the driver of the car was now very anxious to leave the scene. The Land-Rover parked in front of the gate precluded this option.

The injured were despatched to hospital where they were met by more police officers who would keep a bedside vigil. The remaining participants, workers, minders and the car driver, were formed into groups and placed under precautionary guard.

'The guy in the back of the car refused to get out,' said Inspector Woodward, 'but since we had a death on our hands we weren't in the mood to argue so we let him stay there.'

Eventually, detectives and other police specialists arrived and the riot police returned to their base. Satisfied on the farm manager's assurance that the actual Roma and Ukrainian workers had had no part in the mayhem, they were despatched to the fields and the day's work belatedly commenced.

It took several hours to sort out what had happened and take a preliminary view on why it had.

'Eventually we got round to the guy in the car. He was not best pleased at having been kept hanging around but it was obvious that he was holding himself in since all he wanted was to get away and avoid too many questions; provoking the police wasn't going to help that.'

The inspector seemed amused by the man's predicament.

'Joe Kim,' he said. Inspector Woodward again provided a link and continuity for David.

It was clear that the inspector, having told his tale, was keen to get back on the job. But David was still unsure of

118

the significance of Joe Kim in this and the earlier incident and how it linked to the Chinese criminal groups that they were all convinced were involved in the people trafficking that stood behind the whole immigrant labour scene. Although a picture was building.

As they were leaving the pub, he held back the inspector and asked him the question directly.

'But how does Kim fit in? Why would he get involved on the ground like that?'

The inspector seemed unwilling to divulge anything further.

'As you know, there's a lot of Home Office pressure on the police and Borders people and a lot of information feeding in from the mainstream intelligence organisations. And this is where we think this guy Kim fits. He's probably a lot more than just an enforcer and messenger.'

The lunch wasn't quite the end of things. The telephone calls that had both got David involved in the Lincolnshire Police action and had resulted in the superintendent being nominated to oversee the day's activities had also resulted in him being deposited back at her office for a debriefing. A conversation took place just between the two of them. Although David struggled to understand the significance of some of what he was told, it nonetheless closed off some of the events that he had become aware of.

'This, as you probably know,' the superintendent said, 'hasn't been the only confrontation between the gangs.'

David thought he was going to be told about 2008 again, but he was wrong, for what the superintendent then went on to say was probably just as valuable as anything else that he had garnered from the first part of his day.

'The more recent incident,' she said, 'was different. And explains why we might have seemed to have been rather heavy-handed today. As you saw, Kim wasn't the only Chinese man to come here. There have been more and other visits. The gang we suspect he is working for here is trying to muscle in on the

Somali gang, though I have to say that that gangmaster is worth ten of them.'

The superintendent gave an apologetic grin; the Somali woman had obviously impressed her.

'In any event, another Chinese fixer came to talk to the Somali gangmaster about ten days ago. It was all very low key; the gangmaster is very good at leaning in the wind. This guy did whatever business he had to do with the gangmaster, whether successfully or not we have no idea, but whatever the outcome, she and he finished off their meeting with a bout of vigorous sex in one of the barns at the farm.'

David immediately felt himself to be utterly lost. He had no idea where this latest narrative fitted into the picture that he was trying to build.

'Later enter, you might say, the other suitor for the Somali gangmaster's favours, both business and sexual. Mr Petrov, head of a Ukrainian criminal syndicate, was in town to try and secure a foothold in the local labour supply market before the Chinese got it all sewn up. Shades of a Whitehall bedroom farce, Petrov and the Somali woman also had sex in the barn!'

'I can't believe I'm hearing this!' David said.

'Oh, it gets better still,' the superintendent said, with another grin.

'Descriptions are a bit vague but more Chinese arrived, one of whom was very tall, and finding Petrov they attacked him and his sole bodyguard and apparently killed him. It was all a bit of a mess, but they gathered up all the evidence, clothes, belongings and whatever and spirited the body away. Which of the Chinese actually killed Petrov and what happened to his minder we really don't know.'

'This is … Shit, I don't know what it is. Are you serious?'

The superintendent was.

'The press were right there when the body was fished out of the sea off the Dorset coast. Everything is so instant these days, what with mobile phone cameras and the like, it's hard to get a whole story together before the half of it is on the Internet in Australia or Saudi Arabia!'

David didn't mention that he too had been right there.

In the peace and quiet of his flat David Hutchinson tried to piece together what he had learned. The giant Chinese man seemed to be a thread through all of the events that he had observed or been told about. The picture of mainland Chinese infiltration of the local Chinese gangs and the increase in competition and warfare with the *in situ* East European and Somali labour gangs was clear enough. The separate information that he had got from the police and Susie Peveral about the trafficking of much of the workforce for these gangs was also now much clearer to him.

But precisely how the enigmatic Mr Joe Kim fitted into this picture he was no clearer about. Hints of other shadowy figures, the Chinese woman, visiting with increasing frequency, who clearly had some kind of clout, the links to past figures in the Border Agency – all of this was no clearer to him either.

The police seemed to think that there was a status quo developing among the gangs and traffickers. So why would they still need an instantly recognisable fixer to keep flying in?

It was a question to which David had no answer.

São Paulo Daily News
English-language Edition – Monday, 12 July 2010
MYSTERY OF SÃO PAULO GIRL'S ESCAPE
FROM SLAVERY
The São Paulo Police were recently contacted by the Brazilian Embassy in Canberra, Australia concerning Patience Zhang, aged 25 years, released from captivity in Melbourne, Australia.

Miss Zhang, who claims to be a Canadian citizen, a claim that the federal authorities in Ottawa are investigating, was released in a raid by Melbourne Police on a premises in the famous China Town district of the city. She was being held along with four other Chinese women who claimed through an interpreter to come from Indonesia. Police were called to the premises after reports of fighting among two groups of Chinese men.

Unconfirmed reports from Brazilian officials in Canberra suggest that Miss Zhang was one of a group of young Chinese women who had been trafficked from Brazil to Canada and given Canadian passports. This information, if proved correct, would support the investigations of the São Paulo Police into the apparent disappearance of at least five young Chinese women from their area in the last two years. Both the Embassy in Canberra and the São Paulo Police declined to comment on rumours that they had been given the names of other women who were transported to Australia along with Miss Zhang.

Interpol has confirmed that it is investigating an increase in the trafficking of young Chinese women. So far, women have been identified from the US, the UK and Canada. Numbers are unconfirmed, but are thought to be quite small, and Interpol would give no further information. Evidence is building that all of these women eventually ended up in Australia from where they then subsequently disappeared.

All of the officials that the News *has spoken to declined to entertain any speculation about a link to a recent incident in Hong Kong in which a young Chinese woman appeared to be being delivered to a Chinese businessman. The young woman had been drugged.*

According to the official at the Brazilian Embassy in Canberra, a common theme linking these women is that all were educated, even middle class, and although each, by leaving Brazil, was seeking to better themselves, there was no suggestion that any of them had been offered to the sex trade.

18

Mr Kim was not happy having to rush back to Australia. He had unfinished, albeit interrupted, business in the UK and the call to return to Melbourne to take charge of the hijacking of Alice Hou from the rival group was causing him some concern. While he accepted that Alice was high-value merchandise sought by a specific customer, starting a war with another Chinese gang in Australia was not in his opinion a very wise thing to do. There was too much evidence accumulating that the authorities in Australia, if not other countries, were now very much aware of this emerging trafficking sideline and their interest could lead only to increasing pressure on the gangs. And strife among the gangs, Kim knew, would only accelerate any clamp-down.

But Mr Xu had spoken and Joe Kim was in no position to challenge his boss's orders.

Equally, he was concerned about the frequency with which he was being recorded in the immigration and transits records of Singapore or, as in the case in point, Hong Kong. However, despite his desire not to appear too often on the official radar, his regular movements around the world were well known, reported and disseminated.

Joe Kim was travelling on an Australian passport; not that that fooled anybody. Certainly, the Chinese Government's various agencies who took a particular interest in him all knew his real name, his aliases and the various combinations of the two. Be he Joe Kim or Kim Lee Sung, the intelligence services of the US, the UK and various other countries made an effort to keep each other informed about Mr Kim's movements and in particular these movements were relayed to Australia and thence to the Chinese. Suspicions abounded in Beijing on what Kim was up to on his various journeys around the world, but he was adept at not getting caught leaving too obvious an evidential trail. And with Mr Xu's influence in the Chinese infrastructure Kim also had other assistance to obfuscate his activities.

However, when he arrived within Chinese territory, as at Hong Kong International Airport, the authorities were alerted and became especially vigilant while he remained there.

Thus the Australian Head of Intelligence in Canberra was able to write to the Chinese Embassy: 'We know that he has knocked heads together in Great Britain and forced the various Chinese immigrant gangmasters into line with one of the major mainland Chinese crime syndicates now active in Europe. We also know that his role has changed with the appearance of at least one Chinese woman, of complex origins, who while being registered as mainland Chinese otherwise travels on a UK passport. This woman has started to undertake the courier role that had previously been associated with Kim. And she would appear to have more authority and reach than Kim.'

The urbane Head of Intelligence at the Chinese Embassy was sufficiently used to dealing with Australians to understand what 'knocking heads' together meant. His Australian colleague, in reciprocation of his Chinese opposite number's usual economy of information, was only passing on what he thought necessary to maintain good relations. It was a game of sorts but one with a common purpose, if not a common motivation; to eliminate these influential criminal groups. For the Chinese mainland authorities, such free enterprise as the groups displayed was a threat; for the law-enforcement agencies of the rest of the world, they simply represented criminal activities that harmed the generality of law-abiding citizens.

Li Chen knew perfectly well the identity of the two key crime syndicates. The Chinese's own investigations, which they didn't share with the Australians, told them that both of these groups had fingers in the importation of illegal labour into the European Union, Canada and even the US, and were struggling for supremacy against each other and various indigenous organisations all around the world. What they hadn't been sure about was which of the two Mr Kim worked for, although information was soon to emerge in Melbourne that would provide an answer to this question. What they also didn't know for certain, but assumed, was that both groups had political protectors.

However, none of the people keeping watch over Mr Kim at Hong Kong International Airport had any idea why he was heading back to Melbourne. It wasn't really their business. Their job was to insulate him from any contact with anyone from Hong Kong or elsewhere in mainland China, and to see him on his way in as quiet and trouble-free a way as possible.

Kim knew this. With nothing to occupy him, he spent his time making the job as onerous as possible for his minders.

But his patience wasn't unlimited. Being tall, even in Business Class he hadn't slept very much, and the perpetual attentions of the cabin crew hadn't improved his temper either.

His rising irritation was directed particularly at a couple of the plain-clothed police officers. He had no doubt that that was what they were. Walking when he walked, stopping when he stopped, they followed him back to the area next to the re-embarkation gate after his circumnavigation of the terminal. Their presence would have been obvious to a child. But then they were supposed to be obvious.

Maybe I should have gone into the Duty Free, he thought, knowing that that would have activated some sort of action to either deter him or isolate him and prevent any contact with any third party.

But he also knew that his unforgiving boss in the syndicate

in Shanghai wouldn't take kindly to his playing games with the authorities; he was supposed to be as inconspicuous as possible. What did he need from the Duty Free Shop anyway?

Notwithstanding all of the official interest, Mr Kim was also being kept in view by other, much more discreet observers who would be reporting back that his passage through Hong Kong had been totally sanitised. Mr Xu didn't always trust even his most loyal lieutenants.

As always, Kim wondered what was the point of such close-quarters surveillance. He was at least half a head taller than any other Chinese man that he had ever known. How could he have become invisible in such a public place as an international airport?

Time passed slowly but fortunately the stopover was only short.

Back on the aircraft, where as far as Mr Kim knew he was not under surveillance, he took time to review his brief stay in the UK. As he had anticipated they would, the local Chinese gang leaders had detected much greater pressure from the authorities and the gossip through contacts in the London Civil Service seemed to suggest an increased level of cooperation around the world in response to the mainland Chinese's increased activity. He wasn't sorry that some of what he called the political stuff was being taken off him. He'd been impressed by the slip of a girl who was supposed to deal with the increasingly complex interface with the local gangs. But he wondered whether, remote from China, the power she held from her husband would be enough to impress and gain obedience from the British gang leaders. But then Kim wasn't privy to the true nature of Mr Xu's relationship with his clients and how little they trusted him. Contracting his wife to Xu was key insurance to Shi Xiulu.

'Nobody seemed to know why there was this sudden increase in interest,' Kim was to report to his principals later, 'but it was very much about trafficking the illegal labour; nothing to do with the women trafficking.'

It was this analysis that the women trafficking was as yet not too strongly on the radar of the authorities in the UK that had occupied much of Kim's thoughts on the Hong Kong to Melbourne leg of his journey.

But then he was never likely to have heard of Susie Peveral and her discreet crusading on the issue, or of David Hutchinson, whose subversion from his investigation into trafficking of illegal labour Ms Peveral was engineering.

Kim realised, however, that it was only a question of time. That it was on the radar of the authorities in Australia and Canada he did know, but his sense was that they were scratching about in the dark. That was a situation that his actions in Melbourne would change – snatching the young woman in China Town had attracted too much attention.

Women trafficking had always been the least of Kim's concerns. But the particular client that his organisation was working for was far too powerful and far too valuable to neglect. The fact that the perfect woman, a virgin, was being held by another Chinese group was an inconvenience. Snatching the girl was a risk that had to be taken, according to Mr Xu. The fact that another of the high-value women was present was something that Kim couldn't have foreseen. But her presence was to give the authorities a gold mine of information that could well lead to the shutting down of one of Mr Kim's organisation's rivals.

'There has to be an easier way to earn a living,' Kim said to himself once all the action in Melbourne was over, the dust had settled and he found himself in Echuca with a striking Chinese woman who for once raised other feelings than just contempt.

It was an expression he had picked up from one of the gang leaders in Manchester. Not having a sense of humour, Mr Kim didn't really appreciate the subtlety of the remark; avoiding arrest in Lincolnshire one day and kidnapping a very attractive young woman like Alice Hou a week later seemed to him to be all in a day's work.

And now there was Julie Li!

A week after their arrival at Echuca, Julie had so far failed to get on terms with Mr Kim, but she had begun to get to know Alice Hou. Kim proved to be something of a complex and often confusing character. The day after they had arrived he sent the driver to Swan Hill to hire a car. He then spent a couple of hours apparently driving around the locality making himself familiar with the late-model Holden that he had acquired. The driver remained on the boat to physically prevent Julie, let alone Alice, from even coming on deck.

Somehow as the days went by and Kim was forced to have more and more contact with her, she sensed that something of his distrust was abating and something that she found hard to define had crept into his behaviour towards her. Used to and expecting contempt from Kim, Julie took time to realise that a grudging respect was emerging in the way he related to her.

She guessed he could see that he didn't frighten her.

Alice, on the other hand, seemed to shrink into herself more and more whenever Kim was anywhere near her; in his turn, he either ignored her or addressed her roughly and with the sort of contempt that Julie had expected to attract. The poor girl was totally intimidated by him and seemed increasingly to look to Julie as a barrier between them.

At the beginning of the second week Kim gestured Julie out on to the afterdeck of the houseboat and showed her his Black-Berry. Another email from the dreaded Mr Xu had arrived and Kim was required to show it to Julie.

The afterdeck was larger than the foredeck that they had used to deliver the packaged and terrified Alice. It had a guard rail all round it to protect the occupants of the houseboat from the engines, but it was also sheltered from view from the shore where the vessel had been tied up.

The email gave Mr Kim instructions to give to Julie. Mr Xu came from a rather different world from Julie and it would never normally have occurred to him to deal directly with her.

'We need to get busy,' Kim said.

Even he could see that Alice was looking very jaded and nothing like the fresh faced and lively girl that Mr Xu clearly expected and wanted her to be.

The instructions were to get Alice fit and healthy and to tutor her in various domestic skills.

'What does he mean tutor her in domestic skills? She's been doing the cooking and all the other chores virtually since we arrived. I thought it would give her something to do since I have no idea how long we're supposed to keep her here.'

'Never mind that!'

'What do you mean never mind that! You going to have to tell me how long we're going to be here sometime, for Christ's sake. I have another life as well as this.'

Mr Kim looked bemused and fleetingly anxious. Over the last week or so Julie had realised that talking back to him and challenging him were very effective ways of asserting her independence and forcing him to deal with her. And he knew that, if she were determined to leave him, there wasn't much he could do beyond killing her. That was hardly an outcome that Mr Xu would have appreciated. Somewhere in his complex mind Mr Kim perceived that, despite the shadow of arrest that was supposed to hang over Julie, she would run if she felt that she had to. Julie's real motivation seemed unlikely to occur to Kim, so successful had the petite Singapore police lieutenant been in selling her capabilities

'You'll be told!'

She needed to be told. She had been out of contact with the Australian Security Service for over two weeks now and, although they knew it would take time for her to establish herself, they would have been expecting her to attempt some sort of communication.

'So what do you want me to do? I can take her jogging. That'll do me some good, too. If I don't get out of this tub soon, I'll go mad staring at four small walls and you.'

It was light-heartedly said but again Mr Kim's lack of a sense of humour meant that he picked up literally on what she had said and only concentrated on the idea of Alice and herself running freely around the countryside.

'No way!'

'Jesus, man, we're supposed to groom her until she looks the picture of health and beauty according to your Mr Xu, whatever that means. I could take her to the Echuca gym; I'm sure they have one. You could come running with us!'

From the way that his body stiffened, Julie knew that Kim was getting angry. She backed off.

'OK, go and buy an exercise bicycle in Swan Hill or somewhere. Not in town here. I used to use a gym so I'll try and think up some exercises for her.'

The ease with which Mr Kim accepted her proposal told Julie two important things. One, he was desperate to be seen to carry out Xu's orders, which confirmed her belief that he was frightened of him for some clearly very powerful reason, and two, his lack of imagination as well as sense of humour meant that he could be manipulated rather more easily than she had expected. Or at least so it seemed.

Why the invisible Mr Xu wanted Alice to be brought to a peak of fitness and health Julie didn't bother to think about. She had to play along with Xu and Kim until something more concrete emerged on what was behind the whole women trafficking activity. Only then would the police and Security Service have the evidence to take action against it.

Her confidence in her understanding of Kim didn't last.

'I sent the driver away so I'll have to go and get the exercise bicycle,' he said the day after their discussion. 'So I'll have to leave you on your own.'

It was not a situation that Julie had been expecting.

131

And it was clearly a problem to Mr Kim. Alice, who was in earshot at first, looked expectant and then anxious.

Julie could see Kim's difficulty.

'OK,' she said, 'you're either going to have to trust me or, if you can't, what are you going to do – lock me up as well?'

Built as a temporary summer home, the houseboat, Julie had been quick to notice, had an almost impregnable security system.

Something in the gleam in Mr Kim's eye told Julie that she wasn't going to like the solution to the problem that had now occurred to him.

'Get her clothes off.'

The panic-stricken Alice stripped off her meagre clothes which were snatched away by Kim. Silent tears rolled down Alice's cheeks before something of the defiance that she was beginning to be able to muster showed. But beautiful as her body was Mr Kim showed no signs of even noticing.

'Empty your pockets.'

Julie's tight jeans didn't allow much storage for even the most simple of female accoutrements, let alone any weapon.

When it was obvious what Kim had in mind, Julie offered up her left hand to be handcuffed to Alice's right and her right to Alice's left. Kim's efforts to force them into a more awkward left hand to left hand and right to right posture were thwarted by a snarled comment from Julie. It was a small but useful victory for both their comfort and for Julie's faltering confidence in handling Kim. His revenge was painful for Alice, if, as he clearly recognised, short-lived. The delight with which he applied the tape to her mouth earned him a bruise on his shin as Julie lashed out with her heavy boot. As acknowledgement of this riposte, with a grin, he made a gesture as if he was going to tape her mouth, too – something that was totally unexpected for Julie; it was almost erotic. Mr Kim, however, didn't push his luck as far as actually doing so. The surge of feelings that Kim's unexpected lascivious grin induced in Julie occupied her thoughts until Kim had secured the houseboat and driven off. She had definitely not yet plumbed the depths of Mr Kim!

Alice and she were in for an uncomfortable afternoon but at least she had preserved her cover.

With her mind on the erotic, Julie's senses were perhaps overexcited. She quickly and rather brutally ripped the tape from Alice's mouth and walked her awkwardly into the bedroom. In such close proximity to Alice, the look in the girl's eyes came as a shock.

Julie felt herself being dragged on to the bed. Using the handcuffs to pull Julie's arms around and behind herself, Alice relaxed until her head was resting on her companion's chest. The warmth of Alice's body penetrated Julie's clothing.

What? Julie couldn't believe it!

Julie had seen pain, fear, anxiety in Alice's eyes whenever Kim went near her; what she was now seeing was something akin to pleasure. Alice was happy with what had happened!

Being forced into such intimate contact with Julie was clearly something that Alice was relishing.

God help me! What's this all about?

That was soon obvious.

Alice thrust her body even harder into Julie, her breasts being crushed in the movement as Julie shuffled her body to sustain the pressure. Alice cocked her head sideways and brushed her lips over Julie's. Her eyes sparkled. This was suddenly an Alice that Julie didn't know. She'd metamorphosed suddenly, and in the absence of Kim, from a frightened child into something almost powerful and predatory.

Holy shit. They want her to be a virgin but this is…!

Julie's brain went dead; the implications of Alice's actions had stunned her. There was nothing in her wildest dreams, nightmares more like, that could have alerted her to what was happening.

As Alice started to gently gyrate her body against her all manner of feelings started to surge through Julie.

Holy shit, she thought again. *What the hell am I going to do now.*

Julie stiffened her body again and shook her head gently, but Alice was too far gone in her enjoyment of the physical contact. Her eyes glazed over; released by the intensity of her relief at Mr Kim's absence, Alice seemed concentrated on snatching whatever moments of pleasure that she could.

Our Mr Kim would love this!

Except that there was no way on earth that she was going to tell him. Whatever the complications that Alice's apparent lesbian tendency produced, letting Kim or the fearsome Mr Xu in on the secret was definitely not an option.

19

'Kim's a thug!'

Linda Shen didn't offer her opinion to her husband unless he specifically asked. On this occasion, he had asked. He'd invited Mr Xu to dinner and was updating himself after his wife's most recent trip to Britain. What Mr Shi's business dealings with Xu were, as with all his business arrangements, her husband never explained; Linda was happy with this. Not only did she find Xu one of the most objectionable people that she had ever met, she sensed that her husband was no fonder of him than she was. But business was business and Kim had been one of her contacts while she was away. Her husband always made a point of being as well briefed as he could be before his dealings with any of his syndicate associates. It was one of the few things about him that his wife had a grudging respect for.

'You dealt with him in England. How did you find him?'

There was no point in telling Mr Shi that Kim had only spoken to her when he had to, that his manner was rude and hectoring, and that she found him almost as unpleasant as his boss. She was a woman, albeit a new-generation Chinese woman, what did she expect? Notwithstanding, Kim still managed to be respectful enough to inhibit her from reporting his behaviour back to her husband.

'Kim's a thug. His manner to the people that we were dealing with was harsh, rude and, as far as I could see, very much resented. I think his insensitivity and his limited brain power are a serious problem for us.'

It wasn't what Mr Shi wanted to hear but it was certainly what he feared he might hear. Nor was it entirely accurate. Kim was much more intelligent and complex than Linda had implied, but she realised that her trips to the UK would be much easier for her if she didn't have to keep in touch with the man.

Both the Shis had heard about the various raids on the farms in Lincolnshire and Kim's hasty retreat after the latest one. Mr Shi had also heard about the police raid in Melbourne and Mr Xu's increasing focus on the women trafficking side of his business. As he waited for his wife to say more, he was at least honest enough to acknowledge that he had benefited from the trafficking of high-value women! And he had every intention of further exploiting his wife's capabilities, even if he was never likely to acknowledge them to her, to his continuing benefit.

'I think that there must be better ways of working with the people in Britain without Kim and Xu. Their approach is too crude.'

Her husband agreed, again not that he would have said so, but he in his turn felt the beginnings of a grudging respect for his wife's power of analysis. That they might make a very good working partnership as yet was a thought too far for his rather austere, self-focused and masculine mind.

As a consequence, he didn't share the knowledge that Mr Kim had apparently gone to ground after the Melbourne raid, presumably on Mr Xu's instructions, which relieved Mr Shi of the need to consider Kim in his plans any further. It also gave his wife an enhanced and leading role, but he had no plans to tell her that either until the need arose.

Mr Shi didn't trust his wife with organising dinners for his business associates. Food was one of the areas where he knew that his wife was never going to meet his requirements. How could she? Born and bred in Manchester and fed on junk food during her brief career in Edinburgh, she had no more idea about putting together a traditional Chinese meal than any

136

other of the ex-Canadian, UK or Brazilian purchased trophy wives. It was a weakness in the trafficking system that was recognised by both sellers and buyers. Her mother-in-law, with whom she had immense difficulty in communicating, was always drafted in when something special was needed. Why feeding the objectionable Mr Xu with something special was necessary was beyond her comprehension.

Being instrumental in bringing her to China, Xu regarded Linda Shen with a contempt that he only reined in because of her husband's powerful patronage and unforgiving nature. A misogynist by nature and incapable of any sort of physical relationship with a woman, Mr Xu's dealings with her were minimal and, much to her amusement, confined to the most trivial or banal matters. Wheelchair bound though he was, she felt no pity for him and generally avoided any necessity of helping him manoeuvre himself around the confines of her home except in circumstances where he was obliged to ask her to. She was well aware that seeking her help did nothing to endear her to him.

When one such passage occurred between Xu and herself as the latter arrived, with his principal henchman, Li Qiang, Linda was struck by the contempt that showed in her husband's face. As the expression converted into a frozen smile of welcome, she realised that the contempt was not for her but for the man that he was greeting. Her feeling that her husband was no more a fan of Xu than she was was very clearly confirmed.

But Mr Xu in his turn understood his syndicate associate very well. What made Mr Shi superior to him, apart from his much greater wealth, was the sort of subtle underlying class distinction that was understood by everybody, if not always acknowledged. Xu was a facilitator – he made things happen for people like Mr Shi and his other associates and clients; he got his hands dirty, no questions asked. He wasn't a principal and never would be, however successful or rich he became.

The dinner at the Shis' was a very good dinner. Linda watched and listened as her husband managed the conversation around to the outcomes he was seeking to achieve. She was very impressed, despite herself; complex negotiations were something that she had been trained for and which she was good at and she recognised her husband's skill. Encouraging Xu to concentrate on the high-margin end of women trafficking came over to the man himself as an endorsement of a sound business opportunity. Sensing that Mr Shi was not really interested in participating in this activity, Mr Xu was only too happy to take it on without him. Freezing Xu out of the high-cash-flow labour trafficking came over to him as sensibly exiting a risky and hazardous business activity that was under constant pressure worldwide from a whole range of authorities. Xu saw himself as better off not engaged in this area. Mr Shi's capabilities as a salesman and negotiator were recognised by Li Qiang but he felt no obligation to risk his colleague's anger by pointing out what was happening. The rationalisation that women trafficking was low risk and hadn't yet attracted the same interest from the various authorities around the world as the labour trafficking had made enough sense to Mr Li for him to manage his conscience. None of the diners had yet realised that this rationalisation was no longer true.

'That was well done.'

Linda's remark was made in the relaxed after-dinner atmosphere that signalled that her husband was well satisfied with his evening's work. Aware that she had contributed significantly to this success, he mellowed his manner sufficiently for his wife to recognise the softening.

She accepted his nod of appreciation with a flashing smile; the thought that they might make a good working partnership moved a step closer towards his conscious mind.

Already possessed of an heir, Mr Shi's lovemaking was infrequent and erratic. Surprisingly for a man of his nature, it

138

was, however, never rough or forceful. This night his wife struggled to maintain her detachment from it; his lovemaking was also very skilful.

20

While Julie's problems multiplied as a result of Alice's un-expected display of feelings towards her, and as her companion settled herself comfortably against her, she still had time to review how things had developed and about her working relationship with Mr Kim. How long his shopping trip would be Julie had no idea.

If he really didn't trust her, he would have just killed her and found another way of handling Alice. That seemed self-evident to Julie.

But what motivated Kim was still the most important issue for Julie. Although she had no idea what hold his Chinese masters had over him, his seeming fear of them didn't strike her as entirely rational. But what was clear to her was that she had to manage every contact with him as an independent event and not carry the conclusions from one contact on to the next. It was going to be challenging and wearing but, she decided, the safest way forward. Necessarily cast adrift by her new Security Service bosses, Julie had no choice but to get along with Mr Kim.

Thinking back to the meeting with him a few days after her introduction to him at the Queen Victoria Market, she recog-nised that that was the beginning of the working relationship, but at the point that they were at in Echuca it was also still work in progress.

Mr Xu wouldn't have called himself a traditionalist, although he would have admitted to being old-fashioned. His initial reservations about employing Julie Li stemmed first from her being a woman and then from the too neat a way that she had come to Kim Lee Sung's notice. A traditionalist simply wouldn't have employed a woman; being old-fashioned, his thought processes required that he be given evidence of her capabilities, not just be expected to rely on a description of them.

But Mr Xu, anchored in Shanghai by a body whose lower half no longer functioned, was dependent on Kim to provide the evidence that tested both Kim's own advocacy of Julie and her true capabilities. Setting up a process for this verification before Julie was accepted was typical of the caution that Mr Xu applied to anything new or beyond his experience. Only when she finally played her part in the kidnap of Alice Hou was Xu as confident in her as one of his essentially suspicious nature was ever likely to be

'Treasury Gardens.'

A circle on a map that Julie had left on the seat at the Spring Street breakfast restaurant a couple of days after Alan had procured her contact with Kim, along with a flyer for a lecture at a one-day exhibition of Aboriginal art at the gallery next door, told the Australian Security Service date, time and place of the next contact.

'Track Julie, not Kim,' was Alan's instruction to the watchers.

In terms of city parks, the Treasury Gardens were a fairly modest oasis in the middle of an area dominated by the Victorian Parliament and other official buildings. They were readily accessible by tram or Metro, but arrival by either required Julie to show herself fairly obviously unless she chose to approach the Gardens other than via the city centre.

She did; Kim assumed that she would.

Why did they have to play these stupid games? Julie asked herself. Why didn't they just tell her to meet them at Cook's Cottage; it was a tourist magnet, so they'd hardly be noticed.

But of course she knew that the point about the Treasury Gardens rather than the Fitzroy Gardens was that they were very open, with only a limited number of trees to hide behind.

Skirting around the city centre to approach the Gardens from the east challenged Julie's still-rudimentary knowledge of the geography of Melbourne. But it was only when she was well down Lansdowne Street that she detected both of the men following her. They weren't Security Service, she was sure of that; she was most unlikely to have detected them if they had been.

Ambling unhurriedly on to the grass, she headed for one of the broader trees and put it between her and the men following her. Staying within the tree's shadow she accelerated towards a bench at the edge of the Gardens that backed on to Spring Street and awaited developments.

It was then that she saw Mr Kim walking up the Spring Street towards her. It was also then that she saw the first Chinese man hurriedly break out from the small area of bushes beside the government buildings and scurry in her direction. Sensing that he was no threat, she ignored Kim.

How the second Chinese man got to her so quickly she didn't have time to consider; she was immediately set upon by both of them.

Grabbing at her shoulder bag gave the attack an appearance of an attempted robbery. Julie held on to her bag with her left hand and with an instinctive burst of aggression bred of her regular karate training she kicked the nearest man to her heavily in the crotch; he backed away, his silent mouthing in agony telling Julie that he would be much more cautious in any further attack. Surprised by Julie's powerful reaction, the second man hesitated, braced himself and squared up to her. As Julie clutched her bag more tightly to her the man feinted, moved forward and then hesitated again. Then he cast an

142

enquiring glance past her, shrugged, turned and ran off. The first attacker limped painfully after him.

The flicker in the man's eyes alerted Julie, but as she turned she was too late to see Mr Kim's gesture of dismissal.

'Very good!'

Julie could read nothing into the slightly mocking statement, nor into Kim's face as he made it, but she sensed that he hadn't been expecting her reaction to be so vigorous and as a consequence she had passed some sort of test. Kim showed no interest in whether she might have been injured in the attack.

The obviously contrived nature of the episode led the Security Service watchers to the same conclusion as Julie; she was being tested out. Since Mr Kim didn't abandon the meeting, it was assumed that she had passed the test.

Kim gestured Julie to follow him.

If Julie hadn't been able to fathom why Kim was testing her in the Treasury Gardens, the purpose of the time that she next spent with him in a pre-booked room in a hotel on the other side of Spring Street was very clear.

The room was equipped with a dining table and two chairs and set up with a laptop computer, so it was immediately obvious that she was to be interviewed again. Gesturing her to sit at the table in front of the open laptop, Kim reached across her and with far more dexterity than she would have given him credit for he opened up communication with an elderly but hard-faced Chinese man who confronted her in surroundings that spoke of luxury but gave no clue as to their whereabouts. The man's immobility immediately attracted Julie; he seemed only to be able to move from the waist up. Since he was sitting close up to webcam, she couldn't see that he was in a wheelchair. Whether there was anyone else in the room with the man Julie had no way of knowing.

'Miss Li,' the man said, 'my name is Xu, but you need not bother yourself about that. This is the only time that you will see or speak to me.'

The expression that fleetingly scurried across the old man's face suggested that even this was more contact than he would have preferred to have had.

Julie said nothing. Xu probably didn't even notice. He simply continued with what he intended to say.

'Mr Kim says that you are being hunted by the British authorities. My contacts tell me that the search for you has spread to Australia and that you are in danger of being arrested and returned to the UK for trial. This is an outcome that I would not want to occur. Your knowledge of the UK Immigration Control systems will be very useful to me and I do not wish to lose it.'

The first thought that developed in Julie's brain was how unbelievably pompous the old man seemed to be despite his near-perfect English; the second thought was that she didn't believe a word of what he had said about wanting her useful knowledge of UK Immigration. How could he have exploited that in Australia?

She didn't move. She just stared back at the screen, fully aware that Xu could see her every change of facial expression. The gentle noises behind her suggested that Kim had stretched out on the bed and was switched off from what was going on.

'But before we avail ourselves of your expertise we have a task for you. You should pay particular attention to what I am going to ask you to do. Kim will not trust you until you prove that you can be trusted. Mr Kim's distrust can be very painful to those who attract it.'

Julie didn't doubt it; that Mr Kim had a sadistic streak she could easily imagine.

What Julie was asked to do led her to an attic in Little Bourke Street and a modern riverboat at Echuca. The importance of Alice's virginity and the need to protect it was never mentioned. The need to ensure that Alice was fit and healthy equally wasn't mentioned explicitly. As far as Julie could discern, Alice was merely a commodity to Mr Xu, albeit a valuable one. What she would be required to do once it was time to move on from Echuca didn't figure in her instructions either.

However, there was clarity on one point.

'If we have any reason to doubt your loyalty, or if you seek to contact anybody other than those people you are instructed to contact, you will be killed.'

It was a statement made in the most chillingly conversational manner that Julie had ever heard. She had absolutely no doubt that Mr Xu meant it and that Mr Kim would willingly kill her if he was required to do so.

No response was called for from Julie throughout the whole of the interview.

As the link was severed and the laptop screen went blank, Kim unwound himself from the bed, gave Julie instructions for the Little Bourke Street action and then gestured her to the door.

It was only some minutes later as she walked through into the atrium of the buildings fronting on to Collins Street and settled to a strong coffee that she relaxed enough to go into a panic.

Jesus, fucking Christ; what have I got myself into? I'm a trained investigator, not some modern-day version of Wonder Woman.

But if *she* didn't know what it was all about, the urbane man who had been sitting on the other side of the chairman from Alan at her original security service interview, and who had been listening in on the conversation she had just had with Xu, had a far better idea. The Australian Security Service, briefed by partners in the UK and China, had a clear enough view of some parts of the trafficking activities that Julie was being drawn into; what they didn't know was how it all hung together, how it was controlled, who the key players like Mr Xu actually were, and, what was driving the kidnapping of the middle/professional-class and educated women. That this

145

marginal activity was linked to the mainstream of labour and sex-trade trafficking they knew full well. How far these linkages went in terms of the Chinese mainland criminal fraternity, and, more importantly, how far they reached into the corrupt underbelly of Chinese officialdom, was a question that Julie's activities, it was hoped, would give the beginnings of an answer to.

The problem for the authorities in Beijing and elsewhere was that the apparent role of the trafficked high-value women, which appeared to relate to circumventing China's strict immigration and emigration rules, just did not seem to merit the elaborate processes by which they were being captured and trafficked to China.

The consensus among the elite group of public servants around the world, which now included Susie Peveral, was that they were clearly missing something very basic. The clues were there. The UK immigration system was accumulating a growing log of movements between China and Britain, not just of Mr Kim, but also of Linda Shen and a number of other young Chinese women. The concentration was on the movements and the activities that followed in the UK; it would take time for people to think back up the linking train of events that preceded the movements. In the complex web of security, people trafficking and like activities, joined-up thinking was extremely difficult to achieve. The common theme of money was recognised, even if it wasn't yet clear which of the manifestations of illicit money acquisition and management was the key one here.

The one prevailing feeling that remained with Mr Xu after his conversation with Julie, or at least his monologue in front of her since she didn't open her mouth, was undoubtedly good old-fashioned scepticism.

'Kim will need to watch that one very carefully,' he said to his companion.

'And you trust Kim?'

The question was in Mandarin. Mr Xu didn't distrust Kim as much as most, but generally he didn't trust anybody.

'No.'

The chuckle from Xu's companion, who had been sitting in on the video-conference out of Julie's sight, said that he understood the old man all too well. The members of the tight syndicate of commodity suppliers that they were a part of undoubtedly didn't even trust one other.

'Our client has set a deadline.'

It was two weeks later; Julie, Kim and Alice Hou were still in Echuca.

Mr Xu didn't like working to deadlines; it led to mistakes, to taking risks, to taking things for granted that shouldn't have been. But the client in question was rich and powerful. Xu knew that, so did the man now pacing backwards and forwards silently on the expensive Tibetan carpet that was Xu's pride and joy. Li Qiang – even Xu wasn't sure whether this was his real name – was a key member of Xu's business group. A very senior public servant with the ear of some of the most important men in the Communist hierarchy, he lived a double life with an ease and composure that the more intense Mr Xu could never have aspired to.

'The woman, Julie Li, has been instructed to prepare the merchandise. I haven't given Kim any deadline. He needs to stay out of view for a time; the British are pressing the Australians to pick him up over some unrelated labour import- ation activities. He's aware of the pressure the Australians are under. That'll give him an incentive to get the girl ready quickly without any stated deadlines.'

Mr Li wasn't interested. This was a client that had to be satisfied. He gave Xu the deadline.

'It can be met. He is a man of patience; he will want the merchandise in good condition.'

147

Li Qiang didn't appear to hear. Seemingly engrossed in Mr Xu's collection of Qianlong-era porcelain, he became very still. Arguing with Xu didn't make sense.

'It will be met!'

It was an unequivocal statement that the client expected Mr Xu to take as a fact.

'Then you must keep the police from interfering.'

Julie would have recognised the cold hard way in which Xu made the statement. Li Qiang shrugged. In common with Mr Xu, he was probably beyond intimidation.

The People's Police in China was a major problem to the criminal groups that Mr Xu and Li Qiang worked with and were a part of. In fact, they were a problem to a whole range of people in the new China where corruption and political manipulation were rife and the efforts of the Communist authorities to stamp it out were hindered as much by the depths of penetration of the corruption as by their inability to know whom to trust, even among their own.

The challenge for the UK and Australian Security Services and law-enforcement agencies in dealing with the Chinese was to identify the uncorrupted officials to deal with without alerting the corrupted ones. It was an issue that had taken on a greater urgency with the decision to employ Julie, whose life could be on the line if information got into the wrong hands.

21

It was six hours before Kim returned. It was obvious from his body language that he was in a foul mood. It eventually transpired, much to Julie's amusement, that this was more to do with his need to ask Julie to do something for him than with the nature of the request itself.

On being released, Alice was dismissed from the room and locked in the bedroom. At Julie's insistence, she wasn't hand-cuffed again and her clothes were returned to her.

'Outside!'

Kim's demand was irresistible.

They sat out on the rear deck in the semi-darkness. Julie was cold. Her sweatshirt provided inadequate warmth and Kim had given her no time to get a coat.

'I was picked up by the police.'

Julie was surprised.

'What? Why?'

She experienced mixed feelings. It wasn't an action that she would have expected. Taking Mr Kim out of circulation would have stalled the whole project. Unless something major had changed, the Australian Security Service would never have authorised such a thing. But a sense of relief was firmly suppressed. Much as she would have liked to have given up on the whole activity, she knew that she still had a job to do.

'I'm Chinese.'

Kim spat the words out.

It didn't seem a likely reason to Julie, so she assumed that it was his way of covering his embarrassment at what had happened to him.

'They're looking for you. Echuca is just the sort of place where the police would expect you to hole up, apparently.'

Julie was even more surprised; this seemed even less likely. Maybe something really had changed.

'But you convinced them that you didn't know anything about me?' she said.

'Maybe! I still have to take my driver's licence to the police station tomorrow.'

'So?'

'So I don't trust them. There's something not right. They didn't ask where I was staying in Echuca. Why didn't they do that? Do they already know?'

Julie had no answer. Pulling Kim in and then letting him go didn't make much sense to her either. She assumed that the police action wasn't spontaneous. In which case, why had the Security Service put them up to it? Was it a message; a coded enquiry about herself? She had to assume that it was; it was the only reasonable explanation. That meant that she had to somehow show herself but it had to be convincing to Kim.

Kim had his own problems. He was in a quandary of his own making, having dismissed the driver days ago. If when he went back with his driver's licence, whether they knew it already or not, they would want his current address. He realised that to avoid suspicion he would have to give it and expect it to be checked. That would expose Alice to the possibility of discovery and rescue if the police came to visit.

Only Julie could ensure Alice's security, if he wasn't there. But Mr Kim still couldn't bring himself to completely trust her. Yet he knew that he had to; he needed her cooperation. The logic was there; but the underlying niggle of the neatness of Julie's recruitment still troubled him, as he knew it still troubled Mr Xu.

'Did you buy an exercise bike?'

Changing the subject wasn't going to help much but Julie needed to keep up the pretence of innocence.

Kim's scowl clearly said that he hadn't.

'You're going to have to buy one.'

His lack of enthusiasm for this suggestion to her as a solution was rather obvious. The exercise bike was becoming an end in itself.

Possibilities for Julie began to surface. With only one car, three people and the need to keep Alice hidden, the dilemmas were piling up on Mr Kim thick and fast. Julie knew that she had to help Kim, since she was no closer to understanding what the plans were for Alice but she also had to make contact with her bosses.

'I can take you into town and then go on to Swan Hill. You can get a taxi back to the wharf.'

'Sure.'

It was an obvious solution. Julie noted the tight-jawed way that the word was extruded from Kim's mouth. It was if one part of his brain didn't want to say it but another part was forcing him to. The trust gap had still to be bridged. She would have to see to it that, whatever transpired during the day, his trust would be increased.

How the hell was she going to do that? she asked herself.

'OK,' was all she said to Kim.

Next day Kim seemed more reconciled to Julie's plan.

It didn't take Julie and Kim long to tape Alice's ankles and wrists together and tape over her mouth. The look of betrayal in Alice's eyes seared into Julie's brain but her priority was to build Kim's trust. A look at Kim reassured her that he hadn't seen the young Chinese woman's anguish. His contempt for Alice meant that he barely looked at her as he went about the business of restraining her.

Kim had wanted to get an early start the next day so he was irritable and unapproachable, but as Julie was beginning to read him rather better again she sensed that he was also anxious. Since he shared only such information as he thought she needed to know, she was unaware of the surge of emails that he had had from Britain and the pressure on him from there to resolve the outstanding issues of his last visit. He, in his turn, was also unaware that moves were in hand to remove him from the British action. Like Kim himself, Mr Xu shared only the minimum of information that he thought necessary.

Equally, the last thing Mr Kim thought he needed was a raised profile with the Australian authorities; it was as much this as the unfinished business in the UK that was making him edgy.

And the last thing that Mr Xu needed now was for Kim to be distracted from the task of delivering up Alice Hou in prime condition, since that was now his primary and only task.

'Let's go.'

Leaving Alice locked in the houseboat's windowless shower room, the two set off for Echuca.

Kim's nervousness increased as they drove into the centre of town. The police were expecting him. The Security Service was tracking him. The presence of Julie with Kim was noted and contingency plans rehearsed.

Events for the Security Service had suddenly taken a more positive turn. Having been spotted in Echuca by his unusual height, Kim had from their point of view absolved Julie of any urgent and immediate need to make contact; they knew where she was. Had she known this she would not have been surprised therefore that their car had been fitted with a tracking device; they had every intention of continuing to know where she was.

But Julie herself still felt that she had to make contact with the Security Service; Alan had been most insistent that she did so regularly, if infrequently, even if she had nothing to report.

Having delivered Kim to the door of the police station, she drove off immediately.

Julie had no intention of going to Swan Hill. Vague as her

knowledge of the local geography was, she realised that she had a better chance to engineer a contact with the police and via them, Alan, her controller in Melbourne, by going to the larger town of Bendigo.

Her driving as she left Echuca was erratic and occasionally illegal.

Good.

It wasn't long before she had attracted the attention of a police patrol car. Patched into the police radio network, Alan, from the comfort of his office in St Kilda, read her mind accurately.

'OK, let's make it look authentic,' he told the Victorian Police.

Australian country roads are generally good quality and rarely busy. That was something that Julie had been told by one of her Melbourne café acquaintances. She was soon over the speed limit.

Nothing happened for a few kilometres. Then it happened quickly.

'Jesus! Two of them. Where the hell did they come from?'

Slithering on the loose gravel on the outside of a bend, Julie hit a bush and then bounced over a rock and came to a none too elegant a halt as one of the police cars pulled up beside her. A faint twinkle in the eyes of the officer who approached her told her that he was a party to the game in play.

'Miss Li,' he said with a wide and engaging grin.

'Miss Kershawe, perhaps,' said his companion, a diminutive Chinese woman sergeant.

They made their way in a convoy of three to the police compound in Bendigo, the sergeant travelling with Julie.

What!

The sergeant had produced her handcuffs.

'The local press usually have a couple of apprentices around the place. They take photos and daydream of scoops, no doubt.'

153

'In this day and age?'

'Country town,' the sergeant said, 'not Melbourne.'

She was obviously not a fan of the big city.

No press photo was taken. But the quality of the mobile phone video that was taken was good enough to identify Julie Li. The Security Service wasn't the only people who had covered the possibilities when Julie set off from Echuca. Mr Xu was not pleased but he ordered a waiting game. He did not pass the information on to Mr Kim.

Sitting in front of a police laptop computer, the encrypted conversation with Alan didn't take long. His Greek-god looks weren't so obvious through the electronic media as in real life; Julie's expectation of not seeing Alan again hadn't been met but the stresses of the role that he had got her into had dissipated any of the feelings that he had generated in her in the Melbourne coffee shop.

'Kim is under pressure. The Brits are very keen to get hold of him. Apparently, some pretty important trafficking deals have gone wrong and opened up a can of worms with the UK authorities. Not our problem, but being on edge makes Kim dangerous.'

(When she eventually came to hear of this, Linda Shen, in the comfort of her luxury nursery and the gurgling company of her infant son, would hardly be able to suppress a grin of satisfaction.)

'OK. So something's wrong. I sensed he's nervous about what we're doing at the moment; but I didn't think of him as a bloke who would worry over much about anything other than his immediate problems. Somehow this Alice Hou is really important to them; why I haven't a clue. I'm supposed to be getting her fit and healthy. How you do that with a woman who's frightened witless I've no idea.'

Julie was no more going to tell Alan than Mr Kim about Alice's reaction to herself. Alan told her what she needed to know:

154

'At the Chinese end of things, something's brewing. The top brass are very aware of what they call the importation of high-class Western Chinese women, albeit in penny numbers. They also know full well that some pretty important people in the upper reaches of Shanghai and Beijing society could be involved. That's the difficulty. We still can't be sure who is a good guy and who is a bad guy.

'The people we believe we can trust have theories on why the women are being imported. We know that so far fewer than ten have made it. But the stories are conflicting. The very people who are telling us this are interrelated politically, and in God knows what other ways, with some of those suspected of having purchased one or two of the women. Even our most reliable Chinese colleagues can't be sure where the linkages and patronage reach.'

'Alan, you're not telling me anything. Alice Hou is clearly destined to be sent to China – why probably doesn't matter at the moment. What does matter is when that will be and how do we prevent it?'

'I think the Chinese would like to see Alice delivered to Hong Kong or Shanghai. That gives them the opportunity to deal with things in their own backyard.'

Having no knowledge of the banker who had been arrested at the Hong Kong airport and the circumstances surrounding that, Julie was rather taken aback by this statement. But, if anything, what was clear from Alan's new information about the delivery of Alice was that she, Julie, was going to do the delivering!

She said so.

'That's a bridge to cross when we get to it. For the moment, we need to get you back into play with Kim so that you can find out when the delivery is going to be.'

Julie was only too well aware that this was the case. Alan shut down the laptop link.

Having consulted with the sergeant, Julie crept out of the

back door of the police station and quickly bought a step-up platform at a sports shop; Kim hadn't given her enough money to buy an exercise bike. Recovering the car from an out-of-town car lot where it had been deposited by the police, Julie set off back to Echuca.

Julie was unaware that her arrest had been observed, so all she thought she needed to do was construct a suitable story for Mr Kim. The dent in the front of the vehicle gave her the basis for an explanation as to why she had taken so long and would also focus Kim's attention. The last thing he was going to want to do was to expose himself too clearly to the car hire firm; the damage was unlikely to be reported. But he was going to be very angry!

Even so Julie didn't hurry back to the houseboat; she savoured her freedom for as long as she could.

Why his driver's licence wasn't satisfactory Kim wasn't actually told. It was tossed aside on the desk of the senior sergeant while he and his colleagues took their leisurely morning coffee break. Mr Kim uncharacteristically fretted as he waited for whatever supposed checks to be made.

'Quite a character this one,' the sergeant said.

The Echuca Police had already done their checks.

'Keeps interesting company.'

Kim's recent activities in Britain and the rather ruthless way that he had solved some of the interrelational problems among the Chinese labour gangs in the UK had been summarised for the Federal Immigration Department and forwarded to the Victorian Police.

'So what's the bugger doing here in Echuca?'

The senior sergeant knew but he wasn't supposed to share his knowledge with his colleagues.

'Hired a houseboat with a Chinese woman.'

None of the officers supposed that Mr Kim was indulging in an illicit affair; a less romantic individual they could hardly imagine.

156

After the sergeant judged that the arrangements made with the Security Service had had time to be worked through, he picked up the driver's licence and went through to the interview room. His conversation with Kim largely focused on his points score that left the Chinese man only one offence away from having his licence suspended. It was a useful, if unnecessary, means of warning Kim to watch his behaviour. With Mr Xu always making the same point, Mr Kim was unlikely to put a foot wrong in the immediate future.

The houseboat seemed quiet and deserted when Julie eventually made her way back to it. Set against the overriding quiet of the section of the Murray River where they were moored, it unnerved her for reasons that she couldn't explain. Her relationship with Mr Kim had changed; it was more equal, but whether that was going to make the next phase in the action any easier she was doubtful. Mr Kim on edge was a far less attractive prospect to deal with than the enigmatic one that she had first known. And Mr Kim was on edge, having had to endure the incomprehensible football commentary on the taxi's radio on the journey back from town.

Julie moved carefully on to the afterdeck and listened. There were faint sounds from within.

For goodness' sake, she told herself. Of course it was quiet – Kim was hardly going to be discussing the latest sporting news with Alice.

The entry door was unlocked. This wasn't usually the case.

A moment of panic overtook her. What if he had come back and taken Alice away? He could easily have hired another car.

People's National Daily
English-language Beijing Edition – Monday, 26 July 2010
TRIAL OF ARRESTED BANKER

The banker arrested in June 2010, while meeting a young Chinese woman arriving from Melbourne, was put on trial at the Number One People's Intermediate Court in Beijing.

He is charged with several offences relating both to his banking activities and to the importation of prohibited goods. The People's Judge ordered that the nature of the goods imported should not be made public. The banker, whose name is also being withheld until further investigations into his links with criminal gangs in Shanghai and Beijing have been completed, is also charged with an offence under Chinese immigration laws.

The young woman, who was also arrested at Hong Kong International Airport as an illegal immigrant, is understood to have originally come from either Argentina or Brazil. The People's Police claimed that she is the seventh young woman that it is aware of over the last two years who has been trafficked into China after a complicated journey from their countries of origin via the USA or Canada and Australia to the PRC. While it is alleged that these women were kidnapped and forcibly transported to the PRC, evidence only exists on the present whereabouts of two of them. One woman is alleged to be married to an industrialist in a northern city that the police wouldn't name. The second is thought to be married to a businessman in Beijing who is reported to have links with senior members of the Communist Party hierarchy. The police have also refused to name this man. As a result of the arrest of the banker in Hong Kong, investigations are now under way to discover whether these marriages were forced on the women in question.

The possibility that the other young women may have illegally entered China for the purposes of enforced marriage has been raised with the Ministry of Internal Affairs. The People's Judge in the trial of the banker is expected to defer

158

consideration of the charges under the immigration laws until the Ministry has made its own investigations.

If the banker is found guilty of charges of illegal banking activities and of prohibited importation, he is expected to be hanged.

22

David was surprised to find Susie nervous. Susie Peveral, high-flying Assistant Secretary fully in command of her world, was the last person that he would have expected to be nervous. But, with her lust for David turning into something deeper, she was desperate not to put a foot wrong, even over the most innocent things.

'It's not exactly my thing,' was his response to Susie's invitation to a concert at the Barbican Hall.

Since, however, he virtually lived over the top of the concert hall, he agreed and invited Susie back for drinks afterwards.

They both knew that drinks weren't all that was on the agenda.

The concert was as hard-going as David had expected. It was in the lift to his flat that David noticed Susie's state of mind.

The sex was more sedate than it had been on some previous occasions but no less satisfying for that.

Her lying in his arms after the repeat performance that was becoming their trademark, David, with the cynicism bred of experience, waited for Susie to open the conversation on illegal immigration or people trafficking of women, or whatever her current preoccupation was. She didn't – at least not directly.

'I think I'm going to have to go to Australia.'

Maybe David's likely reaction to this statement was what was making her anxious.

Since Australia seemed to be popping up in his investigations in ways that he was beginning to find baffling, somehow Susie's pronouncement didn't surprise him.

Her next statement did.

'It would be great if you could come with me.'

Once she'd made the invitation, she relaxed. Perhaps that was what she was nervous about.

'I'm due some leave. We could lose ourselves somewhere in the wide open spaces of Oz and …'

David kissed her quiet. He was tired and he knew that, if she persisted, they would be at it again and he doubted his strength to satisfy her for a third time.

He distracted her.

'And have sex in a billabong under the shade of a coolibah tree,' he muttered.

Susie's carefully controlled demeanour was lost in a bout of giggles that ebbed and flowed for nearly ten minutes. The giggling was yet another surprise of the evening, generating unexpected images of his pigtailed schoolgirl sister for David. He held Susie tightly to him until she subsided. Then, little girl-like too, she curled herself up beside him and before he knew it the gentle rhythm of her breathing was all that he was aware of.

At no time did it occur to David that he wouldn't go with her to Australia.

The Australia–China axis was the key to much of what was beginning to emerge into the full light of his investigative day. But it was also raising more questions than it answered; questions, he suspected, that some would not want to be answered.

Over breakfast the conversation that they didn't have the previous evening resumed.

'There's still one more step in the chain to investigate,' David said. 'The link to China always seems to be via Australia or an Australian Chinese man. And, as you predicted, at every turn I keep stumbling on this business of women being trafficked for

161

something else than the sex trade. Everything else I think I have a handle on.'

'Yes.' The high-value women trafficking was very much Susie's 'thing'. 'We just got some information from Brazil. A woman from São Paulo who was trafficked to Canada, initially in the usual way of paying the traffickers to get to a better life, has alerted the Australians to several more of her ilk who have been transported there but have disappeared from view.'

'Have you heard about this from other sources?'

'Oh yes, David, it's confirmed. The Home Office and Border Agency have got something going with the Australian Security Service, can't say more, and the Australians have names for at least three other girls who were spirited into Australia and have gone to ground there. And there's a link both to the mainland Chinese and illegal labour trafficking that you have been investigating, as we know.'

The mayhem in the illegal labour trafficking that had followed Joe Kim's and the mysterious young Chinese woman's visits had spilled over into such violence that the Home Office was reluctant for David to continue his official investigation for the moment. Since he felt that he had probably obtained sufficient information to produce a preliminary report, an approved digression to Australia seemed very attractive.

Among the mandarins, the opportunity this presented to delay or bury a report that seemed likely to jangle nerves with the Chinese Government was quietly but silently welcomed. Even Susie recognised that protesting about this inevitable Whitehall response would be unfruitful. A business trip to Australia with David to pursue the only aspect of the work that really interested her she was sure would be worthwhile.

23

After his weekend with Susie, David was exhausted, amazed and fascinated all at the same time.

He knew why he was exhausted! His amazement and fascination represented a jumble of feelings that, in a rare fit of self-analysis, he put down to his growing attraction to Susie and to his respect for her intellectual capabilities as well as her physical ones.

'So I've got a free trip to Australia,' he remarked to his shaving mirror. 'She really means to get stuck into this high-class women trafficking thing then.'

Unfamiliar with the hidden ways of Whitehall, David nonetheless assumed that Susie must have had tacit approval from a higher level for what she was doing – not that there was much officialdom above her.

His preliminary report was stored on his laptop and safely backed up. He had hurriedly dumped his brain on to his computer after Susie had left and while he could still recall the details in sufficient clarity of their disorganised conversations.

Jesus, he had thought as he was doing it, *I doubt if I could shag and prepare an inter-departmental brief at the same time!*

Of course, Susie couldn't either, but it was her chameleon-like ability to switch from lovemaking to the Chinese role in people trafficking, without missing a beat, that so attracted David.

Interesting they've got an insider in the Chinese game in Melbourne.

Susie had been careful to avoid saying anything that might indicate both who 'they' were and how they got their nameless insider into place. But her bed companion knew enough to make some educated guesses.

Our Mr Kim has fingers in many pies, David thought, *as I interpret what Susie wasn't telling me. Somehow the Aussies, or she, have got some sort of agent hooked on to him.*

Shit, that sounds like a guarantee of a short life!

Although Susie had no idea that Linda Shen had taken over the link role to the Chinese gangs in Britain involved in illegal labour trafficking, her instinct that Mr Kim was key to the women trafficking was entirely correct.

'Follow Mr Kim. That's what she seemed to be saying,' David confided to his kitchen at large as he conjured up his breakfast.

But he had another trip to Lincolnshire first as his police contact there had some information that would fill in the final gaps in his report.

Train travel in the UK was something of a mixed feast, and East Anglia and Lincolnshire weren't always in the premier league when it came to consistent performance. Based on his experience in obscure places in Africa and Pakistan, David had come to hate trains.

The first thing that David noticed was the cosmopolitan mix of people who were travelling. And when he noticed that he had seemed to have attracted the interest of a group of Chinese youths, he was beginning to think that it was because he was about the only white Caucasian within their vision.

He was wrong. He hadn't seen the frantic surge of activity at the London station before departure or been aware of the barrage of mobile phone calls that had been exchanged as his progress to the rail terminal had been shadowed.

He was picked up in an unmarked police car. The driver's grunt alerted David.

164

'What?'

'A load of Chinese men got off the train and into a couple of mini-vans. I'd say they were following you and now us.'

'They can't be. How could they have known I would be on that particular train?'

But the policeman was right: they were following them; he'd just done a couple of manoeuvres to check.

The police driver was on the radio. It was probably too late.

Perhaps sensing that they had been detected, the first of the mini-vans suddenly accelerated and tried to pass the police car. The driver wasn't successful but the van did manage to get alongside.

'Hang on.'

Knowing the road better than their pursers, David's driver suddenly started to pull across the line of the van. He accelerated. Holding his position he was almost inviting the van driver to smash into his side. The road took a tight left turn. Still holding his line and still accelerating, the driver swerved at the last minute. The rear of the vehicle took a couple stomach-churning wiggles before it straightened out. The police driver's grunt was a mixture of satisfaction, anxiety and then resignation.

The satisfaction was obvious; it was a brilliantly executed piece of aggressive driving of the type taught at police anti-kidnapping classes. The anxiety was more understandable; the mini-van careered on in a straight line and crashed over the verge of the road and disappeared down an embankment. The driver had no way of knowing the extent of the injuries that the van's occupants would necessarily have sustained.

The resignation signified that the second mini-van was still following them.

The driver was on the radio again.

'Settle down, sir. We'll just have to outrun them for the moment.'

Jerking the stinger into place after the police car had passed the roadblock required split-second timing.

The Chinese driver of the mini-van was clearly expecting some sort of ambush when he hadn't been able to catch the car he was chasing. His instinct to brake caused the van to slither sideways into a line of bollards at the side of the road. The bollards didn't do the van's bodywork much good but they did arrest the vehicle without serious injury to its passengers.

David Hutchinson was in Inspector Woodward's office.

'The Somali gangmaster was asked some apparently innocent questions about you after your last visit and about today's meeting with her. She didn't see any reason to lie. It didn't take the Chinese too long to work out what was happening. The rest was intuition, train timetables and simple planning.'

The inspector had cancelled the meeting with the Somali gangmaster. He now had more things to ask her, but his trust had been destroyed by the car chase incident.

David asked the obvious question.

'But what was that all about?'

'They were planning to warn you off.'

'Warn me off what, Inspector?'

'You're a journalist. Journalists asking questions all over the countryside excite suspicion.'

'All over the countryside – again, what does all this mean?'

'It means, Mr Hutchinson, that they have unintentionally confirmed the link for us between the ubiquitous Mr Kim and the local Chinese gangs.'

'How come?'

'According to the Somali gangmaster, when she said that you were coming the Chinese man she was dealing with checked names and details. There had clearly been a lot of emailing and mobile phone calls after your first visit and the questioning that you were clearly involved in. Out of the four Chinese you saw that day only Kim was a principal; the others were the driver and two bodyguards. When the woman fed back you were returning, only Kim, or someone in his confidence, could have understood the significance. The rest was the usual reaction of the local Chinese gangs.'

'Hell,' said David, 'they're a lot better organised than I would have expected.'

'Big money,' was all the inspector said.

David didn't challenge the analysis.

The incident gave David a useful hook to lead into the conclusions of his report.

The preliminary draft was delivered to Susie Peveral's office the day before they flew to Australia. Unvarnished and as yet not in its final 'diplomatic' version, it gave Susie some interesting reading as they headed south.

David, who had upgraded Susie to Business Class, looked on with amusement as her facial expression displayed a whole range of reactions. The report was clearly what she had wanted.

The second part of David's investigation, which would be much more difficult, was less likely to lead to such a definitive report, but for Susie it was more about getting the women trafficking issue further up the main political agenda.

24

The houses on the northern, New South Wales, shore of Lake Mulwala would have reminded Julie Li of Sandbanks in Dorset. Visits there to her godfather were among her fondest memories. With the same sort of mix of TV personalities, football and other sporting celebrities, the similarities were compelling. Whether Sandbanks had a darker side she would have doubted. That the Lake Mulwala settlement had was as yet beyond her knowledge. But, based on the fact that one of the most isolated houses belonged to a Chinese businessman whose normal address was in Shanghai and the assortment of nocturnal comings and goings, the locals would have certainly suspected that it had.

And they would have been right.

Permanently manacled at the wrists and ankles, Janice Liang, supposedly late of Calgary, Canada and earlier unwilling travelling companion of Alice Hou, provided domestic services of all varieties to a range of Chinese men who came and went from the isolated house at irregular hours.

'She's not a virgin.'

The painfully intrusive and contemptuous medical examination that Janice Liang, Alice and their other companions had been subjected to on first arrival in Melbourne had separated Janice, April Cheng and Patience Zhang from Alice, who was the only one seemingly innocent of any sexual encounters.

In the complex market that the girls were being trafficked into, the price for Janice, April and Patience was no lower than that for Alice or the half-dozen or so girls who had gone before them. Contrary to the prevailing Western wisdom, virginity was a specialist taste among those in the market for wives; sexual experience was just as highly prized.

Protected by his reputation as a fashionable private consultant, making such inspections on young women was not uncommon for Dr Wu. The young of the Melbourne Chinese community were no more and no less promiscuous than any other group of young people. Dr Wu's assistant, a man with huge gambling debts and a fine disregard for the ethics of the medical profession that supported him, reported the findings to Mr Xu's agent in Melbourne. Mr Xu set about marketing Alice. The fact that at the time she wasn't his to market hadn't presented itself as a problem to him.

'Convincing the buyer won't be that difficult,' was Mr Xu's opinion as he had made his plans.

He already had had contact with at least one of his clients with an interest in acquiring a partner of known sexual purity. The loss of Patience Zhang in the raid on the gang holding Alice Hou had been an irritation, but a subsequent ambush of one of the gang's vehicles also saw the transfer of Janice Liang into Xu's 'protection'. The potential repercussions of his actions didn't unduly bother Xu; he was confident that Mr Kim would be able to deal with any.

However, the girls still needed to be held somewhere until a buyer could be found. With the Australian authorities having gone up a gear in their efforts to identify, follow through and break up the trafficking chain 'storing' the goods was an increasing problem. Working in isolated groups helped, but Mr Xu's habit of hijacking the best girls from competing Chinese gangs if he thought he could make a good profit rather undermined this policy. The subsequent warfare was something that had started to concentrate official minds. And debriefing the released Patience Zhang had been particularly helpful.

169

Although it wasn't very far from Echuca to Lake Mulwala, Mr Kim maintained his overall control of what was going on at Mulwala by mobile phone. He had never visited the area and had very little knowledge of the lake and its particular features. Mr Xu's cell system meant that Kim only knew the man in charge at the remote house and even then only by a name that he knew full well was false.

The mobile phone conversations were careful and coded, but since Mr Kim's recent arrest in Echuca the authorities were now at least able to listen in and to gather what gems of intelligence they could.

'We will need to move your merchandise within the next two days,' Kim said in an early-morning conversation.

Julie had noticed Kim's habit of making his calls early, assuming that she or Alice weren't yet up and about. It was usually around seven o'clock. But since Alice was responsible for breakfast and cleaning chores, Kim's assumption was often wrong. As an evening waitress in her more recent past she found getting up early a struggle. It was Julie who generally had to force her out of bed and who as a consequence was able to take her time in the shower while she eavesdropped on Mr Kim as he talked outside on deck.

God, I wish he wouldn't keep switching between English and Mandarin!

Interpreting half a conversation was hard enough without worrying if you'd understood the words properly. On this occasion, Julie need hardly have worried.

'We're going to have to move from here,' Kim announced to Julie once their meal was complete and Alice had been despatched to other domestic duties.

Julie waited for the inevitable instructions. She had already learned that Kim didn't do explanations and to ask was to invite his anger. And his anger was now never far from the surface. Irritatingly, Julie had to rebuild trust with the man on an almost daily basis. Nonetheless, if they were to move on, she needed to know as much as possible about when and where.

'We need a different car,' Kim said.

'You want me to return this one and get another one?'

'Yes, you stupid bitch. You put the dent in it; you can sort it out with the hire firm.'

'OK, OK.'

Julie couldn't believe her luck.

'I'll go to Bendigo, different renting office. But I'll need to know for how long and where we're going.'

'Get it for a month. We aren't going off-road.'

It wasn't much help, but annoying Mr Kim still wasn't on the agenda.

Getting arrested again for speeding, however, was.

Several hours later just as it was getting dark Julie was back on board the houseboat. The police might not have known where Julie, Alice and Mr Kim were going but their tracking device again would give them a good chance of being close behind when they arrived.

'Today?'

Mr Kim had identified the premises of a well-known local farmer on the Victorian side of Lake Mulwala as a place to meet. Access to the farm was off the beaten track but achievable from two directions. It was just the sort of rendezvous that suited Kim's purpose.

'Before the match.'

Kim had already established with the leader of the group holding Janice that the farmer was an Australian Rules fan and a supporter of Carlton and would be well away from the rendezvous area when they arrived.

Time and place were fixed. The Victorian Police had a few guesses about the details aided by the abysmal record of the farmer, who was recognised from the phone transcript and known to them for his inability to restrain his aggression once drunk. And getting drunk was a regular habit on match days, whether Carlton were playing or not. The police took some precautions in case they had wrongly interpreted the telephone conversation, which included alerting their colleagues in New South Wales to the possibility of action on Lake Mulwala, since the lake was not actually a part of Victoria, and prepared themselves for what was to come.

They didn't have to wait for long at the Echuca end. Bundling Alice quickly into the station wagon that Julie had hired before any Saturday afternoon idlers along the historic wharf might wonder what was wrong with the young woman being half carried to the vehicle, they drove off towards the highway.

Even during the winter months there was still a range of pleasure boats that cruised the waters of the lake. Essentially formed by restricting the flow of the River Murray, Lake Mulwala was man-made and as a consequence something of a tourist attraction. Large areas of the lake were navigable, hence the pleasure boats, but, equally, large areas were not – at least not to the commercial vessels as a result of the huge number of dead trees that grotesquely populated these areas. These remnants of the forest that had been flooded formed a bizarre backdrop for boat trips but posed a major hazard to those unfamiliar with the lake. Iceberg-like, the root structures and lower limbs of the trees below the waterline made straying off the marked channels unwise. However, for locals, navigating through the exposed trees away from the marked channels was a skill that was widespread and used and abused as the need arose.

And as Mr Kim approached the rendezvous point on the Victorian side of the lake in good time, the priority for the kidnappers of Janice Liang, the pseudonymously named 'Heng Sun' included, was to get across the lake as quickly as possible.

'They're on the move!'

172

It wasn't possible for the New South Wales Police observers to get too close to the remote Chinese-owned house as its grounds were open and extensive and provided little cover, but once the group of three people had embarked in the rigid inflatable it was easier to keep them in view without creating suspicion.

'We'll let them out into the main channel and then follow.'

The police patrol boat nudged its way from behind the jetty of a house adjacent to the one under observation.

'Looks like three on board. Two seemed to be active in managing the boat; the third seems to be passive in the well of the inflatable.'

At the distances involved, it was enough to confirm that Janice Liang was on board but restrained.

As a large tourist riverboat ambled its way in a long loop to show off the various houses that none of the gaping visitors would ever be likely to be able to afford, the second police patrol boat headed out from the Victorian side, cutting off access to a large area of the bank, much of which was not available to public access anyway. They watched as Heng Sun directed his steersman to head into the edge of the dead forest area.

'He's heading out of the channel.'

The inflatable edged away from any of the tourist-frequented parts of the lake and towards the Victorian shore. Equally and initially imperceptibly the inflatable increased its speed and headed further into the danger area.

The clatter of a helicopter began to dominate the normal quiet of the lake, its clear police identification showing on its underbelly.

'He's off!'

The officer in the patrol boat that had followed the Chinese group across the lake didn't seem surprised.

The inflatable had taken fright at the sight of the helicopter, but it was only when the steersman wound up the two

173

outboard engines and headed into the morass of tree stumps that it was apparent that the fugitives knew exactly what they were doing and where they were going.

A chase was on. But it soon proved to be a one-sided one.

The inflatable sped away, skimming the surface, its bow clear of the water, seemingly mocking the more cautious police steersman. He had no choice but to follow. Beginning to weave an erratic course between the tree stumps, the fugitive inflatable had a head start. Seeking to cut the vessel off, the police steersman accelerated into an equally erratic and convoluted passage through the dead forest. More substantial than the trailer-loadable inflatable, the police patrol boat drew more water as a consequence of its much more powerful and larger outboard motors. But in the restricted confines of the dead forest it couldn't use its superior capability. The inflatable easily out-distanced it.

The juddering crunch that projected the police boat into a half-circle and brought it to a standstill justified Heng Sun's confidence in entering the morass of dead and broken trees.

As the inflatable reached open water on the Victorian side of the lake, its scything telltale wake spreading out into the forest on one side and the shallows on the other, the second police patrol vessel signalled that they had lost contact with the Chinese party.

It was many days before the joint police investigation could put together a complete picture of what happened next.

25

'Linda Shen?'

It was almost a smile of recognition; that worried her.

And had she known of the level of interest in her comings and goings to and from Britain and within, she should have been worried.

This was the fourth visit that she had made to Britain in almost as many months. The police and Border Agency might have admired her devotion to family in Manchester had they not known that she never in fact visited any of them. Having been steeped in the public-service ethos from her police and Border Agency days, spinning a story for the immigration officers went against the grain and usually put her on edge for a few hours after her arrival. But thoughts of her hostage son ensured that she adhered to her role.

The flight from Shanghai had given Linda plenty of time to think about what she was doing, why she was doing it, and the rights and wrongs of it. Her anger and bitterness at being press-ganged into marriage far from home had long since given way to a grudging and necessary acceptance of a life of luxury that otherwise would have been totally beyond her. She preferred 'press-ganged' as a description to 'kidnapped' even if the latter was closer to the truth; it didn't make her seem quite so much a victim. Nothing material was denied to her; her husband, like most of the Chinese men that she had met saw their world very much in terms of possessions, including their wives. Procured by Mr Xu specifically because she not only had an unblemished British passport, but also because she was supposedly intelligent and well versed in British culture and administrative practices, she had soon gained her husband's reluctant and un-admitted trust. She was just the sort of working companion he needed, even if his inherent arrogance and male-oriented outlook made him unable to recognise this openly.

But Mr Shi was increasingly disconcerted to find himself on occasions acknowledging his wife's capabilities and deferring to them, if only subconsciously.

High over Eastern Europe on her way to London, Linda was ready to admit that her life wasn't that bad. She found the separation from her son irksome and on occasions extremely painful, but she reasoned that back in the UK she would have had to work to support him and would have been equally absent from his life for long periods while he was cared for by his grandparents. That was not to say that she didn't acknowledge that she was being crudely blackmailed into what she was doing because of him.

But now that the obnoxious Mr Kim had been removed from the scene she knew that her activities in Britain would be easier to manage.

Serving her husband's interests was ostensibly her prime purpose for visiting Britain. And she would have been the first to admit that Kim had indeed successfully knocked heads together and that her husband's syndicate's grasp on a significant amount of organised crime in the West Midlands, Manchester and East Anglia was well established. It was Linda Shen's subtle and careful encouragement of the local Chinese groups to overreach themselves by expanding into new areas of activity like computer fraud that had come to the attention of the British authorities. With her knowledge of how things worked in the UK, she ensured that there was sufficient transparency about these new endeavours for the police experts to detect them and to eventually deal with them.

'So what crime have I committed?'

Sensing the beginning of the descent into Heathrow, she tried to pull her thoughts together. From her training she knew that conspiracy in various forms was the principal thing that she might be guilty of; however, she was not involved in those things that her husband was doing that caused harm to people.

Crap! Guilt by association!

Much to her initial mortification, she realised that her moral standards had been undermined both by what she was doing and the new luxury that she had rapidly become used to. Something of her husband's simplistic view of the world had rubbed off. The little subversions of the local Chinese groups that she was supposed to be supporting salved her conscience, but until a real opportunity to escape from China emerged she wasn't going to be doing anything to rock her husband's boat.

She was met at Heathrow.

The face over the crumpled sign was smiling. She had never been confronted with the inevitable ill-written 'Linda Shen' sign *and* a smile. Her first reaction was relief. Her usual minder was not there to meet her. Then came the questions. Why not? What had happened to him. Who was this new guy?

'Linda Shen?'

She eventually decided that it was nervousness rather than deference that the man was displaying. She didn't bother to wonder why.

And a suspended sentence for assault in exchange for a minimum of two days of keeping his eyes and ears open was worth a smile to Li Chang.

'OK, Mr Li,' Linda said, once the man had introduced himself. 'Change of plan, we're not going to Birmingham; we're going to the Big Smoke. Ever driven in London?'

Li Chang thought it better to be honest. He hadn't.

'OK, I'll drive.'

The report to the Border Agency was confused and disjointed. Li Chang had no idea why Linda had first driven around the City of London before parking and then walking, or why she had just stood idly in front of various banks and other financial institutions. She said nothing and did nothing, and after half a day headed out to a country house hotel in Kent hoping that everybody who wanted to know she was in Britain now knew.

'I have a new minder. Why?'

The conversation on her satellite phone from the hotel's extensive garden was irritable and revealing.

'What new minder?'

Mr Shi's question was enough for both of them. Which bit of British officialdom had made the substitution didn't bother either of them, only that it had happened.

'Do we call it off?'

The plural escaped Mr Shi, but he was concentrated on whether the risk was too great to continue with the London-based activities that he had planned. The irritation that his wife detected stemmed from the fact that he couldn't make the decision on his own: he needed her input. And she knew that.

They didn't call it off.

Li Chang accomplished the trip from the Kentish hotel to Canary Wharf more easily than either of them had expected considering the early-morning traffic. Linda Shen needed him to be occupied and herself to have maximum freedom of action. Knowing that parking at Canary Wharf was no easier than in the City, she directed him to drop her in a particularly complex area of the district and directed him to a car park at the other end of the built-up area.

Li Chang was in a dilemma. He had no choice but to move off after she had got out of the car and no opportunity to see where she was going.

Linda had no problem with the UK authorities knowing what the bulk of her visit to the banking heart of London was all about, but she had some private arrangements to make on

178

her own behalf and that of her son that she didn't want anybody to be aware of.

The private arrangements didn't take long.

The arrangements on behalf of her husband equally didn't take long.

'This is nice!'

It was the sort of inanity that Linda knew that the over-brained Chinese banking types that she was now dealing with would expect from a mere woman.

The view from the offices of the small Russian bank was indeed spectacular on a clear cold day.

Having made herself intentionally memorable in an abundance of black leather, she knew that she was having a disturbing effect on the young banker. She didn't care. It was important that her husband knew that she had been there and completed what was for her a new and entirely different task.

A member of the Shi extended family placed there like a number of other young bankers with similar ties to mainland China, Mark Shi knew what was going to be expected of him. Why else had he been placed where he was?

'Your uncle greets you,' Linda Shen said formally.

The next twenty minutes were intense, unscripted and only on record encrypted into Mark Shi's computer. No transaction was attempted but codes and the means of recognising them were discussed and revisited until Linda was satisfied that the young man was clear on what he had to do and how and when he would have to do it. The system of part-electronic and part-human intervention was something that her husband had successfully developed and sold at substantial profit to his fellow businessmen.

Checking her watch, Linda knew that she had another ten to fifteen minutes to kill before seeking out the minder. Her day's activities had gone well.

'Another motorway failure,' she said to her companion. 'What must people think here?'

The spate of motorway bridge and other construction failures was a big issue in China. Poor-quality materials and skimped workmanship were widely blamed.

'The Russians have stopped buying steel for construction works,' Mark said guardedly. 'That's bad news. It brings the issue into the public domain.'

And what Mark Shi knew that his visitor didn't was that her husband was one of those guilty of thinning steel reinforcing rods and weakening the mix for pre-mixed concrete. The audit trail back to his company had yet to be established, but Mark was sure that it would be. Sometimes he didn't mind being tucked away far from home!

26

It was the much maligned farmer on the Victoria side of Lake Mulwala who found the car. Checking fences along the edge of his property was something that he did periodically. When he first sighted the burnt-out wreck he was immediately irritated; he knew it was trouble.

'What you think this place is?' he demanded of the dead car as he dismounted from his tractor.

Fly-tipping was always a problem in remote areas like this track.

He was a Pole of long residence and his English still retained something of the fractured verb-less quality that it had had as a boy when he had first arrived in Australia fifty years earlier. His fondness for his drink was legendary, as was the accompanying belligerence, but Carl was respected nonetheless as a hard-working and honest man who would give his last cent to help someone in need.

'Jesus!'

When Carl got to within a couple of metres of the car, he could feel the heat. Wisps of smoke idled out through the shattered windows; the pungent smell of burnt rubber was all pervading.

The car hadn't long stopped burning.

Wary that it might reignite, Carl fetched the fire extinguisher from his tractor and approached the driver's side cautiously.

'Mother of God!'

Starting back, the Pole crossed himself instinctively.

181

Taking another more measured look, he realised that the body inside the vehicle was so badly burned that he couldn't tell whether it was a man or a woman.

Climbing back up on to his tractor to get the best reception he called the police on his mobile phone.

With the metal too hot to touch, there was nothing that he could do but await the arrival of the emergency services. And as he waited he tried to build a picture of what might have happened. The track where the car had been left wasn't a regular road – it was a part of his farm – but with the fields cleared of gum trees and sloping down to the lakeside he found it hard to understand why the fire hadn't been seen. He was grateful that the conflagration hadn't spread to the surrounding scrub.

He said the same to the senior sergeant when the police arrived.

The police commandeered one of the bars of the local pub. Carl repeated his story two or three times until the detective inspector in charge was happy that he had got all the information that there was. The farmer's information was minimal; the police soon found that there was much more to be learned on the ground around the burnt-out car.

As specialist officers from Shepparton and Bendigo supplemented those from Yarrawonga, a picture began to emerge of the activity on the banks of the lake and in the area surrounding the vehicle.

As darkness fell, DI Lynsky pulled the main elements of the combined teams into the pub. The Chinese sergeant from Bendigo joined the briefing; the DI made no effort to introduce her. The Australian Security Service would, however, be fully informed about what had happened.

'OK.'

The senior crime scene officer gave a summary of their knowledge to date.

'Fact,' he said. 'We have identified three vehicles at the scene with the possibility of a fourth parked a little way off.

182

Unfortunately, the farmer who discovered the burnt-out car parked his tractor where we think this fourth car was stationed. He couldn't have known.'

'A boat,' he continued, 'was run up on the bank about ten metres from the vehicles. Something heavy was part carried, part dragged from the boat to the group of vehicles.'

'Supposition,' said DI Lynsky. 'Something from the boat, which we are assuming was the one that our New South Wales colleagues chased across the lake, was loaded into the car. The information we have from the Feds and the spooks is that this was probably a kidnapped Chinese woman.'

The reference to the Security Service raised the interest of the rather weary officers present but no explanation was given. The Bendigo link officer said nothing.

'More facts,' the crime scene officer said. 'The way that the ground was trampled suggests that there was some sort of fighting around the three cars parked close together. There's a jumble of trainer, shoe and boot prints, some of which are small enough to have belonged to women, but, the ground is so churned up that it would be hard to be certain. Some of the female prints suggest movement as a pair; what that means I couldn't say. The clearest set of individual female prints also suggests that she was either injured or had some other restriction on the way she walked. That's it so far.'

The chatter around the information wasn't very intense; there were too few facts. As they began to disperse, the DI's mobile phone rang. He waved them to stay and withdrew to take the call.

'From the engine markings,' he said when he returned, 'the burnt-out car belongs to a leasing company in Bendigo. It had been hired by a woman call Julie Li.'

The short intake of breath from the Chinese sergeant registered with Inspector Lynsky.

Julie was getting thoroughly tired of her clothes. Mr Kim had

183

allowed her to bring only a few changes of underwear; her top clothes, although worn into comfortable familiarity, were getting dirty and scuffed and generally degenerating. Alice was similarly placed but in her stressed-out state she was probably unaware of what she was wearing.

In any event, it didn't take Julie and Alice long to get dressed and packed. It was eight o'clock when they left the houseboat and headed east out of Echuca on the Murray Valley Highway. The rendezvous time was ten o'clock, not that Kim thought to mention that to Julie. Alice was handcuffed and her coat buttoned up over her body so as to imprison her arms. Kim saw to this himself. Slumped on the back seat of the 4x4, a woolly hat pulled well down over her head, she was a picture of misery.

The look of betrayal that Alice directed at her wrenched at Julie's heart yet again, but there was nothing she could do. The only way to get to the root of the trafficking activity was to follow it through to its source and to the criminals behind it. Julie had long since given up panicking over how she was going to do this.

'Not a word from you,' Kim growled at Alice. 'And you,' he said to Julie. 'Only speak when spoken to.'

Julie was happy with that.

The journey to the rendezvous point didn't take long. They were early; that was Mr Kim's way. It was soon obvious to Julie that Kim knew exactly where he was going and had obviously reconnoitred the spot. The farm track was rough and initially not very wide, but it was the deliberate way that Kim headed for a cleared area with access right down to the water's edge that triggered her thought. The low scrub and stunted gum trees provided cover, but the area was secure more because of its remoteness from the main road and any habitation. It was soon clear to Julie that the spot had been chosen carefully and because of its access to the lake. Why they needed access to the lake she had yet to find out, although the background noise of outboard motors was beginning to plant a message in her brain.

Mr Kim carefully turned the 4x4 around in the turning circle to face back down the track. He equally carefully searched the area within about fifty metres of the clearing, still keeping Julie and the car in sight, before getting back into the vehicle.

'He's done this sort of thing before,' she said to herself as they waited.

Alice, whose rapid breathing was beginning to worry Julie, seemed to be unaware that they had stopped, let alone where they might be.

'She'd better be OK,' Julie said in another aside to herself.

Suddenly Mr Kim braced himself. His attention had been focused on the lake; confirming Julie's rapidly forming thought that they were there to meet somebody arriving from across the lake. But it wasn't the lake that had attracted his attention.

Alice's breathing still hadn't slackened.

However, Julie didn't have much time to worry about her; she didn't catch what Kim had said but it was clear from the way that he was reacting that something unexpected had happened. And a look from the car window told Julie what it was.

Mr Kim's forethought in getting to the meeting point very early had paid off. He might not have been explicitly expecting anybody, but clearly he had been prepared for the possibility of an ambush. It seemed that that was what was now happening.

Two motor vehicles had suddenly appeared on the track in front of them. They were moving quickly. One, another Toyota 4x4, slithered to a halt to the side of them, getting as close to the access point to the lake as possible. The other smaller car did a rapid U-turn blocking the track and their exit route.

'Oh shit!'

Julie had no doubt what Mr Kim had said this time. His exclamation related not to the two first cars but to a third that stopped a distance away. Kim obviously recognised this rather more upmarket vehicle.

'What?' asked Julie.

With the rigid inflatable nosing its way towards the bank, Kim didn't have time to reply.

A woman and three men from the newly arrived cars moved into the space between the water's edge and Julie's party, clearly intent on preventing the inflatable from reinforcing them. Two of the men faced the lake while the woman and the other man began to position themselves defensively opposite the now-surrounded 4x4. Kim unfolded himself from the driving seat; where he produced the sawn-off shotgun from Julie never knew. He laid it on the passenger seat as he moved around the vehicle to face the four Chinese. Who was in the BMW, which in its turn had turned round to allow it to make a rapid getaway, Julie couldn't see.

'Jesus!' Julie said softly to herself. 'Do I get out or stay put to defend Alice?'

On the lake the inflatable described a tight arc and cut its engine. The steersman allowed it to drift parallel to the shore until it was opposite the group awaiting it at the lakeside.

If she counted herself, Julie noted that the two parties at the foreshore were evenly matched. Whether their opponents – which was what Julie saw them as – were armed she had no idea.

A rapid discussion in Mandarin among these opponents took place, with the woman clearly taking the lead. Julie got out of the car and skirting the rear stood by the door next to the now-alert Alice. She didn't have much confidence in her fighting skills but she'd decided she had a better chance of being useful outside the car rather than inside it. If it was possible, Alice looked even more terrified than before. Mr Kim moved to join her, choosing his ground she supposed, his eyes not on the group but on the occupants of the inflatable. With the window down, the shotgun was easily accessible from the front seat of the 4x4.

Julie wondered what he was expecting to happen. She was

too tense, however, to wonder why Mr Kim hadn't openly advertised that he was armed. The explanation probably lay with the unknown occupants of the BMW commanding the scene; Kim had no way of knowing how hostile they were likely to prove.

A sharp crack, instantly followed by one of the Chinese men pitching backwards from the force of the rifle shot that had struck him between the eyes, changed the dynamic. Even if Kim was expecting this, Julie certainly wasn't.

'Jesus!' said Julie, not sure what to do.

Kim muttered something about the odds and moved towards the man nearest to him. Knives were out as both of the male Chinese thugs turned to face their much taller opponent. The steersman quickly paddled the inflatable closer to shore but, as the flailing and stabbing group surged around the 4x4, Heng Sun followed the action with his rifle but didn't dare fire again. Julie was forced away from the car as the brawl became more intense. Mr Kim seemed to be able to keep his two attackers at bay with more ease than she would have expected. Pausing to watch, she realised that he was able to use his superior reach to good effect. One of the men was already disarmed but neither had been able to grapple with Kim. Someone more expert in street fighting than Julie would have noted that the two men were getting in each other's way and would have been more effective if they coordinated their efforts more effectively.

Alice's scream concentrated Julie's mind.

While the fighting continued at the edge of the lake, with one of Kim's attackers reduced to the use of only one arm, the Chinese woman had made for the back door of the 4x4 and was dragging Alice out. Something of what was happening began to dawn on Julie. Alice was being snatched back by the group from which Kim had stolen her in Melbourne.

All sorts of dilemmas surfaced for Julie, but Alice's anguish overrode them. She had a role to play. Defending Alice was a part of that.

Another rifle shot rang out. With only the fighting group in her sight, Julie didn't see that it was aimed at deterring the occupants of the BMW from joining the fray.

By the time that Julie had sized up the situation, the Chinese woman had got Alice over to her own 4x4 and was pushing the resisting girl into the back of it. With Kim fully occupied, some action was required of her. Concentrating on getting the now-screaming Alice into the vehicle, the Chinese woman had her back to Julie.

Clasping her hands, Julie smashed them down on to the woman's neck. She staggered away from Alice and fell to her knees. As Julie moved to drag her away or strike her again, she was struck on the side of her head by a fist. She just had time to see the two remaining Chinese men grab at the woman and awkwardly drag her to the car that was blocking the road. Tracked by the rifle they drove off after the BMW, which was already on its way back down the track. A panting Mr Kim watched with a savage grin on his face; he made no attempt to prevent their escape, knowing that Alice was safe in the attackers' abandoned 4x4.

Julie sank to her knees, her head pounding out a thought-deadening rhythm.

'You OK?'

It wasn't Kim who had asked. As the scene around her came into focus, Julie saw that the inflatable had been beached and a second young woman trussed into a coat like Alice was being manhandled from it. Julie saw that the woman's mouth had been taped over.

Heng Sun asked his question as he helped to load this new captive into the 4x4 alongside Alice. The muted squeals of recognition and Alice's excited announcement told Julie that the new young woman was Janice Liang, one of the four girls kidnapped from Canada.

'So that's what this is all about!'

As she nursed her aching head, Julie began to put things

188

together. Janice had obviously been held somewhere on the other side of the lake and it was now time for Kim to move both of the women on, but where to now? Was it to another safe house or was it to their final destination.

With the aid of the steersman and a can of fuel from the inflatable, the dead Chinese thug was loaded into the 4x4 that Julie had hired and it was set on fire.

'Give them something to think about,' Heng Sun said with a grin.

Julie assumed that he was referring to the police. It gave her something to think about as well. Taking off in a vehicle that had no tracker device was something that she hadn't envisaged, although she didn't see this as a deliberate ploy, just an act of convenience. And taking off to God knows where at that. Heng Sun was clearly a much more intellectually resourceful man than Kim. It had never before occurred to her that joining up with Mr Kim and his rather basic approach to problems was something of a benefit against the alternatives.

This, of course, wasn't something that was exercising Mr Kim's rather ponderous thought processes, which were more concerned with how the rival gang had known about the pickup and where it was. He had no idea and a very vexed interview with Mr Xu seemed to be in the offing. Heng Sun had his suspicions, which involved Janice Liang, but he was equally unable to answer the question of how. That Janice was anything but what she appeared to be wasn't a thought that had crossed Julie's mind at this point. But the inconsistencies in her behaviour were something that would slowly eat away at her subconscious.

HEDLEY HARRISON

European Times
UK Edition – Monday, 16 August 2010
ARREST OF CHINESE GANG MEMBERS INVOLVED
IN ILLEGAL IMMIGRATION
In a series of coordinated raids, Lincolnshire, Greater Man-chester and West Midlands Police arrested a number of Chinese men yesterday. In separate raids, two gangmasters of Chinese origin were also arrested.

The Chinese men are accused of running a labour import-ation cartel in breach of the Immigration Regulations masked by the legitimate recruitment and management of seasonal agricultural labour. Links with Chinese gangmasters have been established that also reveal regular abuse of the Gangmasters Certification Regulations.

The UK Human Trafficking Centre provided intelligence gathered from a number of unattributed sources.

Links with organised crime in mainland China involving the gangmasters are being investigated. The Chinese Embassy in London has said that it will cooperate with the police enquiries in every way that it can.

An Embassy spokeswoman said: 'The Chinese Government is aware of a growing expansion of Chinese gangs into people trafficking, drugs and prostitution and with the increasing conflict with criminal gangs from Eastern Europe in both Europe and the Americas. The People's Republic condemns these activities absolutely.'

The Chinese men, who have not been named nor their number confirmed, are being held in custody in various police stations in the respective areas.

The police have declined to confirm or deny speculation that the Chinese gangs whose members were arrested were also involved in the trafficking of women for the sex trade. At a recent conference of police officers, Security Service officials and civil servants from the Foreign and Commonwealth Office, the increasing role of mainland Chinese gangs in the UK and

190

Europe in a number of apparently new and very specific areas of women trafficking were discussed. The role of the Foreign and Commonwealth Office in these discussions is assumed to mean that action in cooperation with other countries is on the agenda. The FCO media spokeswoman, when contacted, indicated that no press conference would be called at the end of the discussions. None of the women's action groups contacted by the Times *was prepared to speculate on what these new specific areas of trafficking might be.*

Police in the three forces making the arrests of the Chinese men were confident that they were successfully combating the illegal trafficking of labour but acknowledged that trafficking women into the sex trade was much more difficult to prevent. Again, they were silent on the new areas of women trafficking under discussion.

27

Susie Peveral had been to Canberra before. She had spent six months at the British High Commission soon after she joined the Foreign and Commonwealth Office. She had enjoyed her stay and liked Canberra; it was one of those places that it was hard not to like. She was looking forward to spending time with David Hutchinson there after he had completed some preliminary work he had to do in Melbourne.

Susie, being a relatively tidy-minded and organised person, had formed a great liking for the administrative area of the city and continued to be fascinated by the new Parliament which she recognised as one of the iconic buildings of the world. Settling herself into a double room in a motel in the Forrest area, she took time on the Sunday of her arrival to orient herself before her first appointment of the Monday morning.

The walk to the British High Commission took her longer than she had expected; one thing that had changed since she was last there was the increase in the quantity and speed of the traffic. But the bustle of Canberra was more relaxed, more easy-going, than that of London, or even of Melbourne.

'Susie. Welcome to Canberra.'

She'd had met Tristram Booth in Brazil; they were much of an age. Like Susie, he was another Foreign Office high-flyer. He was definitely a welcome face for her in Australia. He was immensely tall but neat and economic of movement, and Susie had been attracted to him at their first meeting. He had a friendly face that was very hard to describe but that was easy to read among friends and impossible among the diplomatic milieu in which he and Susie lived.

'Tristram.'

She had also met his wife and his then-small twin daughters in Brazil, so her interest was very much as a colleague. And now with David occupying her mind as well as her bed, Tristram's diplomatic capabilities were more what she was interested in.

Well briefed on the labour and women trafficking activities that were the basis of Susie's current interest, he dispensed coffee and biscuits while she admired the view of Lake Burley Griffin and they awaited the arrival of a colleague. A colleague who, Susie was quick to note, was neither named nor otherwise identified.

When Alan arrived, she might have easily seen why Julie Kershawe had likened him to a Greek god. His clean-cut good looks were striking but had a pallidness about them that Susie found less attractive than David's rugged, suntanned and expressive face. Alan, as Julie had also noted, was the perfect spy – competent, self-effacing and forgettable.

'I have just spoken to your associate.' Alan, as usual, didn't waste words on small talk. 'I have to say there's been some reluctance to talk to an investigative journalist back in the office, and the Federal and Victorian Police have asked for certain guarantees, as prosecutions could be pending related to what they are investigating.'

Susie wasn't surprised.

Tristram Booth gave her a reassuring smile. He seriously doubted whether the first Hutchinson report would ever get into the public domain, let alone one on a subject that might cast light on the inner workings of the Chinese political system. Susie's recent conversations with her Permanent Secretary largely confirmed this. Burying his reports was the outcome that David was well aware was always going to be the most likely. A significant amount of what he wrote and photographed ended up that way; but he still got paid!

'The only loose ends that he seems to have are around the trafficking of educated Chinese women,' Alan continued. 'That's the area where we definitely don't want to go public but where we can still be of some help.'

It was a careful understatement.

Neither of the diplomats was privy to the detail of the latest activities that Julie Kershawe/Li was involved in and the danger that she was exposed to. And Alan had been very careful and selective in what he had told David Hutchinson. He knew, however, that in present company he was going to have to say something more.

Again, it was Tristram Booth who responded to him.

'Don't want to upset our neighbours,' he said, gesturing over his shoulder at the adjacent Embassy of the People's Republic.

In fact, the Chinese were anything but upset. David Hutchinson represented an opportunity to the tortuous official Chinese mind. The suggestion to formalise his role so that he could operate in China by commissioning him to further investigate and report on some of the outstanding aspects of what he had been following up in the UK and Australia was instigated by the Chinese themselves, or at least by the Chinese Embassy in Canberra. The proposal was well received by the faceless Beijing bureaucrats. There was considerable sensitivity to the importation of educated and professional women into the Chinese business and political world. Although it was minute in scale, some of the top people in Beijing hierarchy were thought to have a connection to it. A bit of transparency, albeit maybe limited, provided by a reputable outsider was obviously desirable in the circumstances.

It was an outcome that would utterly amaze the Foreign Office China specialists when the arrangement with David and Susie eventually became known.

Both Susie and Alan knew that there was active cooperation with the Chinese on a range of people trafficking issues. They certainly didn't want to disturb the partnership either. But they had concerns about the reliability of certain individuals among the Chinese authorities, political and official, but they also knew that this was too complex a topic for the British or Australians to get drawn into at the present time.

'Hutchinson has gone to Bendigo in Victoria to talk to the Victorian Police about a young Chinese woman.'

The way that Alan said 'young Chinese woman' immediately focused Susie's attention.

'Julie Kershawe – late of the UK Border Agency?'

Susie hadn't expected Tristram to be so fully informed about Julie.

'I believe that she is also being sought by the Victoria Police,' he added.

Perhaps, thought Susie, *he isn't so well informed as he is making out.*

Julie's cover story had been circulated to the areas of the bureaucracies of the UK and Australia that might need to know. The High Commission's inclusion was routine.

'I believe Hutchinson knows where she is, or rather where she was.'

Alan gave Susie a rather sour look that suggested that she shouldn't pursue the topic.

'As I understand it, after going to Bendigo, Hutchinson is coming here before he heads off again to Brisbane.'

Again, Alan didn't make any attempt to explain the purpose of these movements.

Tristram Booth's part in the conversation that ensued as Alan updated Susie on what they knew of the movements of Julie Kershawe, now calling herself Julie Li, and the prime target of their interest, Kim Lee Sung or Joe Kim, was minimal. His was a listening brief. The description of the events at Lake Mulwala took some time to discuss; Alan was both irritated and concerned by the fact that the car fitted with the tracking device had been destroyed and, as a consequence, Julie and

Kim and the kidnapped girls had effectively gone off the radar.

'Julie is pretty resourceful. The Federal Police have briefed both their New South Wales and Queensland colleagues, since the only way they can really go is north.'

Neither Alan nor Susie voiced their common thought that, while they needed to know where the fugitives were, they needed them to be free to make their way to their final destination, wherever that was.

Susie was quick to note that the labour trafficking issues were no longer a topic of interest to either Alan or Tristram Booth any more than they were to her. The fate of a small number of educated Chinese women, however, was assuming far greater importance. The unspoken but accurate assumption within the Australian Security Services that it was the freedom of movement of the women that was key would have accorded with the thoughts beginning to form in Susie's mind.

The last twist in the conversation came from Tristram Booth.

'I've been asked to introduce Susie to my opposite number at the Chinese Embassy. Or rather to take a stroll on the Parliament building roof garden. Knowing him, we might even get treated to coffee!'

The roof of the Parliament building proved to be a simple area of lawn with very little privacy or shade. But the view over Canberra was spectacular and one of the best urban vistas that Susie had ever seen.

The actual building was cleverly built into the hill so that the roof garden seemed almost to form a natural part of the landscape.

'So the public can look down on the politicians rather than the politicians look down on the public; or some such story.'

It was a piece of democratic subtlety that Tristram, as he made the comment, realised would perhaps have been lost on their visitor.

Mr Luo, who for reasons that were never explained liked to be called Julius even if it wasn't his given name, was the First Secretary at the Chinese People's Republic Embassy, which stood with the British and other Commonwealth high commissions on Commonwealth Avenue. A student of British colonial history. Mr Luo had spent some of his early career in Hong Kong working for the administration-in-waiting and then in the Chief Secretary's office. Although very much the voice of Beijing, he was known for his grasp of the British administrative system and for his understanding of what the Chinese would have regarded as the oddities of the British character.

'Julius never refers to us as the English, always the British; I even heard him correct some pompous US Senator on the point. He'd be just as at home in Oxford as here.'

Tristram's briefing to Susie as they sat in the winter sun waiting for Mr Luo to arrive suggested anything but that of the traditional background of a diplomat. He clearly liked his Chinese colleague. Susie pulled her long coat over her skirt, leaving only a part of her legs on show. Something in Booth's description made her instinctively move to modesty.

Mr Luo arrived on time. Susie immediately felt like Tristram that she would like him. The Chinese diplomat nodded to acknowledge the presence of his two counterparts. Then, as Susie watched in some surprise, he walked to the edge of the lawn facing down the hill overlooking Canberra's main shopping and residential areas and, aligning himself with the building, paused and bowed to the distant War Memorial.

It was clearly something that he always did.

'Julius – Susie Peveral, from London.'

Mr Luo had already been briefed so he knew who Susie was. His bow this time was altogether more personal.

'Miss Peveral' – Julius Luo was never going to call her Susie – 'I understand that you are responsible for the high level of cooperation that is going on over this nasty business of people trafficking.'

Susie nodded her agreement.

'The cooperation is about to move into a more complicated phase. We believe that your government and those of Canada, the United States and the European Union are about to introduce much clearer and much tougher regulations on the legitimate movements and resettlement of labour. We believe that the trafficking of working people for profit has to be stopped but not the opportunities for people to move around the world to improve their own economic conditions.'

It was only as the diplomat paused to draw breath that Susie recognised the quality of his English and the absence of the American accent so common among Chinese officials when they spoke English. His last sentiment however, rather surprised her; it didn't quite fit with the often xenophobic pronouncements of his government.

'This problem we can set aside,' Luo continued. 'And the trafficking of women for the sex trade, this is not something that we recognise as a problem. Very few Chinese women are involved.'

The quick pulling together of his eyebrows by Tristram Booth froze Susie's rejoinder. Whatever she knew to the contrary, this was an area that they weren't going to discuss. The rather old-fashioned Chinese sensibilities had to be respected.

'The trafficking of educated and what you would call middle-class young women into China, however, is something different.'

There was heavy emphasis on 'into China'.

More work with Tristram's eyebrows again forestalled any comment from Susie. The Chinese Government were very wary of people from the West coming into their country and bringing in views that would not be acceptable to the Communist rulers. Susie knew this, but it seemed rather simplistic reasoning as a motivation for trying to stop the traffic.

'We are aware that as many as nine women may have

198

already arrived in China. One has been repatriated to Argentina after being arrested in Hong Kong and our Australian colleagues tell us that they have identified four more, one of whom has been arrested. The whereabouts of the other eight is being investigated.'

This Susie already knew, but with the ever present risk of Tristram's frown she said nothing.

'Actually,' Booth said, 'six more. Two more young Chinese women have been intercepted in Queensland.'

Neither Susie nor Mr Luo was aware of this.

The trafficking of educated young women had unravelled further that very morning. Booth had no details, just the basic information and a casualty report.

Wreckage and the body of a middle-aged man had been sighted offshore a few kilometres north of Cairns, in an area that although popular with tourists was largely uninhabited in the winter. The Queensland Police had immediately recognised the wreckage as part of a large ocean-going cruiser. A search for the rest of the vessel and its crew had started immediately. Since there had been at least two violent storms in the area within the last week, the emergency services went into overdrive.

The breakthrough had been as unexpected as it had been welcome.

It was the excited barking of an ageing Labrador being walked along the beach five kilometres north of Cairns, again in an area abandoned for the winter, that alerted the owner. Snakes, even crocodiles, weren't unknown, especially after the sort of rainfall that they had just had. The dog owner was a retired rancher. The noise the dog was making told him that he had indeed encountered a snake. If it had been a crocodile, the animal would have retreated.

'Couldn't believe it,' Walt Wood told the police. 'Crouched under a tree were two Chinese women, girls, hugging each other. Petrified. The dog was barking at a large snake, making runs at it, but it didn't move. I called the dog off.'

Walt could see that the snake would have long made its escape if the dog hadn't kept cutting off its retreat. He wasn't sure whether he knew what sort it was, probably a Tiger snake, but it wasn't an aggressive Taipan.

'Since there's no mobile phone coverage out there I gathered the two girls up and took them back home,'

Their story had been soon told. They had been a part of another shipment of young women, this time from the UK, via Canada and the ocean cruiser to Queensland. Once the local policeman had got the hang of their Geordie accent, the whole story came out.

Four crew members and one other young woman were apparently still unaccounted for and there was not much hope for them.

Mr Luo expressed his regrets at the loss of life in a rather mechanistic way.

'No doubt the Australian Police will learn more from the two young women when they have recovered.'

'OK,' said Susie, recognising that the Chinese official wasn't really interested in the incident.

It wasn't her priority either and she didn't want to waste valuable time with Luo on an un-investigated incident.

'We have still got two women here in Australia heading for or being taken somewhere, we presume up north, but we don't know where, or what the traffickers are planning to do with them when they get wherever it is.'

'Ship them to China,' Julius Luo said.

'Of course,' said Susie, 'but how, where and why?'

'The woman we arrested in Hong Kong, who was being met by a banker, came on a regular Qantas flight from Melbourne. She'd been given a drug that took several days to wear off and which left her with very little memory. The people accompanying her panicked, as did the airport police, so we ended up only with dead bodies. The banker is being tried for other crimes and the judge has given us the chance to find out more by not allowing the trafficking offence to be brought to court for the moment.'

'Are you saying that somehow, somewhere, the two women that the Australian Police are chasing are going to be flown to China on a scheduled flight?'

Susie knew of the Hong Kong incident but she was no less incredulous now even with the greater knowledge that she had.

'It's the only information,' Mr Luo said, 'that any of us has got.'

'But why?' muttered Susie; as always it was the key un-answered question.

Somewhere in her brain she would have probably thought that she knew. What with China's careful control over its own citizens, women with Western passports, if they could have been manipulated to follow the wishes of the corrupt poli-ticians, officials and businessmen, would have been immensely valuable.

But as the three of them drifted by common consent to the Parliament coffee shop, it was a question that remained unaddressed and unanswered.

Susie and David were, however, offered the resources of the Chinese Government in Hong Kong if she felt that a British presence there would help in bringing the trafficking issues to a head. With the sort of remit that she had, she felt that her involvement would be beneficial to the Chinese and the Australians as well as the British. As she was an acknowledged UK diplomat but not part of the Beijing Embassy, basing herself in Hong Kong was thought to be the best option. It also allowed the Chinese authorities to monitor her activities more easily. Mr Luo was careful not to impose any obvious restrictions on David Hutchinson, though Susie was well aware of the sort of oversight of foreign journalists that existed in China.

*

Back at the motel in Forrest the question left hanging at the Parliament building wasn't going to get an answer there either.

'David!'

Susie's delight at the sight of the reclining bulk of David Hutchinson on the bed swept any thoughts of women trafficking, Chinese diplomats and the like straight out of her mind.

It had been mid-afternoon by the time Susie, Tristram Booth and Mr Luo had agreed on how to communicate with the Chinese authorities when she was in Hong Kong; notwithstanding the realities of the situation it was, Mr Luo stressed, to be strictly on an information only basis. Whereupon the diplomat had returned to his Embassy.

'He's not telling us everything,' Susie had said.

'Of course he's not, but neither are *we* telling *him* everything.'

Booth had been right, but Susie wasn't going to rise to his bait and tell him what she wasn't telling the Chinese; need to know, she told herself. Having their own agent in the party heading north, as the Australians were convinced Mr Kim had been ordered to do, was information that it was too dangerous to put into the hands of too many people.

It was two hours later when Susie had completed her shopping foray to the Canberra Centre and, with rising anticipation, returned to the motel.

Tossing her bags and baggage aside, Susie slid out of her coat and skirt and paraded herself in front of David with just enough challenge to get him excited and then slid herself on to the bed beside him, grasping at his erection as she allowed him the pull down her pants.

David didn't bother to remove her stockings and boots, and although shedding a few shirt buttons in his haste to match her nakedness, he didn't, at first, move close to her.

Aware of Susie's inability to distinguish business from pleasure right up until he was inside her, he half expected some ardour-deadening comment about the kidnapped Chinese women as she worked her body into a sweat gyrating beside him. Nothing came. She was just waiting for him to be ready and then to play his rising passion for all it was worth.

In the end, it was he who took the initiative, forcing her legs apart and then together as he entered. He was rough and impatient once the moment came for him and his thrusting produced a mixture of moans and cries of pain as he came to his climax.

When it was over, Susie locked her legs around his waist and refused to let him go until her orgasm came. Thrusting in her turn against his stomach, she felt his sweat trickle down into her soft areas. It was the final trigger.

David rolled on to his back. Eyes closed he let a wave of tiredness sweep over him.

Susie was filling the Jacuzzi.

Humming the traditional stripper music, Susie unzipped and studiedly removed her boots and slowly peeled off her stockings. Excited by her own actions, her body rocked again in an intense orgasm. Rousing himself from the bed, David picked her up and swung her round in one motion depositing her in the half-filled bath. Watching her with the leering look that weakened any resistance to his charms that she might ever have had, and judging his time, he climbed into the bath beside her.

'Idiot,' she said as she clawed herself into his arms as the water in the Jacuzzi surged and bubbled around them.

Relaxed by the sex and the bath, they were ready for their evening.

'King O'Malley's?'

Although the motel had a restaurant, neither would have thought to eat there.

David had been told about the famous Irish pub, but in response to Susie's question it was the only answer that he could give since it was also the only place he knew of.

'Oh, I know a better place than that. When I was here

before I was taken to this place in O'Connor by a rugby-playing giant who worked in the Commercial Department. Apparently, it was a favourite watering hole for rugby players from the Wallabies downwards.'

'Lead on. We'll get a taxi so we can freeze our gullets off by drinking as much Aussie beer as we can get down us.'

The restaurant lived up to Susie's billing. The seafood was good, the beer not to Susie's taste, but the wine suggested by a helpful barman, well aware of the problems of navigating an Australian wine list that didn't include any of the names that someone from Britain would recognise, was very well received.

'Great place!'

David was content – full of the best things that Australian cuisine and vineyards could produce. When his mobile phone rang, he seemed not to want to recognise its tones.

'David!'

Susie was never quite switched off. For her, the imperative of a mobile phone ringing was not to be ignored.

David listened. It was clear that that was all he was expected to do.

'Well?'

After several minutes of silence and a few more mouthfuls of wine, Susie's curiosity got the better of her.

'That was the police in Bendigo.'

Of course it was! thought Susie irritably.

'Ever heard of a place called Dubbo?'

She hadn't.

'It seems that Mr Kim used his credit card at an ANZ bank in Dubbo.'

28

David's trip to Bendigo had proved successful once the police were satisfied about his interest. Detective Sergeant Chou Yun, having touched base with the British High Commission and the Australian Security Service, briefed him on what they knew about what Julie Li and Mr Kim had been doing in the Echuca area. It wasn't much.

DS Chou Yun had called back after their brief conversation with David the previous evening.

As she lay beside him, something in David's tone inhibited Susie from indulging her desire to get as much of her body as she could in contact with his.

'So what happened when they left Echuca?'

Susie was concentrating. They were back in real time and the arrangements made with Julius Luo the previous day slipped to the back of her mind. DS Chou Yun was updating David more fully about events before Mr Kim had been detected in Dubbo.

Mindful again of the possibility of future prosecutions, the sergeant was careful about what she said.

'We decided to let them go and to follow them.'

DS Chou Yun didn't actually say that the Bendigo police had been ordered to let them go.

'Go where?'

'Apparently it was to a meeting with some other Chinese types on the shores of Lake Mulwala.'

The sergeant didn't stop to explain where the lake was.

'There was a big fracas involving maybe eight people including our Mr Kim. We think it might have related to the endless warfare between the Chinese gangs in Melbourne. What was left after the fighting was a burnt-out 4x4 rented by Julie Li, with a body in it.'

'Could you tell whose body it was?'

'We're satisfied that it was a man, so not Julie Li. That was a relief. As far as we could tell, the man was of typical height for a Chinese, so it wasn't Mr Kim.'

'OK. So what has this to do with the women trafficking activity?'

'Well, from the description given by the people arrested previously after the fighting in China Town in Melbourne, it was a very tall Chinese man who made off with one of the women who had been trafficked from Canada. We believe that Kim, and Julie Li, have this kidnapped woman with them.'

All of this seemed to fit with what Susie had told him after she had reviewed her high-level discussions with Julius Luo. Mr Luo was going to make arrangements to ease their path for a trip to China for Susie to act as a go-between for the Australians and the Chinese in Hong Kong and for David to go to Shanghai.

Mr Luo hadn't had to work too hard to get approval for David's trip.

Susie had rather unnecessarily explained the Chinese sensitivities to David. They were very resistant to the involvement of outsiders in their affairs. Relations with Australia were structured in a very 'keep your distance' way, yet they knew that they needed to cooperate closely on the issues surrounding people trafficking. And they needed to be in contact with the other countries involved. But relations with Britain always posed special problems.

Hong Kong was China's window into the outside world. It was a kind of neutral ground. The Chinese wanted most of what had been going on in the British days to continue but couldn't lose face by admitting that or implying that they weren't in control. The old Hong Kong lived on in many ways, quite a few of which were unofficial, and totally deniable. So a Brit who was ostensibly there as a representative of the Australians, and not the British, ticked all the right boxes.

As the conversation with the sergeant ended, David realised that he was alone in bed. He could hear Susie talking on her mobile in the bathroom.

When she returned, it was her turn to update David. She didn't say whom she had been talking to.

'The Australians are going to let Kim and his companions – Julie Li and the two trafficked women – out of the country. Hong Kong is the most obvious place for them to go. The Chinese are going to let them into China, though the Embassy and the Australian Security Service sense that this is causing political difficulties. They believe that there's some unrelated political game going on inside the Chinese establishment. But it's important to them to be seen to be in line with the rest of the world on the issue of people trafficking. They are looking for some means of proving their transparency to the outside world.'

David had a nasty feeling.

'That's why our Julius Luo wants you to go China and to Shanghai. But it was also why he needed to protect his back by getting top-line approval. That he now has.

'They want you as an independent witness, or perhaps more as a means of sanitising what goes out to the rest of the world.'

'No way!'

'Yes, Her Majesty's Government demands it. Besides, it seems that you have a high reputation in China.'

'Bullshit.'

Susie's giggle faded into the bedroom where she had unfinished business; there was no chance that David wouldn't do the investigation required of him!

29

The humidity of Shanghai was something that newcomers noticed but soon became used to. Equally, the high summer temperatures were noticed by those brought up in northern Europe but taken for granted by those of more southerly origins. The smog was irritating, but, for those with means, avoidable. The three young women seeking the synthetic climate of the Super Brand shopping mall in the Pudong district were among these last.

They were into shopping; it was something that the non-working wives of the new elite of Shanghai did. And these three, all of whom hadn't been living in the city for very long, had yet to become jaded by the idleness and pointlessness of hunting through racks of designer clothes that they didn't need to buy. It was an experience that had been beyond their wildest dreams until seemingly a few months before when they had all been whisked away from their dreary and soulless existences to be deposited in China, married and cast adrift as the wives of the new super-rich. If you had asked two at least of the three what they remembered of their lives before China, they would have been hard pressed to conjure up images of their South American childhoods. However terrifying and inexplicable had been their journey in time and place to the present, the memories had been erased with casual ease by the undemanding lives of luxury that they now were living. They were both newly made pregnant, and what futures they saw in front of them were becoming increasingly rose-tinted by the day. For these two, boredom was an inconvenience that it was going to be easy to cope with. With good money spent for them, what would eventually be demanded of them, beyond procreation, they had yet to find out. But payback would inevitably be demanded.

For the third young woman, things were different.

She was not pregnant. Married to a successful businessman and intimate of a number of Communist Party officials and government ministers, she lived in even greater luxury than the other two, and had all that she might have ever wanted. But she had not been able to settle into the life forced on her in the same way as her two shopping partners had. In her private moments, she was still haunted by girlhood dreams of there being something more to her life, even if she still couldn't quite put her finger on what. Her new husband would have simply said that she was just that much more intelligent than her companions. But then he himself was that much more intelligent than his peers and for him there definitely was more to life than importing Western Chinese girls for breeding purposes in the face of an imagined dearth of suitable home-grown marriage partners. For him and his business partners, these new wives were a bridge to the West and a way to circumvent the increasingly severe restrictions being placed on him and his ilk. Business success brought ambitions that were anathema to the Communist leadership.

'So when are you going to England?'

It was the younger of the more complacent two girls who asked the question. They were speaking Spanish. It was something that they always did; it was a small unconscious rebellion that allowed them a degree of privacy that wasn't normally available in their new lives. At home, they were required to speak English or, increasingly as their proficiency improved, Mandarin.

There was curiosity behind the question but no envy. With the hormonal distortions of pregnancy the young woman was finding it hard to see past the current pleasures of her existence. Travelling abroad was the last thing that she would have wanted to do.

'Next week, I think.'

The discontented woman answered a little nervously partly because her Spanish was rudimentary and partly because of their location. The central thoroughfare of the shopping mall was crowded with lunchtime shoppers escaping the rigours of being a part of the world's fastest-growing financial power-house. The group was forced together and into the hearing range of the ever-watchful group of bodyguards who accompanied them everywhere. Mindful of their different, Western, concepts of freedom, the husbands of the three women provided this protection an on almost round-the-clock basis.

The pregnant women saw nothing unusual in this. Security was everywhere in China; violence was endemic in the countries that they had originated from. However, it was the constant presence of these bodyguards, loyal only to her husband, that fed the third young woman's feeling of dissatisfaction. That, and the growing anxiety that she wasn't going to be able to carry out the tasks that her husband was sending her to Europe to undertake.

Rose Zhu – her husband, Hu Ziyang, actively encouraged her to use the Western form of her name – had come to China like the other two women effectively as a package, in her case bought and paid for by Mr Hu. It was a transaction that involved her in uncertainties and terrors that she had been less able to rid her mind of than the other two; she was owned, whatever status was being accorded to her by Mr Hu. He, being a good judge of character, had far more confidence in her than she had in herself. Like Mr Shi, Mr Hu was slowly beginning to understand and exploit the capabilities of these new wives.

And knowing from her childhood and her early adult life that nothing was for nothing, she had waited to find out what the price was going to be for the life of married luxury that she had so unexpectedly been introduced to.

'I have to wait for someone at Hong Kong to accompany me to Britain,' she said when they were again able to put distance between them and the minders.

Just one bodyguard for another, she thought.

But she was wrong.

The woman who met her at the pre-arranged time in the coffee shop of the Hong Kong International Airport was indeed accompanied by a minder, but the man had clearly been told to keep his distance. The minder wouldn't be accompanying Rose; his role was to see that she and her new companion definitely boarded the aircraft to London.

'I'm Linda.'

Linda Shen had been well briefed by her husband and had a sense that Rose Zhu was also something of a free spirit like herself. Not that Mr Shi had described Rose in anything like these terms; it was Linda's own interpretation that was confirmed almost immediately when she and Rose readily got on comfortable terms with each other. At no time did she share anything of her own background with Rose. Linda recognised very quickly that her husband had subconsciously rather than consciously moved on in his relationship with her and was acknowledging her skills and experience, and his trust, by asking her to undertake a totally different role with Rose Zhu. She was not going to jeopardise this new relationship and the benefits for her and her son that she thought she could derive from it.

'I don't trust Mr Hu,' was probably the most important part of Mr Shi's message to his wife.

Mr Hu was a fellow businessman and a customer for one of Mr Shi's latest schemes to circumvent the Chinese Government's financial controls. Linda had met him and had recognised that he was intellectually more in her class than her husband's. She had no doubt that Mr Hu would be able to double-cross Mr Shi if he put his mind to it, but in response to her husband's more open approach to her and her role, she had decided that Mr Hu wasn't going to be allowed to get away with anything. So when she met up with Rose Zhu she was on her guard.

Rose herself had been every bit as carefully briefed as Linda had.

'You have two things to do,' her husband told her.

Hu Ziyang was superficially a rather jovial man whose solid stoutness and pleasant social manner belied his sharpness of brain that was both revered and feared. Capable of both ruthlessness and cruelty, he had bought Rose purely for the access she provided to the UK. A marked man in the eyes of some factions of the Communist Party, he was unable to travel freely out of the country. A shrewd judge of character, he had investigated several of the Western women available and had chosen Rose because of her intelligence and her thoughtfulness. He had no doubts about her capability to carry out his plans or of his own ability to ensure that she didn't escape from his grasp when in Europe. And, although he had no idea that the person designated to accompany his wife by Mr Shi was his own wife, virtually all the contacts that she would otherwise make in Europe would be through extended family members.

One of the things that Rose had to do was sell some rough-cut diamonds to a dealer in Antwerp.

'He will be expecting you. He will have had emailed photos of the diamonds. All he will need to do is inspect them, verify them and then give you a receipt. The price and means of payment are already agreed '

Linda only found out about this first part of Rose's tasks on the flight to London. Having no confidence in the security of emailing from the aircraft she decided not to report this unforeseen aspect of the trip to her husband. If he was going to trust her, he would have to trust her.

The diamond exchange was easily enough accomplished.

Neither woman had ever been to Antwerp but the trip opened up possibilities in Linda's mind.

As she waited for Rose to complete her transaction in the sort of street-side café that she had never come across before, Linda had what she later described to herself as a crisis of conscience.

'What am I doing here?' she silently asked the world around her. 'I'm actively helping him to make yet more illegal money! Why don't I just go round the corner to the nearest police station and hand myself in and tell them everything?'

Perhaps for the first time Linda realised just how far-fetched the story that she would have to tell would be. Kidnapped in Britain. Shipped to Canada and across the Pacific Ocean to Australia partly in a box? No Belgian policeman would understand her English probably, let alone give credit to her story. She'd have to wait until she was in England; her former Border Agency colleagues would certainly understand her story.

'But would they believe it? Why didn't I try to escape? Surely the life of luxury and my acceptance of it would throw doubt on my credibility?'

For Linda, denying her the opportunity to take her son when she went on her trips was the key issue. But would the British authorities see it as such a powerful control weapon? Surely, they would simply apply to the Chinese authorities for protection for the child. However, Linda knew how it would be.

'They'd always decide in favour of a man!'

Her son belonged to her husband in Chinese eyes; she was nothing.

As she drained her coffee cup, Linda was aware of another feeling. It didn't replace the pain that thinking about her son always brought to her but it was powerful.

'Actually, I'm enjoying this!'

It was a thought that she was conscious had been there for some time; certainly she was aware of the feeling of satisfac-

213

tion after she had brought the two schoolgirls back to China Her dealings with the villainous Mr Kim and the gang leaders in England had been successful, despite her being a despised woman; that had made her feel good, too.

Her thoughts didn't get any further. Rose had re-joined her But once started she knew that somewhere in her brain this feeling of value and achievement would mature. She was going to have a hard time rationalising it against the sordid reality of what she had been forced into.

'But,' her Border Agency mind assured her, 'you haven't yet done anything that a judge would accept as proven as unlawful in the UK.'

Mr Hu had shown Rose two photographs. One looked like a college reunion; three rather disordered rows of smiling men all grinning broadly. Some were sporting baseball caps – a thing that Mr Hu hated – others were bare headed. As her husband ran his finger over the photograph, Rose had a feeling that the capped and un-capped young men were deliberately arranged in particular groups. She couldn't imagine why they should have been.

The second photograph was a panoramic wildlife scene taken in Africa. A pride of lions lounged in the obvious heat of the day next to a group of zebra. Some of the zebra were feeding; some were clearly alert, head up and on guard.

'You will arrive on 27 August,' Hu said. 'It's important that you hand these two photographs to my cousin at the Allied China Bank in London Wall that day.'

The Bank's address was written on the envelope containing the photographs.

'What could be easier?'

Rose was chilled by the tone in which her husband asked the question. There was somehow a threat in the innocent query that terrified her.

She didn't tell Linda any of this when they arrived at

Heathrow from Antwerp; only that she had a meeting at the bank in question.

For Mr Hu, the trip to Antwerp was a way to realise the value of some diamonds that he had been given while his companies were building a major infrastructure project in Zambia. The fact the donor was now sitting uncomfortably in a Zambian jail didn't seem to bother him.

And it was a way to preserve the profits from his business activities. A realist, Mr Hu, like Mr Shi and many of their business colleagues, anticipated that one day the Communist regime would be swept away, hopefully peacefully, and he would be able to enjoy his capitalist wealth in his own country.

With the outflow of private capital from the People's Republic actively discouraged when the sources of the capital were perhaps not as transparent as the Chinese Government would have wished, access to electronic banking was fundamental. And with the photographs that Rose was carrying having the capability to be read in conjunction with a particular date in numerical terms, Mr Hu's nephew had all the information that was necessary to make transfers to the various offshore bank accounts far from China that he had set up for the head of his family.

Rose Zhu, of course – as she and Linda Shen emerged from the Heathrow immigration queue – had no idea about the transfers that she was initiating. Linda nodded towards Rose as the latter passed seamlessly into the hands of the inevitable minder and then set off to the brief meeting with her husband's nephew, following which she embarked on an expensive but totally innocent shopping trip. The most injurious accusation that could have been levelled against Hu was of an extravagant indulgence of his new and very pretty wife.

Left in the VIP car park awaiting the limousine that was to take her into Central London, Linda herself smiled sweetly at her own minder, confident in the knowledge that he, unlike Rose's attendant, was her man not her husband's.

And while Rose exhausted the spending allowance that she had been given, Linda recovered her UK mobile phone and made a number of transactions and searched a number of websites. The consequence was the evidence that she had been seeking that confirmed that Julie Kershawe had indeed gone to Australia under a cloud. It was a piece of unfinished business from Linda's previous visits to the UK that had left her dissatisfied.

'Julie is as honest as any woman I know. There's something not right here.'

That she was making enquiries didn't go unnoticed and a number of rather more secret emails from the Border Agency and Security Services brought Linda not only to the continuing notice of the authorities in Britain but also now to those in Australia. With the protection of Julie Kershawe/Li being paramount, the reports on Linda were embargoed for transmission to the Chinese authorities.

30

The two women queuing at the check-in at Brisbane International Airport had the security officials scratching their heads. Muslim women were not unknown, although they were often students who tended towards a more corrupted and westernised form of their traditional dress. But these two women were absolutely traditional. However, a recent fracas with a Saudi princess gave the officials pause before they approached them.

'We're supposed to be looking out for two Chinese women; how the hell can we tell what these are?'

The senior Federal Immigration officer was irritated enough by the instruction – watch out for the two women, verify them, don't make any fuss, just put them through the normal processes and let them carry on with their journey. He didn't have time for this; stopping people entering Australia was more his business.

The lesser immigration officer, who was of Chinese origin, grinned. The two women checking in were Chinese. The Chinese features and the Muslim dress would normally have simply said Uighur to him, but the instructions from Canberra were specific.

'It's them,' the Chinese immigration officer said.

The check-in clerk showed him the passports.

The whole charade was being observed.

'What now?'

There was nothing more for the immigration officers to do.

Mr Kim, trying unsuccessfully to look inconspicuous on the concourse, was uneasy. The Muslim dress wasn't his idea, but Julie Li was adamant that it was the best way to hide Alice's features. Looking around him he could see no other Muslim women; he felt that his objection was justified. They did stand out among the usual run of travellers.

However, from her experience during a student prank Julie knew that there would be a reluctance to interfere with them dressed as they were.

Alice, wearing a brown burka that reached to just above her ankles and pale trousers, led the way with Julie, in the all-embracing black so frequently seen on television, following. The impression of mistress and servant was implied by the definitions in the passports which the immigration officer took with him as he led the two women into a backroom. Kim noted that their luggage continued on its way to the aircraft. In recognition of the sensitivities of the Muslim community, their passports were clearly going to be checked in private.

Alice stood in the corner of the cramped immigration office, her senses dulled by the drugs that Mr Kim had given her; she was hardly aware of what was going on.

'The Chinese authorities will let you through Hong Kong,' Alan had said.

Despite her earlier expectation of never seeing Alan again, Julie had been pleased to see her Security Service colleague; it gave her confidence that someone was watching over her. She'd always known that she was likely to have to go from Australia to China, but it was only as Mr Kim spelled out the arrangements for her that she understood that she would be going on her own with Alice. Kim made a point of telling her that she would be watched every step of the way and any variation from the plan would be noted and action taken.

Mr Kim's emphasis on action being taken left Julie in no doubt that the dreaded Mr Xu and his cohorts would have no hesitation in killing her if they thought that she was creating problems for them.

'We'll be met at Hong Kong and tickets will be available for us there to fly on to Shanghai.'

Julie filled Alan in on Kim's plan. She confirmed Shanghai as their stated ultimate destination and how things would be handled in Hong Kong, to be sure both that she had them clear and that the various authorities involved were fully in the picture. Alan undertook to update the Chinese.

'What happened to the other girl you picked up at Lake Mulwala?'

Julie was surprised how well informed Alan was.

'She was handed over to a couple of Chinese thugs at Warwick. I assume she'll be going separately.'

Julie noted Alan's lack of concern about Janice. It rather confirmed her feeling that there was something not quite right about Alice's erstwhile companion. Her confidence and her lack of the mind-numbing anxiety that afflicted Alice had impressed and surprised Julie.

'All I know, Alan, is that Kim has different instructions about her from Xu.'

Even Mr Kim had seemed to sense something different about Janice.

'Kim treats her far more respectfully. I guess it's because he doesn't frighten her like he does Alice.'

'OK. We'll talk to the Chinese.'

When he did, he got nothing from them beyond the clear impression that they weren't telling him everything, but they also weren't surprised to hear how Janice was being treated.

The immigration officer took Julie and Alice back into the check-in area and then through to the departure lounge. It was an unnecessarily lengthy journey; Julie realised that their departure was being advertised to those watching.

Mr Kim noted the manoeuvre, as he was supposed to do, and left the airport.

With Julie and Alice now in transit and detached from the trafficking organisation in Australia, things were about to change dramatically for the Chinese groups running it. With information on the bulk of the chain now being available to the Federal Police, an endgame strategy was in place and awaited only a signal from Canberra for a four-state police operation to swing into action. The signal depended both on the confirmation by the Security Service that Alice was on her way, which had been given, and contact being made with Janice Liang and the party holding her. This had yet to occur.

'At least we now know what this is all about,' Alan remarked to his superiors at a subsequent presentation. 'And why our Chinese colleagues are soon keen to stamp it out.'

The residents of Coolangatta had never seen anything quite like it. Used to the boisterous and unruly surfing community, who were capable of raising a riot during the surfing season on almost any pretext, a car chase through their streets was definitely a novelty.

Mr Kim left Brisbane Airport and headed south on to the highway, initially unaware that anybody was taking any interest in him. But he was being tracked.

'Oh, shit!'

The realisation that he was being followed first by an unmarked car that made no attempt to disguise itself turned to anger and then concern as the chase was taken up by a blue light-blazing patrol car. Kim accelerated. The police car accelerated. He was definitely being followed.

Cutting in on a family Holden bumbling along between Surfer's Paradise and Currumbin, Kim swerved then swerved again to correct his steering. The semi-trailer that he was trying to avoid honked loudly and the driver made an unmistakably angry gesture at the following police driver.

More used to driving on UK roads, Kim forced himself to ignore the shock of the near miss and push his vehicle harder.

However, the chase wasn't going to last long. Coming up behind a nine-axle truck, he was forced to slow down. This was something way beyond his experience; he had never encountered such a vehicle before, let alone attempted to get past something as long. Cramped by the police car, it soon became obvious that his only way of escape would be by taking the risk of passing the truck at a point where the police car couldn't follow him.

Mr Kim was sweating. The road curved. Vehicles roared along it from the opposite direction. He knew he had to take his chance. When it came, he was just too slow to accelerate. Cutting in on the truck before he impaled himself on a fast-approaching petrol tanker, he felt the slight nudge as his back wing grazed the truck's front bumper. The car spun.

Watching a blurred panorama of the road verge and the traffic passing in the other lane, Kim jerked at the steering wheel and for a moment the vehicle seemed to straighten itself out. But it was heading for the verge and a coppice of dis-organised gum trees. The roadside embankment took the force out of the car's motion, Kim flew forward and then back as his seatbelt kept him from exiting the vehicle through the wind-screen. Stunned by the force that threw him back into his seat, his head crashed against the rest; he didn't move.

'He's OK!'

The arriving patrolman's concern faded as he urged a groggy Mr Kim out of the car and to stand against its side. Kim's usual fight had gone. Handcuffed and arrested, he soon recog-nised the pointlessness of resistance when he had recovered himself.

Three days later Mr Kim was on a flight himself. The judge in the federal court in Melbourne, after hearing all the argu-ments, decided that the severity of the charges that had been laid against Mr Kim in Australia was marginally less than those that had accumulated in the UK, Canada and the US, and shipped him off to London. However, he did keep a lien on Kim for when he had served his time in these other countries.

Janice Liang, whose hidden strengths had begun to emerge during her captivity at Lake Mulwala, had quickly worked out that Mr Xu's organisation was based on a cell system in which none of the individuals had direct contact with one other. Communication was only via the cell leaders to Mr Xu or one of his trusted lieutenants. Mr Kim, Kim Lee Sung, was one of these more trusted lieutenants.

However, for the moment there had been a setback as far as Janice was concerned. Despite the interruption at Lake Mulwala caused by local rivalries and the loss of face in Melbourne that resulted from Alice's seizure and her own, Janice had assumed that transferring her to Kim's group and joining Alice Hou was a part of the plan to get them both to Shanghai. That Shanghai was their destination was one of the positive things that had come out of her imprisonment by the lake. Seemingly, however, getting the two girls together was only an interim arrangement.

So what is this Kim guy's role then?

Despite the bouts of sex with her captors at the lake that she had signalled her willingness to take part in, she had learned very little. That Kim gave the orders in Australia, that he was away a lot in Europe and he was much feared amounted to very little useful intelligence.

All that shagging was for nothing!

Janice suppressed the notion that she had enjoyed a lot of the sex.

The two thugs who had collected her at Warwick were contemptuous of her and as a consequence lax in their security of her. At no time did they secure her feet and she easily loosened the ropes that bound her wrists.

What a bunch of useless amateurs!

As they headed back out of Warwick towards New South

222

Wales, Janice sensed that the two men were worried. Concentrating on the driver she realised that he was constantly checking his mirror.

We're being followed, she thought.

Making an exaggerated series of movements that advertised that she couldn't use her hands, she pulled herself against the seatbelt until she could see in the passenger-side wing mirror.

They were being followed; and it wasn't by a police car.

In fact, as became clear when they reached a relatively straight and deserted stretch of road, they were being followed by two cars.

A sudden blast of noise as the first following car accelerated and pulled alongside alerted Janice to some impending action.

'It's those bastards from Lake Mulwala,' she said aloud.

The car was trying to force them off the road. The second car was accelerating but not pulling out. The jarring crunch from behind told Janice, and her minders, that they were also being rammed. She slipped her hands free of the ropes that bound her wrists.

As she realised what was happening, it was clear to Janice that she didn't want to be captured by the Melbourne gang that were now pursuing them. That would be a major setback.

A consultation between driver and passenger that was so rapid that Janice couldn't catch what had been said at least told her that the two men realised the position they were in and were intending to fight back.

A violent jerk of the steering wheel at the approach to a bend forced the car alongside them off the road. Where it ended up and in what state Janice never knew and at the time really didn't care. They had shortened the odds. Thrown sideways by the driver's action, she stayed below the level of the back seat. It seemed to be the safest place until things sorted themselves out again.

It was a good decision. As the back window shattered above

223

her, the passenger let out a strangled grunt and pitched forward. It was an amazing piece of marksmanship. There wasn't much of the back of his head left. The odds had lengthened again.

A succession of laboured grunts attracted Janice's attention. The driver was taking desperate counteraction. As the car swerved all over the road to confuse the gunman in the following vehicle, the handgun of the Chinese thug in the passenger seat slithered down into the well at Janice's feet. She grabbed at it and released herself from her seatbelt. It was another change in the odds.

Nothing happened for a few moments. Unseen by Janice, the following car had drawn back to give the passenger a clearer and steadier target. The shot crashed into the back of the headrest. The driver let out a scream and lost control of the car. It was another astonishingly accurate shot.

'He's not dead,' Janice muttered as she realised that the driver was clawing at the steering wheel trying to get the vehicle under control.

He didn't succeed.

Janice threw herself up on to the back seat as the car failed to respond to the frantic efforts of the stunned driver. Out of the passenger side window she saw a densely packed line of gum trees. Shooting off the road into a partially cleared area of forest, the car careered down the slope. Janice swung around behind the driver and braced herself. Her movement wasn't any too soon.

Snagged on a tree stump the vehicle reared up and crashed over on to its roof. The scream from the driver Janice later realised occurred when he was catapulted through the windscreen carrying the largely ineffective airbag with him. Crushed as the car then fell on him, he died instantly.

The second scream that Janice heard turned out to be herself as she was thrown against the back of the front seats, struck her head on the car roof and felt the tearing slashes of the remaining shards of glass in the back window as she was thrown out.

Skidding over the body of the dead driver and the leaf-strewn ground, the upside down car slithered slowly into another tree stump and stopped.

Jesus!

Janice didn't stop to wonder what deep memory had thrown up such an exclamation. Battered, bruised and bleeding, she was as rigid as a board in her fear. It was only in the seconds after she relaxed that she found that she was still clutching the minder's handgun.

The smell of petrol pulled her back to reality. Her immediate fear was that the car would explode. Getting away was her only priority.

She instantly sought the shelter of the trees to her right as she scanned up the slope to the road. At first, she could see no movement.

Then, as she crouched in the mess of leaves and young gum trees, her senses focused and she saw that someone, also gun in hand, was cautiously making his way down through the cleared area of tree stumps towards the wreckage.

'He must be the shooter,' she told herself, the memories of the precision of his marksmanship steadying her.

The man was now abreast of her and was easing himself forward in a crouching body motion with the gun held two-handed at the ready. He peered into the mangled remains of what had once been a rather classy four-wheeled-drive Toyota.

Janice knew that he would soon realise that she wasn't there. She needed to act. Mindful of the crackling rustling sound that dead gum leaves make, she raised herself upright and then on to her toes. The man was three or four metres away and when he came around from the front of the mess of buckled metal he was bound to see her.

Down the side of the hill and in the trees, the sound of her shot seemed muffled. As the man pitched backwards from the force of her bullet, Janice started up the hill, still trying to keep within the shelter of the trees. The last thing she wanted was to be confronted by the man's companion and the next to last thing was to find that the driver had seen or heard what had happened and taken off.

Neither thing happened. He hadn't stirred from his vehicle. Still skirting the trees right up to the road, Janice approached the car from behind and in the man's blind spot. She ripped open the door and pushed the gun into his face before standing back.

'Out!' she said.

She gestured the man out of the car, hit him on the back of the head with her gun and kneed him down the slope all in a few split seconds. A truck was approaching over the brow of the undulation of the road three hundred metres away. Janice wanted to be in the car and moving before the truck driver could think that there might be something wrong.

Several dozen Chinese people, mainly Australian nationals, were arrested in the next few hours and days. The whole apparatus of the organised people trafficking was rolled up. It was quick, clinical and effective. A chain reaction started that reached back and linked into the UK, Canada and the US. April Cheng, the fourth woman in the group that included Alice and Janice, was located and taken into protective custody in Mildura in Victoria. No other trafficked women were located.

The Queensland Police quickly closed out the site of the car wreck to reporters and issued a media statement that gave only the barest details of what had happened.

The reactions in mainland China varied from intense satisfaction to panic. Various levels of Chinese officialdom experienced one or other of these emotions. Mr Xu, however, was not one of those who panicked; nor was he one of those who initiated a tactical close-down of their activities. He'd sat out more than one attempt by the Chinese authorities to put an end to the sort of illicit business activities that he indulged in. This, however, was not a good time for those officials whose loyalties had been subverted by Mr Xu; debts were called in. From past experience, it wouldn't take long for Mr Xu's brand of normality to reassert itself.

Meanwhile, on the flight to Hong Kong, Janice sat next to an interesting and entertaining character, an Englishman, in the certain knowledge that the seat allocation was not accidental.

HEDLEY HARRISON

Melbourne Gazette
Continental Edition – Friday, 27 August 2010
PEOPLE TRAFFICKING ROUND-UP
In an action coordinated by the Federal Police and Immigration Service, police forces in Queensland, New South Wales, Victoria and the ACT moved to close down major people trafficking operations that have ramifications in mainland China, Canada, the US, the UK and South America.

As reported in The Gazette *on 1 July 2010, the Victorian Police interrupted a trafficking movement of young Chinese women. Four of the young women were destined for the sex trade; the fifth, a Canadian citizen of Brazilian origin was returned to her country of birth. The police at the time were tight-lipped about both this last young woman and a sixth who had seemingly disappeared, indicating that the circumstances surrounding their presence in Australia were more complex.*

In a statement in Canberra, the Federal Commissioner of Police said that three branches of the people trafficking business were being actively addressed. The illegal importation of girls and young women for the sex trade was a problem that the authorities had been battling for years.

'This is the most widespread and difficult trade to suppress,' the Commissioner said.

The trafficking of both men and women seeking a better life was also a long-standing problem rife with exploitation by criminal gangs. The traffickers were becoming more sophisticated and were exploiting the various regulations in the Europe, the UK and elsewhere often riding their illegal activities on the back of the legal movement of economic migrants.

'Again this activity, which has been highlighted all too often by the tragedies taking place off the Australian coast, is difficult to contain,' the Commissioner continued. 'However, with the cooperation of the Indonesian authorities, this is a battle we think we are winning.'

228

'The key feature,' the Commissioner went on to say, 'about all of these activities, and particularly the third, is the involvement of mainland Chinese criminal gangs. The Beijing authorities have alerted us to a new and unusual trafficking activity which they have not yet been able to completely identify. The trafficking of educated young women of much higher value to certain interests in China has become a concern, partly because the gangs masterminding the movements are suspected of having corrupt relationships within the Chinese administrative machine but more particularly because the movement is into China not out of it.'

The Commissioner was picking his words carefully. Immigration into China is controlled much more rigorously than into most countries. The reasons for this are political, although sources at the External Affairs Department did make the point that with the massive excess in the male population the issue was sensitive.

The numbers are small, although the profits are enormous. The Commissioner outlined the actions being taken – which he described as 'mechanical' – to remove the organisations and resources that have been used to move these special women from particularly Canada and the UK to Australia.

'The trafficking route, with the help of the Canadian authorities, has now been identified. A number of Chinese Australian citizens have been arrested and charged. Several safe houses of various sorts in various locations have been seized and closed down. So far, only two women have been rescued and returned to their countries of origin. This, in turn, has led to further arrests in Canada, the United States, Brazil and Argentina.'

In response to The Gazette's question, the Commissioner declined to comment on the nature of the Chinese end of the trafficking route. A representative of the External Affairs Department at a subsequent press conference emphasised the sensitivity of the issue with the Chinese. She qualified her

229

remarks by saying that issues of corruption were currently in very high profile in Beijing and that the Australian Government was anxious to support the Chinese authorities in any way that they could.

31

David Hutchinson had been to China before. He had travelled widely in the carefully managed way that Western journalists were normally permitted to travel. Getting visas had taken rather longer than expected, and some careful negotiations between Susie Peveral and the Chinese First Secretary, Mr Luo, in Canberra had been necessary. Julius Luo, being more knowledgeable about journalists of David's ilk, wanted guarantees from Susie about what he might write about after the visit was over. Being an observer while the Chinese authorities closed down a people trafficking activity that had tentacles stretching into some normally inaccessible places was one thing; writing analytical articles when back in the UK was something else completely. The Chinese certainly wanted to be seen as transparent and whiter than white in an area that had imposed significant strains on relations with the Western democracies, but background stories and speculations about a society that could produce such a rigid political control system yet have so little control over determined individuals were never going to be welcome.

David, despite the intimate explanations from Susie Peveral that he had had, still wasn't clear exactly what, out of a minefield of topics, he was supposed to write about and where it was to be published. The only thing that was clear was that both the UK and Australian Governments expected him to deliver. It was an entirely new situation for him; his work had been censored in the past but generally it was because he deliberately crossed lines. Here he didn't know where the lines were that he shouldn't cross.

It's always the same in higher politics, David thought to himself. *As usual, the real issues have got lost somewhere in the game playing and position taking.*

Janice Liang knew who the man sitting opposite her was; she had been briefed by Mr Luo. David had no idea who she was.

Janice was feeling pleased with herself. She was also feeling rather battered after her incarceration by Mr Xu's Australian henchmen. Not only had she managed to retain her cover throughout a very stressful and lengthy period spanning three continents, she had successfully escaped the clutches of Xu's organisation and directly and indirectly caused a very substantial part of it to be closed down. She had every confidence that the Australian authorities would successfully complete the job. She also had a much clearer idea of the identity of some of the officials and politicians who were profiting from the trafficking activities.

If David had known who Janice was, he might well have speculated in a way that would have given Mr Luo serious cause for concern. But, in the Business Class comfort of a Qantas jet, David was no longer troubled by the reasons for his going to Shanghai. He had expressed his reservations in the appropriate places and had basically been told to get on with it – to lie back and enjoy it. Responsibility for the trip had been acknowledged on high in both London and Canberra.

Never ever having travelled Business Class before, Janice was only too happy to sit back and enjoy the unaccustomed luxury.

David, at first, hadn't been so easily reconciled.

'I don't like this,' David had said earlier to Susie in bed in their motel room.

'For God's sake, David, all you've got to do is go where they tell you, see what they want you to see, and say nice things afterwards.'

But David still had a sense that there was something dishonest about what he was being asked to do. He had even spoken to another friend in the Foreign Office, but what he was fed back was that relations with the Chinese Government were more important than almost anything else. If the Chinese wanted an international journalist as an independent witness to a piece of internal political theatre, that's what they were going to get.

'Shit, David, and you accuse me of taking my business to bed with me!'

Susie's dismissal was accompanied by a sharp dig of her nails into the soft flesh of David's inside thigh. It was the sort of power statement that she liked and he was getting used to. He had learned to respond forcefully.

Taking her breasts in his hands, he used them to lever her on to her back. A slow sigh of contentment told David that that was what she had wanted. Once she did switch off her business brain, Susie's sexual urges came quickly and very physically. It was something that Susie had demonstrated in their earliest encounter backstage at the O2 Arena and she had never lost the taste for the sort of edgy sex that she found David so good at.

When the taxi came to take him to the airport, David was exhausted from a non-existent night's sleep and the most athletic sex that he had encountered from Susie to date. He was off to Brisbane, Hong Kong and Shanghai; Susie was to be corralled in Hong Kong when she eventually went to China.

'The Chinese Embassy here aren't too happy about my going at all,' she said over a hurried breakfast, 'but that's probably because I hitched up my miniskirt for Julius Luo and showed him far more leg and boot leather than he's accustomed to seeing.'

David could imagine Susie giving Luo the come-on if she

was being frustrated by his stonewalling. Equally, he was as aware as she was of the tortuous nature of Chinese diplomatic relations.

'Won't get much of that sort of thing in China, I guess?'

'Don't you believe it, David. I'd look out for a honey trap or two if I were you!'

If his fellow passenger, the young Chinese woman now exchanging the insignificant opening chatter of a conversation with him, was a honey trap, David would never have recognised it.

Content with Susie for the moment, David was happy enough to ease the tedium of the journey by engaging with Janice. As he was going to China, he reckoned that he needed to be able to get on with the Chinese and talking to the woman seemed like a harmless and inconsequential way of doing that.

Janice was happy enough to get the conversation going; if she kept it light-hearted, it would make her life much easier later.

She was going to see a lot more of this Westerner and she needed to at least be on relaxed terms with him.

David, in his turn, wasn't going to forget her. Subconscious comparisons of her rather gaunt good looks with Susie's aristocratic prettiness would see to that.

Mr Xu was an old man in a country where old men still held the bulk of the power. He never talked about the old days. His credentials as a Communist were highly questionable despite being the friend and even confidant of many prominent Party figures over many years. He always survived whatever the fortunes of these people turned out to be. He wasn't openly and obviously corrupt; it was more that he was adept at making use of the State's resources that he was charged with managing. There was always something in it for Mr Xu – he saw to that.

What that something was, varied.

At the very lowest level, Mr Xu was able to indulge his taste in Italian opera at virtually no expense to himself and his wheelchair had pride of place in the restricted areas of several national theatres. The villainy, the unrequited love and the grandiose pretensions of the heroes of Puccini, Rossini and Verdi offered no irony to Xu, even as he revelled in the intricacies of the plots.

At a higher level, the numbers of favours out there to be collected were probably beyond Mr Xu's count, if not Li Qiang's.

Li Qiang had been Mr Xu's political secretary during his days of senior officialdom. Now that the old man had been long retired and well settled into a life of luxury and relative ease, Li Qiang had steadily ingratiated himself back into the role of Xu's chief of staff while still retaining his senior post at the Ministry.

Mr Xu didn't trust Li Qiang in the way that he almost trusted Mr Kim but he knowingly allowed himself to become dependent on him, with the insurance that he had both detailed records of Mr Li's illegal dealings on his behalf and the loyalty of the man's driver. Mr Xu had determined that, if he ever had proven cause to distrust his henchman, Li Qiang's life expectancy would be sharply reduced. Li Qiang knew this and he, too, had taken out insurance!

So Mr Xu didn't really care who owed him favours; he had the capability to call them in at any time. And as the Australian authorities effectively closed down his whole organisation in their country Xu knew that the need for damage limitation in China, Canada and the UK would result in many of these favours being required.

But for the moment it was business as usual – his latest acquisition was already in Hong Kong awaiting onwards transmission to her buyer in Shanghai.

The coded telephone call from his man at Hong Kong

International Airport had come through just before Li Qiang arrived late on the Tuesday afternoon. The Chinese Intelligence Service heard the message, knew it to be a message, but had no way of knowing what it meant. Events at Hong Kong Airport, however, had some way to run yet but Mr Xu would not come to know that until much later.

'When are you seeing our man?' Mr Xu asked.

Having spent time in both London and Canberra, Mr Xu liked to converse with his subordinates in English to show off his command of its idiom, which was considerable. Although crippled in body, his mind was as sharp as ever and even Li Qiang would on occasions marvel at the shrewdness and perceptiveness of his eighty-five-year-old boss.

'In one hour.'

There was something cold and intimidating in the quiet smile of acknowledgement that Mr Xu gave his chief of staff. Used to such expressions, Li Qiang thought nothing of it and in due time set off for his appointment. He was on his guard – he always was – but a threat from Mr Xu was not uppermost in his mind.

The door had barely closed behind him before Mr Xu was talking in rapid Mandarin to someone who was clearly expecting his call, knew what had to be done, and was simply waiting for the signal that he was now receiving.

Li Qiang was not a native of Shanghai. He came from a small provincial town in western China where his father had been a Communist Party boss of considerable and rather baleful influence. When his father had been hanged for corruption in one of the many upheavals that followed the end of the Maoist era, his son had been sent to a government school to be brainwashed into being a powerful and ambitious public official. Having had very little in the way of a moral framework in his upbringing, he had failed to notice early on in his career that there were boundaries to virtually everything in his life and crossing them had consequences. Put to be tutored in the Interior Ministry by Mr Xu, who knew all about boundaries and the risks and rewards of crossing them, Li Qiang very soon became both an indispensable part of the Interior Ministry machinery but also of Mr Xu's burgeoning criminal empire. The lax and corrupt state of Chinese society in the days before the economic boom – a time of exceptional opportunity for anyone with the courage to take advantage of it – was quickly recognised by Mr Xu. He had that courage. The subsequent development of the capital and manufacturing base in the Chinese economy was manna from heaven for Xu and his ilk.

Li Qiang thrived, grew arrogant, made people dependent on him wherever he could, and totally underestimated the scope of Mr Xu's shrewdness and vengeful nature. He was unmarried, and thus there were no restrictions on his greed, his single-minded self-interest and his innate cruelty.

Nonetheless, still with something of a country boy's wonder at the glories of Shanghai, old and new, Mr Li was always happy to be visiting the French Concession area and particularly the Xintiandi shopping district. He rarely bought anything – there was very little he needed; he just liked to marvel at the conspicuous consumption that was all around him in the various shopping areas.

And he liked to take coffee in the new and rather glitzy Starbucks that had instantly become the centre of the world for legions of young, rich and often idle Chinese, the offspring of the Li Qiang generation of grafters turned middle-class consumers. Starbucks coffee shops were more egalitarian and gender neutral than the older coffee shops – this was the reason why the Chinese youth liked them – and were places to be seen in. They were also places that were hard to hide in, which was why Li Qiang had chosen the one he had.

Not that Hu Hengsen had any intention of hiding; he was too arrogantly confident in himself to ever feel that he might need to. In his early thirties, prosperity personified, he sat at

237

the back of the Starbucks shop staring at the minute cup of coffee in front of him with distaste. More than ten years older than the average devotee, and the only person present not wearing jeans and some excruciatingly Western T-shirt, Mr Hu looked about as out of place as he might have done in a zoo. The youngsters chattering and texting on their phones all around him attracted no interest from him and he attracted very little from them. Their two worlds hadn't collided; they had simply passed each other by. Only Mr Hu's two minders, who occupied a table between him and the swirling mass of people at the counter, met the youngsters' occasional amused gazes with a glowering silence.

As he entered the coffee shop, Li Qiang looked at this odd scene with some amusement. The rendezvous had been set up as an almost childish attempt to get Mr Hu off balance. It didn't work.

'Mr Hu?'

The barely perceptible movement of the head was as close as Mr Hu was likely to get to acknowledging Li Qiang.

Had class distinction still existed in China in the old terms, Hu Hengsen would have been among the super-elite, a mandarin, an Imperial servant of refinement and remoteness; to him Li Qiang was a peasant-bred nobody.

'Yes?'

Mr Li knew what the question meant and he was only there to provide the answer.

'The package has arrived in Hong Kong,' he said. 'It will be delivered to you within the next two days. The package will be brought by a courier who was recruited in Australia and who will return to Australia as soon as delivery is made.'

'No.'

Mr Hu's negative was not what Li Qiang was expecting. There was no obvious need for further conversation; the contract between Mr Xu and Mr Hu was clear in its details and lodged safely with a third party. And it included an agreement to there being no variations. Li Qiang was momentarily at a loss.

Mr Hu explained. 'Afterwards, the courier may go back to Australia.'

'Afterwards?'

Li Qiang suspected he knew what Mr Hu meant by 'afterwards' but knew that his employer would want to know exactly from Hu's own mouth.

'After the ceremony. The courier will be at the ceremony and then allowed to go back to Australia. And I will want clear evidence of the courier's safe arrival in Australia.'

Mr Li suppressed the obvious questions. Clearly, the Xu organisation was not trusted – why should it be? – and the witness of an independent person at the ceremony and the security of that person leaving China was a simple enough precaution. But for Mr Xu and Li Qiang it was a risk that Mr Li at least would have preferred not to take.

As Mr Hu reached rather obviously into his inside jacket pocket, Li Qiang knew that at this point he had no bargaining power.

The noise level in the coffee shop had been steadily escalating as the brief conversation proceeded. The music suddenly turned from the latest hit single of China's number-one pop group to an old Beatles favourite. The gathered youngsters went wild. It was an obvious moment for money to pass.

Mr Hu withdrew his hand from his pocket and passed an envelope to Li Qiang. He made no effort to hide the transaction. No one, not even the minders, was paying attention to him and Mr Li.

And then Mr Hu was gone. How he managed to leave the coffee shop through the heaving mass of young people with the minders, without causing so much as a ripple, Li Qiang never really understood.

Li Qiang pocketed the envelope. It contained one hundred thousand US dollars in high-value notes, down payment from a quarter of a million dollars. How a young woman, even a virgin, could be worth such a sum of money Li Qiang didn't bother to wonder.

As Mr Hu and his small entourage swept out of the shopping mall and into an illegally parked car at the back entrance, the minders noted the three men in rather ill-fitting suits who were lounging in the open area outside Starbucks. Careful observation told the minders that these men were no threat to Mr Hu.

The terrified shop assistant who later reported the body in the refuse bin in the yard at the back of a newly opened jewellery store was incoherent in her description.

When the police recovered the body of Li Qiang, they were quick to note the single bullet wound at the back of the head. They were equally quick to put the death down to a gang-land killing of the sort that was almost endemic in the new Shanghai. That Li Qiang was a senior official in the Interior Ministry ensured that only a minimum of details reached the media.

As the investigation got lost in the depths of the police and Interior Ministry bureaucracies, it was clear that Li Qiang was on the payroll, not only of the State and Mr Xu but also, in a freelance capacity, a number of other organisations equally as nefarious as that of Mr Xu.

He was hardly missed.

'Welcome!'

The young man who entered Mr Xu's apartment and employment as his new chief of staff was the grandson of a long-standing and trusted friend. Xu had had enough of public-service types; he of all people should have known how unreliable they would be.

Two days later the sum of one hundred thousand US dollars found its way into Mr Xu's Norfolk Island bank account.

240

32

When the final stages of the transfer of Alice to China had been discussed, Mr Kim hadn't approved of the burkas that Julie Li and Alice Hou were wearing on the flight to Hong Kong. He thought that they would make the two women too conspicuous. And he had an entirely justified suspicion that that was what Julie was intending.

'Conspicuous? What's so uncommon in a couple of women in burkas?' Julie had said.

Of course in the UK and Europe she was right. In Australia, it was rather less common. Hinting at a mistress–servant relationship with her drab black and Alice's more colourful attire, Julie was not only fulfilling Kim's worst fears – she was also signalling her independence from him now that she had taken over full responsibility for Alice.

She and Alice were noted at the airport and on the aircraft and reports were made to a number of interested parties. And whatever Mr Kim thought of her plan Julie knew in advance that his opinion was going to be ignored. The poisonous Mr Xu had finally brought himself to contact her directly and had approved of what she was planning; a fact that didn't help her already fractured relations with Kim.

It hardly mattered.

The Hong Kong flight was busy. As David Hutchinson settled into Business Class under the watchful eye of Janice Liang, Julie and Alice settled into their seats at the back of the aircraft. Julie blocked any access to Alice in the window seat, as a good Muslim servant would have done. Alice was now recovering from the drugs that she had been treated with for most of the last few days, and her despair was beginning to overwhelm her. Her whole world had been in turmoil for so long that she had almost forgotten what peace of mind was. If she had been capable of coherent thought, she might almost have welcomed the drugs as a means of shutting herself off from the horrors of her existence.

Alice had been aware of the presence of Janice Liang in her company for a few days, but in her drugged state and her permanent fear of Mr Kim she had been unable to re-establish the close relationship that the two had had on the voyage from Canada. Often bound and taped up together, Alice had developed feelings for Janice that were almost like hero worship at first but which soon became an affection verging on infatuation. Seemingly never afraid, Janice had probably done more to help Alice through the journey than anyone or anything. In much the same way, Julie's gentleness in the face of Mr Kim's violence had also induced the same schoolgirl crush type effect, so fragile and vulnerable was Alice's state.

'Jesus, Alice,' Julie had said to herself more than once when Alice's affection had spilled over into physical contact, 'if I understand even a half of what's going on here, you're going to be in dire trouble if you can't control your feelings.'

Now on the flight to Hong Kong as they tried to play the parts of Muslim women, Julie's thoughts were in a turmoil of their own. Seeing the world through the black slit of the headdress she was wearing prompted thoughts of Tariq al Hussaini and the bittersweet times that they had spent together and the Rag stunt that they pulled.

'Tariq, you bastard,' she said under her breath.

But the venom had gone out of the statement.

Whatever else Tariq al Hussaini had done for Julie, his unremitting selfishness and self-focus, once she had recognised it for what it was, had conditioned her to deal with the complex world she was now inhabiting. In the quiet moments of the night on the houseboat as she relived those last months of her life in Britain, Julie finally realised and accepted that she had been manipulated, not just by Tariq, but by her own lords and masters at the Border Agency.

They're the bastards, she had thought to herself many times. But were they?

As she began to ponder what had happened in Australia, and how she had been manipulated there, too, a small niggling thought started to grow in her mind. Yes, she had been manipulated, but what she had achieved as a result of that, she had achieved on her own. She had been successful in everything that had been expected of her, when in their unguarded moments the likes of Alan and his Security Service colleagues had clearly been anxious and uncertain of a satisfactory outcome.

The whole operation to date had been successful; she and Alice were on their way to China and the surveillance had worked throughout. That had been entirely down to her.

And the really hard part that was about to start was also going to be down to her. In China, she would certainly be reliant on her own resources – at least, as far as she knew.

Jesus, they went to all this trouble to set me up in the eyes of the Australians and Chinese because they knew I could achieve what they wanted; me – and not just because I look like a full-blood Chinese woman!

But she had no time to savour how good that made her feel. 'Julie!'

The obvious fact that she wasn't in Britain or Australia now, but was actually on the way to China, finally pushed all the speculations and self-satisfaction from Julie's mind.

Shit, I really am on an aeroplane to Hong Kong with a woman who is about to be basically sold into slavery and I'm running bait for the Chinese Security Services and Christ knows whatever bunch of … what?

243

'Julie?'

Bait – bullshit! – all you've got to do is hand the woman over as planned and get yourself back to Australia. You've got the return ticket in your bag.

She refused to acknowledge the surge of panic that wanted to spread through her body. She had been on her own all the time. If anything went wrong, she would be stranded in China; that was the deal. OK, so it wasn't just completing the handover; she had to keep herself visible to the Chinese authorities and invisible to everybody else. And after her experiences at Lake Mulwala and in Queensland she was far from clear who everybody else was. But, in reality, nobody among the array of officialdom supposedly backing her up knew that either.

'Julie!'

Alice's hand lay on Julie's arm seeking some sign of comfort as the bleakness of her existence began to impinge again. She felt the shudder that ran through her minder and she almost withdrew the hand.

Through the slit of Alice's burka headdress, Julie could see her anguished eyes. She had been drugged and restrained and told nothing – the last few days must have been an unimaginable nightmare for the poor girl. With the baleful presence of Mr Kim ever in her vision, Julie had been unable to alleviate her suffering. Alice had been terrified almost to rigidity and Julie had been able to offer no reassurance.

As the closing stages of the captive's delivery to China developed, Mr Kim had become more and more aggressive and even more unpredictable. It was a relief to both Alice and Julie when he had gone, but it had left Alice in a state of shell shock that she seemed incapable of overcoming.

'Alice?'

As always First and Business Class passengers were allowed off the flight first; Janice Liang was among the very first to scurry

244

up the ramp from the aircraft to the arrivals area. Seasoned flyers like David Hutchinson didn't hurry. Experience told him that there was no point in hurrying. The need to hurry was a concept unknown to the designers of airport people management systems and Hong Kong, he knew, wasn't going to be any different. Besides, he had nearly two hours to wait for the Shanghai flight and one airport was much the same as another.

The usual long walk up and down stairs to get you back to where you started from began. Hong Kong was among the world's newest and most modern airports, but it still seemed necessary to walk these miles to get nowhere. As he was funnelled into the lanes approaching Immigration and Passport Control, an unexpected variation to the norm confronted him.

'Now what?'

David had seen the small group of two policemen and a young woman in a pale-blue uniform shuffling to intercept him.

'Mr Hutchinson?'

The dazzling smile of the young woman as she addressed him did nothing to allay his immediate concerns. It wouldn't have been the first time that he had been arrested and expelled on arrival in a country irrespective of what his expectations of welcome might have been.

'Would you come this way, please?'

The smile got more dazzling as the impossibility of refusing became apparent to David.

If the public walkways and corridors were complicated, the private ones were byzantine by comparison. David was led to a small elevated office that opened from the higher level beside the coffee shop/restaurant and which gave an extensive if oblique view of the main concourse of the airport below them. There were several other policemen in the office, two of whom were wearing bulletproof vests. As he arrived, these two men left.

'I'm Yu Jing,' the girl in blue said with a slight American

accent. 'If there's anything you need…'

The quality of minders was certainly good in China, David thought to himself.

As the two armoured policemen appeared in the concourse below him, David had the impression that he wasn't the object of interest to the police and he had just been got out of the way. It didn't take long to see why.

The two figures, one in the soulless black burka and the other in the more fashionable brown one, moved unhurriedly along the concourse, the black-clad woman supporting the other.

As the two women approached the central shopping area, clearly heading for the toilets, a sudden burst of movement distracted the watchers. The action was initially out of the direct view of the office.

'Sir.'

Yu Jing shepherded David away from the window overlooking the concourse and out to the fringes of the coffee shop, to an area that looked down at the milling crowds not buying anything in and around the clutter of expensive European and American luxury-goods shops.

Why are they so keen for me to see what's going on? David wondered. *Susie says I had to look, listen and then report. Factual, factual and factual*, he reminded himself. *Shit, there's a bunch of polizei out there with enough firepower to storm the Bastille and I have to watch while they arrest someone!*

But watch he had to.

Mr Xu's man got his message to his boss the moment that the flight had landed and he had seen the two women emerge from the arrival gate. The woman in brown seemed to be being supported by her companion, which is what the man had been told to expect. The man's instructions were very clear. He needed to cause a diversion that would ensure that the two women didn't attract any attention.

246

Julie's initial nervousness diminished as they entered the airport building, but when she understood what it was that she had to do, her concerns started to return.

She need not have worried.

As Xu's man pocketed his mobile phone and moved into the body of the coffee shop and towards the stairs down to the increasingly packed shopping area, the circle of police still didn't know what they were looking for. Their own anxiety rose as the police commander realised that, if the diversion that he had been warned to look out for took place in this particular area, he would be in trouble. Two international flights had just landed, both with a considerable number of transit passengers, most of whom, like David Hutchinson, were foreigners; the risks in any incident were going to be enormous.

The scream and inevitable babble of staccato American voices alerted the police and attracted David's attention.

'He's got a gun!'

Since none of the police officers in the immediate vicinity of Xu's man spoke English it was more the tone of the excited cry that alerted them.

A frightened circle of open space instantly formed where the man had been standing, but revealed nothing. The gunman had moved into one of the shops.

Entries to the shopping area were quickly blocked and the police herded the now excited and anxious crowd back into the central spine of the building. Stretching almost out of sight, the central area contained the moving walkways, the various lounges surrounding the departure gates, but also toilets and a range of advertising displays, the invariable paraphernalia of a busy airport.

'Into the toilet, Alice!'

Unaware that a diversion was deliberately being created to provide her with cover, Julie nonetheless was quick to exploit the opportunity it presented. Correctly counting on the attendant's curiosity taking her out into the open area around the toilets to see what the commotion was all about, Julie hurried Alice into one of the cubicles.

'Not a word!'

Alice needed no admonition; she had been largely bereft of speech for the last couple of hours and moved more like an automaton than a person.

The burble of noise in the toilet told Julie that other people had taken refuge there, but the sounds soon became normal for such a place and she sensed that whatever had happened was no longer a course for concern.

The police had been attracted first by a muffled scream from the upmarket dress shop closest to the exits from the concourse and then by the surge of people fleeing from the premises.

The rapid flow of Mandarin from what seemed to be the manager of the shop caused the police to freeze and then to cautiously entered the trading area. The young Chinese girl found in a crumpled heap at the back of the store pointed mutely and in obvious terror to the service area and the back entrance. Xu's man was almost at his car before the police were able to follow and out of the car park by the time that they did.

Had she known that Mr Xu was planning this diversion, Julie might have counselled against it; but of course Xu knew full well that the European ethos of protecting the women and children first wouldn't apply and that she and Alice would be ignored rather than attract notice.

The flight to Shanghai, delayed by the brief hiatus at Hong Kong Airport, was full and the passengers rather subdued.

Whatever that was all about, David thought once he was settled, *you have to admit that the police behaved much as the British police might have done.*

Alice and Julie re-embarked after an otherwise trouble-free stopover.

248

David was seated well to the front of the aircraft. Janice Liang, who this time made every effort not to be seen by him, was sitting about halfway back. She had a few moments of anxiety during the boarding process, Chinese passengers were nothing like as well behaved as their British or Australian counterparts, and she had been forced into Alice's and Julie's range of vision.

'Shit,' said Julie, almost out loud, 'what's she doing here?'

Julie hadn't seen Janice since they were parted in Queensland. Seeing her boarding the aircraft openly and freely was a bit of shock, although Julie wasn't quite sure why she was shocked; she had come to expect the unusual from Janice. With Alice flagging and increasingly dragging on her arm, she had plenty enough to do without worrying about this other young woman. Alice's and her progress was nonetheless reported and received with some relief in Melbourne as well as Beijing.

It would be some time before Julie got to understand Janice's role in the people smuggling saga.

'Sir, welcome to Shanghai.'

As David walked into the foyer of the Renaissance Shanghai Yu Garden Hotel, the last thing that he had expected to see was the young woman from the flight to Hong Kong.

'It's my job to ensure that your stay in Shanghai is as pleasant as possible.'

And perhaps not, David said to himself. *It's your job to see that I see what I'm supposed to see and to do what I'm supposed to do.*

Recalling what Susie Peveral had told him and her amused comments about honey traps, David made up his mind to be very wary of this young woman. There were too many coincidences stacking up. He had no doubt at all that the woman's presence on the flight from Australia had been deliberately set up. He assumed that she was his minder, but whether that was all that she was, the jury was out for him.

'My name is Janice Liang.'

33

For transit passengers, passport inspection on arrival had been cursory. On departure, it had been more thorough and Julie and Alice as well David Hutchinson were duly registered with the Chinese Security Services as being on their way to Shanghai.

Between times and unaware of the distraction created for them, cramped together with Alice in the concourse toilet, Julie had quickly shrugged herself out of her burka and rolled it up into a tight ball.

'Alice, for God's sake!'

Paralysed by being in an almost permanent state of terror, Alice stood rigidly in front of Julie, not understanding that she, too, had to remove her own burka. Julie almost ripped it off in her frustration and anxiety. Stuffing the two garments behind the toilet bowl, Julie gave Alice a quick hug and then a drink from a small bottle that she carried in her rather copious handbag.

Totally unfamiliar with Chinese medicine, Julie had been most reluctant to feed Alice with the drugs that Mr Kim gave her, but having seen Kim's clumsy and brutal technique for administering them she was forced to take on the job herself. Alice still walked a little stiff-necked from having had her head forced back and the bottle of medicine jammed into her mouth from Kim's ministrations.

Equally, having seen the effect of the drugs – they might have turned Alice into a partial zombie but at least she was a

251

biddable zombie – Julie had overcome some of her reservations. However, she couldn't overcome Alice's terrors or her own horror at them.

Alice took the dose of drugs that she had been offered. No longer capable of resistance, she seemed to recognise that they would do her no harm but calm her down to some extent; an extent that would allow Julie to walk her to the departure gate for Shanghai.

Divested of the burka, Julie was back in jeans and boots mode with a tight sweater and fleece; clothes that were appropriate for Melbourne but which she knew would be too much for the summer temperatures of Shanghai. She would at least be noticed, and, as it later turned out, admired by the younger generation of fashion-conscious Chinese nouveaux riches, for whom any Western costume was desirable. Alice's more modest trouser suit, as intended, attracted nothing like the same sort of attention.

Any connection between the two young women finally being funnelled into the bowels of the Air China aircraft and the two Muslim women who had landed from Australia totally escaped the other reboarding passengers.

Briefed by the police, two discarded burkas were spirited away by the Hong Kong Airport Security staff.

When the purser announced the journey time, Julie groaned inwardly. It was almost as if time had gone into slow motion. The closer she got to the end point of her journey, the longer it seemed to be taking.

Yet Julie was happy enough that whatever was going to happen it was going to take her to a conclusion that would at least hopefully save Alice from her fate. Not that she, as the aircraft reached its cruising height, would have been inclined to risk any money on what that conclusion might be.

But the thought that regularly invaded her nightmares – had she been set up as expendable and thus end up in some remote

Chinese jail for the rest of her life rather than back in Melbourne, let alone Britain? – was still there.

Again, she need not have worried. Pawn she most certainly was, expendable she also most certainly was to the Chinese, but not to the Australians. And the Chinese now owed too many favours to the Australians and had too much 'face' to maintain.

God, if I get out of this alive ... she thought wearily.

As always, she couldn't articulate what she would do and as always she admonished herself for being so negative.

In a situation that was now moving from the weird to the bizarre on the way to the totally unbelievable, Julie was also a pawn in a game that she couldn't even have had any intimation of. Hu Hengsen was using her safe return to Australia as a marker of good faith for the payment of the final instalment of funds for the purchase of Alice.

Julie knew that she was taking Alice to be sold to a mysterious Chinese businessman; that was what the whole of Mr Xu's activities were about as far as she knew. What gave Alice value, beyond the rather simplistic explanation given by Mr Kim of her being a virgin, Julie couldn't imagine. Of course, she knew that there was a massive preponderance of males in China as a result of the one-child policy, and the rich, as always, would be able to buy their way out of the problem for their marriageable sons. But kidnapping and forcible delivery of the victim to the businessman seemed to be way too over the top.

Why, why, why?

As she looked at the gentle face of Alice whose almost unseeing eyes followed her every movement, she was ever more perplexed. She was suddenly afflicted by a momentary panic.

Jesus, Alice. If you really are a lesbian!

The image of Janice Liang flashed into her mind. A confident Janice Liang who was somewhere in the aeroplane, she supposed. The brief time that she had seen Alice and her together they had clearly been on good terms. Julie had no way of knowing what Alice's feelings truly were towards Janice, let alone what Janice's feelings about Alice might be, but the idea of offering a young woman with no taste for men to a ruthless businessman who had shelled out God knows how much money for her seemed to Julie to be a real cause for panic, even if it was a panic based on ignorance.

Being obliged to focus on getting Alice to Shanghai and to the businessman in the secret but full knowledge of the Security Services of China, Australia and Britain was challenge enough for Julie. To understand the Chinese authorities' need to both eradicate the criminal practices that were represented by the trafficking and the corrupt business activities that stood behind it, as well as demonstrate to the UK, the US, Australia and others that they were successfully achieving that eradication, was beyond Julie's opportunities for comprehension.

What threat can poor little Alice pose?

As an individual maybe none, so the logical Western mind might think. But Alice was just that, a Western mind, in the eyes of the Chinese authorities. A Western mind founded in Chinese culture; the worst possible import into a country where imports of people were very carefully controlled.

Of course, if Julie had known that fewer than a dozen Westernised Chinese women had been imported and married into the independent but corrupted non-political Chinese elite she might have been even more surprised.

But the Chinese authorities were nothing if not paranoid.

And Alice, like the other trafficked high-value women, had a Western passport that would allow her free movement in the West! The opportunities that this represented to the complex, corrupt and self-seeking networks that underpinned some sections of Chinese society were inevitably anathema to the Communist authorities, yet their ability to counteract the exploitation of these opportunities was often strangely inhibited.

But then some sections of Chinese officialdom were nothing if not corrupt.

Alice dozed and Julie tried to relax. Having now spent so much time on aircraft, Julie was feeling frustrated, jaded and angry all at once. Relaxation was probably beyond her.

If she was going to have to be reliant on her own resources anywhere, it was going to be in Shanghai. It was this thought that was driving so much of her thought processes.

They were to be met at the airport. As she rehearsed her instructions for the hundredth time, Julie's anxiety began to emerge again. She was aware that Alice had been hijacked from another group of Chinese criminals by Mr Xu and Kim. She was also aware that the original group had twice tried to recapture Alice – once at Lake Mulwala and then again in Queensland. In the backyard of the Chinese criminal fraternity she had no idea what might happen, and she cursed the premonition that told her something would.

And these shitty Chinese security people still want me to deliver poor Alice to her businessman!

34

'Listen carefully, Miss Li. Do exactly what you are told and no harm will come to you.'

'No, no, no!'

Alice's voice rose to a scream.

In the crowded area of the baggage reclaim the commotion around Julie and Alice passed almost unnoticed; but not quite. The plain-clothed policeman scanning the mass of people from the supervisor's window high above the reclaim area picked up the movement, recognised Julie as the person he was looking for, and called for help.

Much busier than the reclaim area at Hong Kong, the Shanghai equivalent was seething with passengers when Julie and Alice arrived. Backed against a solid mass of people all waiting impatiently for their belongings to emerge from the depths of the airport system, the man addressing Julie stood behind her but was pressed against her.

Julie couldn't see this man or get a measure of his size. But she could see that another man, much shorter than the one behind her appeared to be, had grasped Alice by the left arm and was attempting to steer her away from Julie and into the crowd.

'Never mind about your bag; you won't be needing it. Just move towards the exit sign.'

'Sod this,' Julie muttered to herself – although still not sure who was supposed to make contact with her, she was clear that it wasn't these men.

She didn't move.

However, she did know who the men were. It didn't need much imagination to work it out. And they weren't Mr Xu's men. Mr Xu's men would have watched and waited all the time that Julie was following her orders. And they wouldn't know that she wasn't until she failed to meet them at the agreed location. The Chinese police or whoever else it was who was tracking her equally wouldn't know that things were not going to plan – how could they?

Shit. It's the bastards who attacked us at the lake!

'Move!'

The man sounded nervous. Alice was beginning to resist the second man and to cry. Things were not going well for the two men.

'Move!'

The sharp pain at the base of her left ribcage told Julie that what she was being threatened with was a knife and not a gun. And she knew that she had to act.

A sudden thunderous roar beside them announced that the adjacent baggage carousel was starting up. A swirling surge of people pressed around them as the waiting crowd moved forward to recover their luggage. People pushed and shoved at each other and Julie realised that the short man had disappeared with Alice.

'Move!'

The man really was nervous. With the swirling and often aggressive mass of passengers intent on reaching the carousel and seizing their suitcases, he wasn't in control of the situation, even if it provided perfect cover for what he was trying to do.

The chaos for Julie, however, was an opportunity.

Realising in the scrambling mass of people that her assailant had no leverage to strike at her, Julie smashed her heel down on the man's foot as hard as she could and wrenched herself from his grasp pivoting to face him. Pitched forward by a middle-aged man thrusting his newly retrieved suitcase into the small of his back, the man now presented a realistic target for Julie.

'Sorry, mate,' she said in sudden and unconscious imitation of her ex-boyfriend.

Bringing her right knee sharply upwards, she crashed it into his crotch. She almost heard the squelching sound as his genitals were jammed back into his body. The man dropped to his knees dropping his knife which was immediately kicked away by a scurrying foot and wordlessly looked up at Julie as he collapsed on to his forearms.

Unconscious of the drama happening in their midst, the milling crowd still scrabbled for their suitcases and clawed their way away from the carousel. Inadvertently clubbed on the side of the head with a suitcase by a retreating businessman as he fell forward, Julie's attacker subsided among the feet of the now diminishing crowd.

'Alice?'

Julie was unaware that her call was uttered at such high volume. She couldn't see Alice anywhere, even as the mass of passengers rapidly dispersed to the various exits from the baggage hall.

Then she realised that she could hear her.

Alice's hysterical screams of 'No, no, no!' served only to energise the thug trying to drag her to the exit and out of the terminal building. Not understanding English, he nonetheless knew that the anguished tone of her screams was dangerous as it would attract attention; violently silencing her, however, would have had a similar effect.

As they were in the Domestic Terminal, the man's route seemed straightforward enough. There should be no more officialdom for him to get past.

'Alice!'

The baggage hall was suddenly empty. The two remaining suitcases circling the carousel, one of which was Julie's and Alice's, were pulled off by a porter.

The thug turned to see who was calling out to his prisoner. He saw Julie but the sudden look of panic on his face told Julie that he had seen something else as well. And, in the moment of inattention, when he turned back to continue his escape, he found himself confronting a policeman pointing his handgun at him in a two-handed stance.

Julie edged forward. The policeman took aim at the thug's lower body.

Julie didn't at first realise that it wasn't this policeman who fired.

A sharp intake of breath followed by a curse that Julie didn't understand signified that behind her someone had been shot. A massive reverberation of firepower rattled around the baggage reclaim area as several handguns were discharged.

The thug at the exit thrust Alice away from him and dropped to his knees, arms raised. It was a motion of surrender; he hadn't been hit.

'Alice, Alice?'

Julie reached the shaking young woman in very few strides and folded her into her arms. It was only when she looked back over Alice's shoulder that she was able to see what had happened behind her.

'Jesus Christ!' she said.

There were four men. One, a uniformed policeman, was standing over a body on the floor slumped up against the side of the baggage carousel. A second man, sitting on Julie's suit-case, was nursing his upper arm; the blood seeping through his jacket sleeve suggesting that he was the man who had been shot and who had uttered the curse. The fourth person, who appeared to have just arrived at the scene immediately took charge.

As more police and medics materialised, this fourth man picked up the now-abandoned suitcase and handed it to Julie as she came forward dragging a 'living dead' Alice behind her.

As the surviving thug was led away, the man who had

retrieved the suitcase gestured for the two women to leave the reclaim area.

'Thank you,' said Julie automatically.

A look of mixed surprise and contempt crept across the man's face.

Snotty bastard! Julie said to herself, the nameless man's body language and facial expressions telling her that he was probably someone high up in the Chinese Security Service who had suddenly got drawn into something rather distasteful.

If she had ever got to talking to Susie Peveral, temporarily of Her Majesty's Diplomatic Service, she would have found that her analysis was accurate. The use of David Hutchinson as a monitor to reassure the outside world that China was dealing with the people trafficking business vigorously and ruthlessly was one side of a coin. The other was to put their best brains to work at sorting out the complex of activities and interactions behind the scenes that they didn't want David to see. Julie's role, to the Chinese, this sour official included, was a part of this other side.

The black 4x4 BMW was parked in the pick-up area exactly where Julie had been told to expect it. The back windows were tinted, though in this instance with the intention of preventing the occupants from seeing out rather than the more usual intention of preventing the curious from looking in.

Julie had no idea where they had been taken to. It wasn't a hotel; it had an internal basement garage and was, as far as Julie could determine, a very luxurious apartment block. The apartment that she and Alice were taken to had no staff, but the bodyguard in the vestibule was clearly there to prevent them leaving. It was getting late and, again according to her instructions, all that she and Alice had to do was to settle in and wait.

Julie found the sudden return to the normal processes of living unreal. It was if all that had happened to them in the last few days had been in her imagination.

It was dark outside. On Julie's urging, Alice took a shower and then she showered herself before they prepared themselves for bed; there really wasn't anything else for them to do. Belatedly, Julie realised that the apartment had no television set. As instructed, Julie didn't give Alice any further medication. Alice without medication was a situation that she knew that she would have to face. By the next morning Alice would be free of the drugs and her reactions were likely to be as unpredictable as they had ever been.

'Mr Hutchinson.'

As Julie and Alice slept in, Janice Liang joined the journalist at breakfast at the Yu Garden Hotel.

David noted the coldness and the careful way that Janice held herself back when the conversation got under way. He assumed that she had been told to be businesslike and not too friendly.

'I'm informed that the young woman we are interested in has arrived in Shanghai. There was an incident at the airport but that has been dealt with. Surveillance of the various parties has been stepped up. We understand that the final meeting will take place in two days.'

Janice had briefed David as far as she was allowed to the previous evening. He knew that he was being used, with the connivance of his government, and that what he would be shown and told would be selective. David's briefings from Susie Peveral, his work on people trafficking in the UK and the information that Janice had given him meant that he was very clear about what was about to happen and what he was to verify as having happened. Anything else was supposed to be unseen by him.

An old *Goon Show* quote shot through David's mind – 'dashed cunning these Chinese'.

Janice also shared some further information that suggested

261

that the Chinese authorities were taking the opportunity presented by the exposure of some of the corrupt businessmen, and the government officials who were protecting them, to close down a whole range of illegal activities. And being China there was also an element of political manipulation going on.

People's National Daily
Shanghai English-language Edition –
Monday, 20 September 2010
CORRUPTION REACHES DEEP INTO GOVERNMENT
*The arrest of businessman Hu Ziyang on charges of theft,
misappropriation of government funds and property has
caused consternation among both government and business
circles. Police with officials of the Internal Revenue department
and the Shanghai Communist Party raided Mr Hu's house on
the edge of the Changning District and his city offices. A large
quantity of papers was seized at both locations.*

*Mr Hu is known to have extensive contacts in the finance,
business and governmental worlds. Starting life as a government accountant, he became a banker and most recently a
bond trader on the US, UK and European markets. The source
of the funds that Mr Hu traded in these external markets is
reported to be a major area of investigation.*

*Mr Hu's wife, Rose Zhu, originally a UK citizen, has also
been detained by the police and her movements between China
and the UK investigated. The British City of London Police
has been asked to provide information on her trips to London,
including any of her travelling companions. The suspicion that
her visits were used as a vehicle to transfer significant funds
out of China was not denied by the head of the international
branch of the Ministry of Finance.*

*Several business associates of Mr Hu and key family
members are being interviewed by police; others remain at
liberty for the present. At a press conference the Head of the
Major Fraud Department of the Ministry of Finance confirmed
that there was evidence that Mr Hu had extensive contacts in
the criminal world, but the suspicion that he had been funding
the trafficking of illegal workers into both Australia and the
UK was categorised as speculation, though not denied.*

*At least three government officials in Beijing and an
unspecified number in Hong Kong have also been arrested on*

charges of corruption. While the extradition status of Chinese citizens in the UK is uncertain, the British police have nonetheless been asked to arrest two bankers in London, one of whom is a relative of Mr Hu. The suicide of one of Mr Hu's cousins in Houston, Texas, in the USA was confirmed by police as being related.

35

The news of the arrest of a number of businessmen and their associates was deliberately withheld from the Chinese media for several days and not picked up by the world media for almost a week. To the Communist authorities, this was a fairly minor piece of media management. Not only did the public at large not realise that a major anti-corruption exercise was under way until it was largely complete, but as a result of the structured way that the arrests had been made, the key players in what were to be the final stages of the crackdown were also kept in ignorance. This secrecy, however, was a major achievement, Chinese officialdom being notoriously leaky.

'They don't even know who the good guys are, let alone who among the Communist elite are bad guys,' Susie Peveral said to David Hutchinson in a hurried mobile phone call. 'The word on the street in Hong Kong is that the canker reaches way up the hierarchy.'

It was a dangerous statement to make, even for a British diplomat, on an open line, but Susie realised that David would need to know just how fragile were the relationships that he might get involved with.

Hu Hengsen was one of those who knew nothing about the arrests. Something of a recluse, he spent most of his time at his luxurious country house several kilometres outside of Shanghai. The anti-corruption authorities were counting on this. Mr Hu, in common with many of the new Chinese oligarch generation, like their Russian counterparts, had close and often convoluted relations both with government officials but also, more dangerously, with politicians. The relationship was mutually beneficial, but a growing awareness among the very highest ranks of politicians that the corruption was beginning to undermine the burgeoning national growth rate and feed discontent that might threaten the Communist grip on power meant that counteraction was inevitable.

Being aware that the Western world regarded the convoluted and corrupt relations between the less scrupulous of businessmen, officials and politicians as unacceptable for a country of China's status, the Chinese President had ordered firm action. Also being aware that the Western world regarded transparency as being as important as integrity, the project to use David Hutchinson as an independent observer was, to everybody's total amazement, established. Keeping him at arm's length from the official British establishment, and holding Susie Peveral in Hong Kong, was insurance against accusations of external influence over the journalist's eventual report.

The Security Service, being more alive to the risks than the often aged and remote Party leaders, had been developing its own countermeasures for some time. Mr Hu was unaware of the extent of their penetration of his business organisation. For some time, the penetration had been benign because the Security Service was in effect riding on the back of Mr Hu's overseas business dealings as a means of gaining intelligence and of building its organisation in Western countries. This had been the most successful in the US and particularly South America where the Chinese communities were more under pressure from local priorities and the assumption that Chinese loyalties were always to China.

This was a myth that Susie Peveral had warned David about.

'There's always an undercurrent in the Americas around the idea that mainland China will always command Chinese loyalties over local citizenship wherever Chinese people settle.

Since most of the Chinese communities in the UK and other Commonwealth countries have origins in Hong Kong or Singapore, this is not a view that is prevalent with us.'

But, as Susie knew full well from her work on people trafficking, there were nonetheless other aspects of the UK Chinese communities that were equally undesirable. One of the reasons why Hu Hengsen was of interest to the Chinese Security Services was that his organisation had established itself very successfully among the Hong Kong-based activities in the UK and Europe, both through his extensive family connections in the former colony and by his corruption of a number of lesser Chinese diplomats and trade officials. And, like his cousin Hu Ziyang, who was now languishing in a Beijing prison, Mr Hu was moving into consolidating his finan-cial position outside mainland China and with it ensuring his own security by engineering the movement of both his own funds and those of his associates in official and political circles. Mr Hu was a business associate of Mr Shi and an extensive user of the objectionable Mr Xu's services. However, unlike his cousin he lacked an emissary like Rose Zhu to facilitate the movements of his money to the fullest extent. This was the deficiency that he was about to try to remedy.

'Mr Hu is very rich. His basic source of wealth was initially largely legitimate and comes from both property development and manufacturing. But, like so many of his kind, he is begin-ning to move into illegal activities, particularly the exporting of his private capital abroad.'

The Chinese authorities were very clear about the distinction between private capital and sovereign wealth and what each might be used for.

Janice Liang had joined David Hutchinson for breakfast at his hotel. It was part of her role to keep him abreast of the events that the Chinese authorities wanted him to verify. The arrest of Hu Ziyang and his associates was something that he

267

needed to know about but was not central to the eventual arrest of Hu Hengsen; it was Hu Hengsen that Janice was concentrating on. The Chinese authorities had special plans for him and were at great pains to keep him in ignorance of what was going on among his associates and colleagues.

This was not an easy task but it was a tribute to the sort of control that the Communist authorities could exert – when it felt it needed to – that it was so successful. The authorities knew, of course, that this success was time-limited.

At no time was it made clear to David why Hu Hengsen was being singled out in the way he was. David's assumption that it might be based on something personal rather than political or business led wasn't too far from the mark.

'Through contacts with at least one Russian oligarch and a merchant bank owned by a group of Hong Kong businessmen, who all appear to be totally ignorant of Mr Hu's plans and activities, he has opened a number of bank accounts in Switzerland, the Cayman Islands and, we believe, Jersey. All of these bank accounts have only nominal sums in them at present but there is emerging evidence that Mr Hu is planning to make large transfers of money held in the PRC – on both his own behalf and, we believe, for others – into them. These transactions, for which he obviously has no approval, and for which he is clearly not planning to seek approval, amount to a significant portion of his total wealth.'

'Hang on, Janice,' interrupted David, 'what the hell has this got to do with people trafficking. People trafficking of what you called high-class women?'

David hadn't been paying much attention since he couldn't relate what this woman was saying to his understanding of what he was supposed to be there for. He had no interest in the financial dealings of Mr Hu, legal or illegal, or in the Chinese authorities' strict controls on the outflow of private capital. He just wanted to do what he had been asked to do and get out of China; it was not one of his favourite places.

'Trafficking people into China is illegal. Immigration can be legitimately undertaken but the rules are strict. People like Mr Hu don't generally live by the rules of the State. And people like Mr Hu don't generally expose themselves to action by the authorities.'

David was getting impatient, but Janice was working through her briefing in her own way and at her own pace and he realised that he was going to have to work at this pace.

'All but two of the high-class women that we are aware of, who have been trafficked, have been married to wealthy individuals and have become pregnant almost immediately. There's a shortage of women in China, particularly these educated and independently minded women, and for these it's a seller's market in the marriage stakes. But this, we are sure, is not the prime reason for the trafficking.'

Once again, Janice spoke in the first-person plural without explaining who this encompassed.

'Such local Chinese women as there are in this category don't usually want to be married, let alone to be subservient to domineering husbands; they want independence and careers of their own. The new breed of successful local Chinese business-man, oligarchs, whatever you want to call them, understand this, but developing a more global vision they see opportunities and benefits in having wives with a broader Western back-ground. Or, more to the point, they want wives with the knowledge and background to move readily between China and the West. Some of these men want to found business dynasties; others want to be rich and powerful on a less restricted stage than China. Our Mr Hu is very much one of the latter. He's arrogant and ambitious and sees the unending Communist hegemony as too entrenched to change in his life-time.'

Janice's use of the term 'unending Communist hegemony' amused David, but she seemed oblivious to the incongruity of her words as an official of that hegemony.

269

David, when he worked over the day later that evening, picked up on Janice as describing herself in the group of independent and career-oriented women. But having been deliberately set up for kidnap and sale in the Chinese efforts to combat people trafficking, she was fully aware of the motivations of women like Alice Hou, which were confused, ambivalent and, in Alice's particular case, complicated by a faltering understanding of her own sexuality and her ability to relate to both men and women. Alice's suitability for the role that Mr Hu wanted her for was something that neither Janice nor David had given any consideration to.

David found it hard to generate any feelings beyond contempt for the likes of Mr Hu.

'One woman we know about is Rose Zhu,' Janice continued, 'who originally came from the UK and who is certainly married but had not become pregnant. But what she did do was make a number of trips to the UK and Switzerland that corresponded to subsequent transfers of large sums of money from Chinese banks. The man to whom this woman is married is a cousin of Hu Hengsen and is generally in the same sort of business with a similar retinue of corrupt officials and politicians to cover his tracks.'

'Except that he obviously didn't cover his tracks too well,' muttered David.

'It's our belief that our Mr Hu is similarly planning to marry Alice Hou and to use her as a vehicle for exporting his, and other people's, wealth from China to the West.'

Janice's confidence in her assertion impressed her listener.

'Jesus,' David said to himself, 'can it really be that simple?'

To the sophisticated Western mind, such simplicity might be suspected to mask something more complex, but David at least knew from previous trips to China and Vietnam that the Oriental mind was capable of seeing things in simple terms but at the same time seeing them as much more important than a European or an American might.

Her continued use of the first-person plural served to confirm for David that Janice was a part of some unspecified official organisation. He also realised that an endgame was in play and that Janice was a part of it. It was this endgame that he was obviously supposed to witness and report on.

Janice's briefing continued into the details of what was expected to happen that day.

Linda Shen, had she been able to hear Janice's background explanation, would have been pleased to note that her multiple trips to Britain had so far not attracted the active interest of the Chinese authorities to the extent that Rose Zhu's had, even if they had made at least one trip together. A more thoughtful and less arrogant man, Mr Shi had been careful to maintain as low a profile as possible with the Communist authorities while at the same time developing a deep mutual-protection regime with a select few officials. Linda had benefited from that. But if the knowledge of her trips to the UK wasn't advertised to the Chinese authorities, they were certainly well known to the UK police and Border Agency and to Susie Peveral, even if the reasons for them were not yet clear.

'So,' David said, 'we're off to a wedding that might not take place.'

'Alice?'

Viewed from behind, the white satin slim-line wedding gown that Alice was wearing looked stunning.

As she turned to face Janice, the tight facial expression and dead blank stare were anything but those of a radiant bride. But then, as the slow-motion sound of Janice's voice and her broadly smiling face percolated into Alice's overwrought and almost non-functioning brain, enlightenment dawned.

Alice threw herself into Janice's arms.

Hu Hengsen, the seriously under-excited bridegroom, and Mr Xu's new chief of staff scanned the arriving guests with

271

curiosity rather than interest. Neither knew who the tall foreigner was. Neither knew who the young woman accompanying him was, although alarm bells tinkled vaguely for the chief of staff when it was apparent that the bride knew her.

How can that be? he thought.

With the ceremony soon to start and with the need to identify as many of the attendees as possible, on Mr Xu's direct orders, he didn't have time to consider how a freshly smuggled young woman who had arrived in China only a couple of days previously could be on such strikingly obviously affectionate terms with someone who was clearly a local girl.

However, his subconscious brain did tell itself to find out who the local girl was when he had the opportunity. There was something too confident, too commanding about the woman. The new breed of Chinese career women intimidated him almost as much as Mr Xu did, but they were often members of the officialdom; that was his worry.

How Janice got the invitations to the wedding David didn't bother to ask. Now in the knowledge that she was almost certainly part of the Chinese Security Services, he was way beyond wondering what Janice Liang was capable of. Equally, he was unaware that the other young woman looking anxiously at Alice as she threw herself at Janice was the mysterious operative that the Australians had planted within the trafficking organisation. But he soon concluded that that was who she was.

Julie Li, who had immediately recognised Janice and the feelings that seemed to run through Alice, moved quickly to drag her away from the two new arrivals. The presence of a non-Chinese man with Janice made her stand out obviously enough without Alice signposting her any more.

The incident made Julie feel uneasy. She had no evidence that Janice was hostile to her and Alice; equally, she had no evidence of who she was and why she was there either, and in the company of someone Julie immediately recognised as a Brit.

Janice's metamorphosis from victim into confident official – Julie being one knew one – didn't exercise her mind as much as it might have done in the past. Her capability to prioritise both her activities and her anxieties had developed considerably over the last few weeks.

The drive out to Mr Hu's villa had taken Janice and David almost an hour. The driver of the late-model Range Rover that they were using was, like Janice, clearly also a Security Service operative. And he was definitely on the alert. For what was not apparent to David.

He had been swept up into the usual all-embracing security regime applied to foreign journalists but he had a sense that he was receiving special treatment because of the role he was expected to play. The authority that Janice seemed to exercise was considerably more than that he would have expected from a routine minder. At no time since he had met her on the flight had Janice offered any explanation of her role or why she was charged with his care. But then David hardly expected her to; that wasn't how the Chinese worked.

'Jesus,' muttered David once they had emerged from the sprawling outskirts of Shanghai and eventually headed into what reminded him of the gated suburbs of several American cities that he had visited. Except that the architecture was anything but American. And it was anything but Chinese as well.

'The super-rich,' remarked Janice in a tone of contempt that was very obvious.

A grunt from the driver focused Janice's attention. They were approaching what looked like a roadblock. A small armoured car and a knot of men in military fatigues were gathered on the wide verge that was a feature of all the roads leading into the exclusive estate. The soldiers were alert and watching warily an exchange that was going on between the driver of an armoured Mercedes that had been stopped and an Army officer.

The conversation didn't last long and the officer issued a sharp order.

After some hesitation, two men climbed cautiously out of the Mercedes. Quickly surrounded by the squad of soldiers, they were led away in handcuffs.

David noted that Janice seemed to relax.

'So what was that all about?' he asked.

'The fat guy is an official of the Interior Ministry,' Janice said. 'He's thought to be in the pocket of Hu Ziyang, our host's cousin. He hasn't been arrested until now because his brother is a senior Party official. The deal was that if he showed up here he was confirming his involvement with the Hu cousins, and he would be arrested so that he couldn't alert anybody at the wedding.'

The Range Rover was waved through once the soldiers at the roadblock had checked the number plate. It was clearly expected.

'Jesus indeed,' said David as they rounded a corner and emerged from the canyon of high walls that surrounded every property. Coupled with the wide verges, the walls created a depressing impression of exclusion and exclusivity.

In front of them at the opposite side of an open area as large as a parade ground was a set of wrought-iron gates worthy of any stately home in Britain. The view up a drive opened on to a white stone-built Adam-style winged house that would have not looked out of place in rural Surrey. The opulence was not lost on David.

The armed security guard at the gate checked the invitation that Janice produced against a list and checked the photographs on the list against the two faces looking at him from the car. The man's orders were to search all cars entering the grounds. He hesitated. The documents and faces matched his list but there was clearly a proviso or restriction applying to them not apparent to the journalist.

Needless to say, David didn't understand the stream of

staccato Mandarin that Janice directed at the guard; he did, however, note the driver's quivering shoulders as he tried to control his amusement. As yet another armoured Mercedes pulled up behind them and its driver nervously tooted, they were waved forward.

'Some woman,' said David, making no attempt to lower his voice.

Janice grinned.

As they parked, more security guards appeared and as they got out of the car they were urged away from the house. They didn't have much chance to get a closer look at the imposing structure. But, reasonably familiar with real Adam country houses, David recognised that, had he got closer, what they were being channelled away from wouldn't have been worth looking at anyway. All over the Chinese countryside imitation European houses were being hurriedly thrown up; most were inferior to Mr Hu's home, but even his dwelling looked artificial and would have offended the sensibilities of most lovers of the genuine article. As they joined the trickle of people heading for the vast back lawn and towards the huge marquee that had been erected to act as marriage venue, Janice hesitated.

I wonder what her problem is? David thought.

A wary anticipation had seemed to come over Janice; she was very much about to enter the unknown.

The marquee was open-sided to give relief from the late-summer heat and divided into two sections, the smaller of which was laid out with rows of plush seats. David had a quick guess at around forty people being expected. Unseen, the larger portion of the tent was equipped as a luxurious dining room for the wedding breakfast. The whole setup again wouldn't have been out of place in rural Surrey if it wasn't for the proliferation of plastic, such as would have been most unlikely in Britain at a gathering with the pretensions of the one that they had just arrived at.

This is very traditional American, David thought with an expression that quickly showed more of contempt than endorsement.

'These people don't believe in the old Chinese ways,' Janice said; the bitterness of her tone was obvious to her companion.

It was then that Alice saw Janice.

Back up the approach road to the Hu residence, the traffic had been permanently stopped by a well prepared roadblock. Working with a copy of the list used by the Hu's security guards, the Army officer was satisfied that all the people listed that he had orders to allow through were gathered in the marquee.

The soldiers formed up and the armoured car was repositioned from the grass verge on to the roadway. The officer gave his orders and the column moved off towards the Hu residence.

After a series of rapid radio conversations with two other groups of soldiers positioned less obviously, the officer quietly briefed the two NCOs with him. Loyal only to the Army, the NCOs seemed unsurprised by the task that they were being allocated.

Back at the marquee several of the guests expressed some comfort at the presence of the soldiers, assuming that they had been organised via the usual secret and corrupt channels. Hiring the military for private functions was a fairly common way for the Chinese oligarchs to project their power.

36

As Julie Li dragged Alice back to her position at the end of the aisle in the marquee, Janice mentally shook herself back into action mode and scanned the gathering. She knew that she was bound to see Alice at some point, but the sight of her looking so downcast and vulnerable was very upsetting for her. But events were now accelerating and she had no choice but to concentrate on the job in hand.

Unwilling to risk being caught carrying a camera or recording gear due to the obsessive electronic security aids that men like Mr Hu surrounded themselves with, Janice had to rely on memory. David as a journalist had been reluctantly allowed more freedom because Mr Xu's chief of staff, in ignorance of David's brief, had assumed that whatever he wrote could be managed in the way that all journalists' copy was managed in China.

Talking quickly in quiet English before they were invited to their seats, Janice identified as many of the guests as she could to the journalist, using his memory to supplement her own. Like David, she had been quick to realise that very few women were present; those that were were there in some menial capacity. It was the only wedding that either of them had ever been to where spouses were clearly not included.

Janice noted that only two people present, apart from Alice and Julie Li, were personally known to her. She was relieved that it was so few; their invitation was on a rather tenuous basis and the last thing that she needed was for it to be challenged. Being who they were Janice was confident that the two men that she had identified were unlikely to know her or to take any interest in her.

'That's quite a bunch,' David said as he stored the names and faces.

As a photographer as well as a journalist, he had a facility for remembering faces and names together.

The canned sound of an electronic organ playing the 'Wedding March' quietly and rather uncertainly announced the proceedings were about to begin.

A Catholic priest appeared at the front of the seated area. Disowned by the Church but still ordained, he had become the tool of many of the rich and powerful members of the new Chinese elite, giving them spurious legitimacy and respect-ability in a society that officially required no such support but unofficially sought it at every opportunity. He was followed out into the open area by a small group of people, all men. The music died and the faint rustle of Alice's dress on the grass as she was led to her place was the only sound as the bridegroom stepped forward.

'That's Hu.'

'Sour-looking bastard,' muttered David.

The bride and attendant arrived in front of the priest.

Julie Li, who was now standing next to Alice, her hand under her left elbow in support, hadn't seen the bridegroom close up. He was shorter than Alice. His dark eyes were like marbles. There was a malevolence about him that struck Julie forcibly. He cast an appraising glance over Alice as he moved into position, and before nodding the priest into action; a look of cruel contempt lit up his eyes.

Shit, thought Julie, *this is the first time he's seen her!*

Mr Hu moved to stand beside his intended bride. As the priest began to intone his ritual, a dull thud reverberated away in the background. Janice heard it – it was if she was expecting it – and tensed up. David thought he heard something but

278

wasn't sure. No one else seemed to notice.

Conscious that he shouldn't just concentrate on the wedding ceremony, David was scanning the grounds that surrounded the marquee. He suddenly focused. With a professional eye for detail and experience in many unusual situations he realised that something was happening out there. There was movement in the trees at the edge of the lawn. With the eyes trained on the bridal group no one among the guests seemed to have noticed this.

Knowing that there were soldiers surrounding the Hu compound, David wouldn't have been surprised that some of them had infiltrated the grounds. But, unlike Janice, he had no idea what the troops orders were.

'Jesus, now what?'

A burst of gunfire had everybody alert.

37

Out of respect for her husband and a desire to cultivate his acquaintance, Linda Shen had been one of the few women invited to the wedding of Mr Hu Hengsen in her own right. Her husband had declined for them both. Rose Zhu, who had quickly come to detest her husband's cousin, had advised Linda against attending. Rose, however, in the seclusion of the changing rooms of the newly opened boutique M&S store in The Bund area nonetheless told Linda all she knew about the intended bride. It wasn't much. But Rose knew much more about Alice's purchase process.

'The stupid bastard paid over the odds because this Alice Hou is supposed to be a virgin.'

Linda, whose own husband was clearly much more forth-coming than Rose's, found this rather odd. Hu Hengsen's sexuality was a matter of much debate around the coffee bars frequented by the trophy wives. But in the way of these things it was a debate more based on ignorance and innuendo than fact. But Mr Hu's sexuality was never going to be an issue, whatever it truly was; like everything else about him, it would be firmly under control and subservient to his business objectives.

Since both Linda and Rose had been purchased in much the same way as Alice, they were sympathetic to the poor girl. For Rose, she would be a useful addition to her small circle. Linda didn't expect to see that much of her.

'He won't even meet Alice until the wedding.'

Linda didn't find this odd, however; unlike Rose, she had met her husband for the first time at her wedding, too.

'That old shitty sod Xu brought her in accompanied by a minder. A woman. It seems that my husband's honourable cousin doesn't trust Xu, who does, and demanded the woman bodyguard attend the wedding as well as a guarantee that she is returned to Australia so that there can be no repercussions,' Rose continued.

'Xu provided a photo of this Alice taken in Hong Kong Airport to prove that she had arrived. It's all cousin Hu has to recognise her by when he arrives at his wedding.'

Linda was beginning to lose interest. She had met both of the Hu cousins and had taken a dislike to both of them. But in Rose's position, based on her own experience in managing her husband, she believed that she could make more of her life than she was doing. And Rose didn't have a child to be intimidated with.

'That's Alice.'

Rose Zhu brought up a photo of Alice Hou on her mobile phone.

Linda glanced at it out of politeness. It wasn't a photograph of Alice alone.

'What?'

Rose was astonished by Linda's double-take followed by a hasty reversion to disinterest. But she was convinced that Linda had recognised Alice; how and from where she had no idea.

Linda hadn't.

Julie Kershawe!

Clearly visible behind Alice in the photograph was her erstwhile Border Agency supervisor and colleague. Julie was in China, on her way to Shanghai. Linda was totally flabbergasted.

What was she doing acting as a minder? Perhaps the things that she had read about Julie and her fall from grace were true? Linda still couldn't believe that.

There was something, though?

She forced herself to think slowly and carefully. Rose was looking at her with an increasingly puzzled expression. Had the problem been to do with Julie's boyfriend? Creepy bastard! But she couldn't put her finger on anything that convinced her that Julie could be a bad guy. There was obviously something that she couldn't have known about.

The photograph was recent; she focused on that. Whatever was going on was to do with Julie in the here and now. But whatever that was, and she was now more than ever convinced that it was something both important and could be potentially threatening to her husband and hence to herself and her son's well-being, Linda couldn't immediately figure it out. And what she couldn't figure out she generally put aside until enlightenment occurred. In this case, enlightenment seemed likely to take time.

'Linda?'

They'd finished trying on the clothes that they weren't going to buy and one of the bodyguards was agitating the shop assistant to interrupt them. It was Rose's man. With a quick exchange of what were less than sincere hugs Rose left.

Later Linda learned that Rose had been arrested by the Internal Ministry police as she had left the M&S store.

Rose's arrest came as a shock to Linda Shen and her husband. Mr Shi was one of those that the authorities were trying to isolate and deal with separately because of their entanglements with senior Communist Party figures. It was bad luck that Rose and Linda chose that particular day to go shopping. Rose's arrest had become imperative and the Security Service agents who took her into custody had no idea who she was keeping company with. Alerting Mr Shi was collateral damage that they would have preferred to have avoided.

'We must see Xu.'

Mr Shi wasn't panicked by what he perceived was going on but he knew that he would have to manage the future projects that he had in train with Mr Xu in order to insulate himself from any further official action.

The telephone call that Linda took while her husband was emailing some of his associates caused her some amusement. He might not be panicking but some of the officials that he had in his pocket most certainly were. Perhaps he should have been. The Security Service computer geeks passed on his emails as soon as they had decoded them. Arresting Mr Shi based on the evidence that the Interior Ministry Anti-corruption Unit now had would be a major coup; his protectors in the Communist hierarchy were going to be too concerned to protect their own backs to be of much use to him. But, as Linda passed on her message, her husband still showed no signs of concern. And unlike Rose Zhu and others of the trophy wives, Linda's role in her husband's money-laundering activities had been minimal and well hidden from prying official eyes.

And like her husband she had contingency plans.

Mr Xu was to be sacrificed. That was a long-held fall-back plan of Mr Shi and his associates. And the authorities were going to let him carry it out.

38

David Hutchinson had been in firefights many times before. However, without the flak jacket and helmet, with 'PRESS' emblazoned all over them, he felt vulnerable. But this was exactly the situation that he was being paid handsomely to report on. He was there to witness and tell the world how the Chinese authorities dealt with both the criminal gangs who were behind the people trafficking and also those members of their establishment who had strayed into the orbit of the criminals. And the deal implied that it would be a favourable report. Nonetheless, a firefight wasn't something that he was expecting, nor was it something that he had been warned of, either by Janice or Susie Peveral.

But as Susie had told David previously when she called him from Hong Kong, the Chinese always took too straightforward a view of things. For a Communist dictatorship, solutions could always be simpler than in a democracy with an independent judiciary. The outcome of the raid on Hu Hengsen's country house was preordained and designed only to give credit and credibility to the Chinese authorities. This was a certainty that made David uncomfortable. And, equally, over the ensuing days it became obvious that people trafficking was only a pretext for addressing a whole range of criminal and corrupt activities that were becoming increasingly politically embarrassing to the Chinese Government.

The outcome that the Communist leadership was seeking was a clear external and international recognition that corruption had been firmly and finally purged from Chinese society.

Only time would tell how successful the authorities would be in achieving their objective.

But in the marriage marquee in the seclusion of the grounds of Mr Hu's house, as the sound of the burst of gunfire died away, no one among the guests could have had any idea what was happening and what was about to happen. David's experience kicked in and he prepared himself for the unexpected. At least everybody's attention was focused.

Except for Janice Liang, none of the guests would have had any reason to expect violence. It was a private wedding arranged by a powerful and influential man; why would there be any violence? Most of those present to varying degrees could rely on some part of officialdom to either protect them or at least to look the other way at the appropriate moment. Even Janice had only been told what would happen in order that she could make sure that David both witnessed the effects of the official intervention but was kept safe from any risk if any interactive violence occurred. The first of these two requirements seemed easy enough, although it did carry the risk of him seeing too much; the second was much more difficult to be certain of.

'The bloody endgame at last,' muttered David, more in recognition of the fact that something had clearly started than in any expectation of carnage.

The tiny Japanese camcorder that he had been given by the Chinese Interior Ministry PR office was surprisingly difficult to operate and he couldn't be sure as he scanned the background behind the bridal group that the soldiers in their camouflage fatigues would show up enough as they cautiously emerged from the trees.

In the event, it didn't matter – the presence of the troops would dominate much of the subsequent filming.

The soldiers quickly formed an arc around the marquee on the open lawn. There was a wary silence broken only by the nervous coughs that covered the anxious eye contact among the officials and politicians. Discomfort levels among these worthies were rising towards panic. The other guests were uncertain and intimidated but as yet not fearful of the soldiers. David was quick to focus on and record the reactions of some of the more agitated individuals as they were pointed out by Janice. His muttered comments into the camcorder would later provide the sort of background colour that the authorities wanted. The fact that there were no names didn't bother the Chinese authorities; they knew who these corrupt officials and politicians were. Generally, the other guests didn't interest them.

Then there was action!

Even through the canvas wall separating the seated area from the dining space, the intensity of the flash and the detonation of the stun-grenade was enough to disorient and render the bulk of the guests momentarily incapable of thought or action. David's filming wobbled until he could get his own startled reaction under control. Unseen, the terrified catering staff streamed out of the marquee and were corralled at gunpoint by the troops.

'Jesus,' muttered David, 'they're not taking any chances!'

The noise faded and the acrid smoke was dispersed by the gentle breeze that had been providing some relief from the stifling temperature in the marquee.

As the minutes passed and the soldiers moved into close range, the shock diminished and the guests began to coalesce into clear and separate groups. Three began to be identifiable.

In a swirl of movement, four bodyguards surrounded Mr Hu. But where were they to shepherd him to? The only way out of the marquee was into the arms of the waiting soldiers! The wedding planners hadn't thought to provide a secure escape route.

'Alice.'

Janice's exclamation was more to direct David's filming to

the bride-to-be than to attract her attention.

Led by Mr Xu's new chief of staff, another and different group of bodyguards – who had quietly infiltrated the wedding ceremony as attention began to be focused on Mr Hu – surrounded Alice. Viciously back-elbowing Julie Li from the young woman's side, and acting with more purpose than Mr Hu's men, the bodyguards inserted themselves into the mass of people now milling fearfully around. Xu at least seemed to have thought of having a contingency plan.

But even as the bodyguards forced Alice into the unintended protection of the disoriented and anxious general run of guests, the dozen or so associates, and payroll officials and politicians of Hu Hengsen, began to separate themselves and to put distance between them and Xu's men and Alice. This third group split into two parties one each side of the central aisle. For them, there was much to be fearful of.

'Clever!' David observed.

Observing this three-way breakup of the guests, David quickly recognised what the Xu party's tactics were. Embedding Alice in the fifteen or twenty guests who were anxiously beginning to chatter together as they were backed against the marquee's side wall meant that the soldiers would have to shoot their way to the young woman to rescue her.

Simple and clear as it was as a tactic, David began to look for a different vantage point. Staying at the edge of the seating area as required by Janice, he had a good view, but he was now between some of the soldiers and Alice and was inadvertently providing her with an additional shield. He needed to move about.

It was a new situation for David. He had reported on many things in many circumstances but he had always been a bystander. Here, although he wasn't strictly a part of the action, he was certainly more in the middle of it than he had ever been before, and he had never been the sole witness to the events that he had had to report on. But there were overtones of some of his past assignments, and as the seeming stalemate developed his mind transmuted the marquee into a tent on the edge of an obscure village in Sangin in Afghanistan. There he had witnessed a meeting between the Taliban, tribal elders and US Marines. Treachery had been expected and a bunch of trigger-happy US Special Forces first surrounded and then shot down the Taliban representatives. It was unprovoked in the sense that the Taliban had, in fact, no offensive intent, although his American press colleagues present refused to subscribe to this view. The firing started as a result of an inadvertent movement by one man whose lack of English caused him to react when reaction was not necessary.

His greatest fear now was a similar misinterpretation of a movement or action.

It was the first time that David had seen the formidable Chinese Special Forces and he hoped, even prayed, that they would be less precipitous in their actions than their American counterparts.

So far they had been.

With the arrival of more troops, the arc of soldiers tight-ened. Escape was impossible. But David knew that some kind of action to rescue Alice was bound to happen. For the Chinese PR exercise to be a success, this was the first priority. Arresting the officials and politicians was secondary in time but nonethe-less as important.

As David focused his attention on the young officer now standing beside the quaking priest in front of the disorganised rows of chairs, he wondered whether the soldier had been told that the whole proceedings were to be filmed. With the officer's automatic weapon trained on Mr Hu and his bodyguards, David was forced back again into memories of another standoff.

The pictures that he was taking of the shattered remains of a Beirut suburb as the Israeli Air Force tried to eliminate a senior Hezbollah figure were already on their way to his newspaper via email. But the fact that he had taken pictures at all was not acceptable to the townsfolk who owned the rubble that used to be their homes. The squad of Hezbollah gunmen who appeared to express the citizens' anger were confronted by a small group of Lebanese police; outnumbered and outgunned but nonetheless confident of their authority, guns were cocked and pointed, with David between the battery of weapons.

'Press!'

The contempt of the Hezbollah leader was manifest but so also was a grudging respect.

Unshipping his camera, David had handed it to a small boy drawn to the scene by foolhardy curiosity, and turned away. He had lost control of his bowels for days – it was the closest David had come to giving up his job.

'Until now,' he muttered.

The priest had turned to the officer and was obviously pleading for no violence. There was no sign that his plea was having any effect.

David's experience told him that stalemates didn't last.

'Where's Alice?'

It was only when Julie Li spoke to Janice that David realised that Alice's bridesmaid-cum-minder had joined them.

Julie was clearly on edge. She gestured at the group of people being herded by the Xu party along the wall that separated the seated area from the dining area. With Alice in their midst they were nearly at the end and out into the open at the edge of the marquee. The soldiers watched and waited. Since there was no way through the cordon, there was bound to be a confrontation. The officer realised that the people being used as shields were not among those that the authorities would have preferred to capture alive. He made a cold calculation.

Julie felt confused. With Alice snatched from her by people she didn't know, she had been completely wrong-footed. She knew that the Chinese authorities were planning some action but she hadn't expected it to be as public or as dangerous as what was now happening. Nor had she expected such determined action to ensure that Alice didn't fall into the hands of the authorities.

Suddenly a surge of bodies separated from the Xu party. Whatever the loyalties of these particular guests might have been, they were all now only interested in distancing themselves from both Mr Hu and the Xu party. Unlike the more obviously compromised officials and politicians, they were mostly family or small-time business associates of Mr Hu and his cousin brought in to provide a neutral but acceptable congregation for his wedding. None of them was especially beholden to the Hu business empires.

As David filmed and stored the details of the unfolding events on his camcorder, groups of the neutral guests were allowed to leave the seating area to be detained briefly by the police. The officials and politicians who were scheduled to be arrested were funnelled towards Mr Hu's house and the awaiting police vans. As the numbers dwindled, the two groups tightened around Mr Hu and around Mr Xu's chief of staff and Alice.

Something had to happen.

With a barely perceptible nod from the officer, David, followed by Julie and Janice, moved to join the priest at the front of the seating area. The remaining area was going to be cleared.

Something definitely was going to happen.

Through a gap in the wall of bodies surrounding her, the sound of Alice's tortured sobs could be clearly heard.

'Wait!' said Julie to Janice.

But the military, having organised the groups, were clearly following their priorities. For practical reasons, it was apparent that the Xu party was now being left until last. Mr Hu and his party were to be dealt with first.

What triggered the exchange of fire neither David nor the

Army officer clearly saw. Mr Hu was gestured to leave the marquee with his bodyguards. With the soldiers partially distracted, there was a surge of movement around Alice. The only clear images were of Mr Xu's chief of staff raising his weapon to fire and the sergeant standing next to the officer opening fire with an automatic weapon.

Janice's urgent cry told David that his worst fears had materialised.

'Wait!'

Julie was quick to respond to David's shout. Janice started moving towards the mess of dead and injured bodyguards writhing on the ground. Fearful that she might get shot in the still-prevailing uncertainty, Julie moved to hold her back.

When they were eventually able to approach, Alice lay in a twisted heap against the wall of the marquee, a small slick of blood surrounding the neat hole in her forehead.

The silence and stillness that followed the shooting lasted for several minutes as the officer and sergeant checked the casualties and the soldiers prepared to remove the bodies. In addition to Alice, three bodyguards and Mr Xu's chief of staff had been killed; two soldiers and two bodyguards had been wounded.

This was not quite the result that the Chinese authorities had wanted. David's filming would show the carnage, but an explanation of what had caused the shootout, or whether it could have been avoided, would be more difficult.

'At least the Army didn't start it,' David said bitterly.

Among Shanghai's officialdom, it was later considered that the decision to confront Mr Hu and his associates at the wedding ceremony was wrong and a PR disaster. This was not a view that was made public, however. With so many key players removed from the scene, the people trafficking – the official pretext for the intervention – would be suppressed, though no one doubted that it would start again. A whole echelon of corrupt officials and politicians would be punished, but again, with so much money slopping around in the economy, David, and the more realistic of the reputable Chinese elite, had no doubt that it would be only a temporary victory. And, as with his report on trafficking in Britain, precious little of what David recorded would see the light of day. However, it would be extensively studied in the secret depths of the Communist bureaucracy; the lessons learned would probably not be the ones that might have been learned in Whitehall. At least, that was David supposed at the time.

Janice and Julie were both distraught in their own ways at Alice's death. When the ballistics evidence showed that it was Mr Xu's chief of staff's bullet that had killed her, Julie's distress turned to anger. Why the Xu faction had killed off its own asset was beyond her – her own high-stress trip through and from Australia now seemed totally pointless. But she was powerless to express her anger, and in any case she was an outsider whom the authorities would want removed from the scene as quickly as possible.

Janice, with a clearer understanding of how people like Mr Xu worked, might have agreed with Julie about the pointless waste of an asset but, for her, Alice's death seemed to be more down to the panicked action of a youthful and inexperienced chief of staff.

What Janice's further response to the death would be Julie and David had yet to find out.

39

The fallout from events at Hu Hengsen's country house created high levels of anxiety, even fear and panic, across a whole swathe of Shanghai's official, political and business establishment.

'Hellfire.'

Linda Shen's amusement at her husband's use of an English expression that was a favourite of hers was tempered by the scowl that went with it.

'What *is* going on?'

Mr Shi, when his wife didn't attend the wedding at the Hu house, didn't go either. Nonetheless, he proved to be one of the few businessmen to break through the wall of immediate silence that the authorities had erected around events. Linda didn't ask what he knew or how he had found out; she preferred to be ignorant of such information. She had always been very careful not to know the names of any of her husband's corrupt contacts.

She did, however, plan her day so that she could visit the Shanghai Yu Garden Hotel; her contacts had told her that a favoured Westerner, a British journalist, would be staying there. The opportunity to meet up with such people came very rarely in China. How she intended to use the meeting, if it could be engineered, she only had rather vague ideas about.

With its usual efficiency in managing the media, the Shanghai Communist leadership had spun the reporting of the fracas at the Hu house as in-fighting among the criminal fraternity. To the Shanghai media, and thence to the media of the rest of China, there was no evidence of any involvement by officials or politicians.

Unlike Linda's preferred ignorance, however, Janice and David knew full well that there were officials and politicians involved. Much to David's surprise and consternation, the police vans spiriting these people away were actually on the road back to Shanghai before the ambulances carrying the wounded.

'This is China,' Janice had said, reading something of David's thoughts.

Alice's death had been a deep shock to Janice. The unfairness of it and the unprofessional murmurings in her head calling for revenge rather than retribution were beginning to disturb her. Contact with David Hutchinson, coupled with her limited experience of life in Canada, was causing her to question the inevitable dismissive official attitude to the killing. Alice's brutal death should not have happened, yet, because her killer was shot down in the chaos, no one now seemed to care. But this killing was personal to Janice and she knew whom to blame for it.

The number of businessmen and corrupt officials and politicians arrested at the Hu house and then in the subsequent follow-up campaign came as a shock to some of the more detached members of the Communist hierarchy. The inevitable internecine warfare within the hierarchy, which, as Susie Peveral had suspected, had made it acceptable for David to observe and report on events at the wedding, had led in the past to inaction and connivance. The more enlightened bureaucrats were aware of unresolved issues of corruption within the Chinese State, but with the most senior Party members often shielded from the realities of everyday life the scale of the corruption and the level that it had reached up to were only just beginning to be appreciated. A vigorous response was anticipated once the immediate fallout had been dealt with.

The lounge of the Shanghai Yu Garden Hotel was deserted. Janice and David had returned the previous evening to be told that they had a meeting the next day with a senior bureaucrat. The invitation, which Janice knew was more an instruction, caused her some anxiety.

'Damage limitation,' she had said to David. 'They'll want to use your report as a means of showing that they were on top of the situation.'

David wasn't sure which situation Janice was talking about. His report was about the whole process of importing high-value women into China; the hiatus at the Hu's house wasn't something that he'd expected to be involved in or saw as fundamental to his conclusions.

Normally the centre of the bustling social activity of the hotel, the lounge had been cleared of people. They were shown in by no lesser person than the hotel general manager.

After two days spent in the gloomy and spartan luxury of an unnamed Army camp following the action at the Hu Hengsen house, the return to something more typical of his lifestyle was very welcome to David.

'That's the report. And the still photographs and videos that go with it.'

Handing over the tiny flash drive to the inevitable nameless official from the Interior Ministry from Beijing before they left the Army barracks had seemed like an anticlimax.

Janice had looked on. The nameless official had ignored her, even though he knew what her contribution to identifying the route of the people traffickers and engineering the final confrontation at Mr Hu's house had been. For him, there was still unfinished business before the trafficking of high-value women into China was finally suppressed. Mr Xu was as yet untouched and so were his backers like Mr Shi. The official, knowing who Janice was, would have expected her to be a part of any continuing action to be taken.

David's unease at the whole reporting project had never been very far from the surface. Nor had it been very far from asserting itself as he had spent time preparing and presenting a version of events at the Hu house, something that he didn't see as relevant to his findings and which he had witnessed only under official insistence. It had been made clear to David that irrespective of the importance that he might place on it, he would have to make more of the handover and marriage of Alice than seemed to be relevant to the main thrust of his report. The intensity of the politics was obvious. His problem was to finalise a version of his findings that satisfied his conscience, contained no untruths, but could still survive the editing attentions of the unnamed men he had been obliged to work with.

The Beijing official at least accepted the report without question, confident that his minions would ensure that the desired spin would be put on David's words.

God knows what will get lost in translation.

In the event very little was. The subsequent political tinkering with the report had been minimal; the most fiercely contested changes that the Chinese spin doctors wanted were about ensuring that the message that they wanted left in the minds of readers was clear and unambiguous.

But now, as the flash drive disappeared into the briefcase of the official, a sense of unreality overtook David. He couldn't believe that he had done what he had just done. He knew that he had produced the report, he knew that he had been at the events at the Hu house, but deep down he was struggling with disbelief. How could such a secretive and exclusive political system as that of the Chinese countenance a Western journalist essentially presenting the facts of a very controversial chain of events exposing the corrupt underbelly of their State? The only way he could understand it was if the Chinese authorities somehow saw themselves as victims of criminal activity that was externally originated and that they were trying to justify themselves to the outside world. There wouldn't be any need for any political spin to be put on that situation.

That'd be a first!

Never again, David thought to himself once again.

But as Susie Peveral had known when she had originally facilitated the deal for David to work with the Chinese, no journalist ever says 'Never again' and means it.

'It's who you are, David,' she had said after their last exuberant meeting, 'not what you write that most of the world will remember. And tomorrow an earthquake or a riot in Tehran will take over and all this will be forgotten.'

'Jesus, Susie, you're no better than the rest of them.'

Nonetheless he had known, and still knew, that Susie's cynical take on the report was true. Like so much of the work that he did, it could still end up as a footnote, however significant he or Susie might have thought it to be.

But as the hotel general manager showed David into the seemingly empty lounge these thoughts disappeared from his mind as he sensed the man's wary deference to whoever was waiting there to meet them.

A group of three men were sitting in an arc of chairs in front of the windows. David was aware of two or three other shadowy figures in the background. As they were urged forward, two of the men stood up and moved to seats behind; the third remained seated but gestured at David and Janice to each take one of the seats just vacated. The smile of greeting was open, friendly and rather more animated than David had become used to from Chinese officials. After his initial greeting, the official took no further notice of Janice.

David was experienced enough to know that, however open, urbane and friendly the man was, it was only his agenda that was going to matter.

Tea was served. The conversation was slow to get started,

for David left it to his host to take the lead. He took his time. The man made no effort to introduce himself, but the all-round deference shown to him identified him as someone very senior in the Communist hierarchy.

'Mr Hutchinson, you will be returning to Hong Kong and then to Australia or Great Britain.'

It was a statement in impeccable English, not a question, but David got no sense of pressure or urgency. He nodded his agreement.

The man then referred to a sheaf of papers that he had been holding and had clearly been discussing when David and Janice had arrived.

'This is very good. I wonder whether …?'

The discussion of David's report that then took place was detailed, thorough, challenging and intense. The conversation told David nothing about the man beyond the fact that he was very shrewd and perceptive; what his personal views were or whether the report was acceptable as well as 'very good' were never addressed.

David didn't really care. As he explained the basis of his conclusions, he had an overwhelming desire to get away from the artificiality of the Chinese bureaucracy. He had had his fill of facts being managed to fit conclusions rather conclusions determined from facts. He no longer felt that he owned the report; he really didn't care what they did with it.

Finally, they were allowed to go.

'Never again!'

And he really did mean it.

40

It wasn't as easy in Shanghai for Linda Shen to elude her driver-cum-minder as it was in London. In Shanghai, it was the minder who had the detailed knowledge, not her. And even dressed down as she had tried to be, she was so obviously one of the elite that sliding unnoticed into the hotel via the kitchen basement entrance would have been next to impossible without attracting notice. Attracting notice was something that Linda was desperate not to do.

'Breakfast!'

She had delivered her son to her mother-in-law with her usual reluctance. Much as she disliked her husband's mother, the old lady doted on the child and the child responded. But Linda was becoming increasingly aware of the potential need to extract her son and herself from the family if, as she firmly believed was becoming possible, her husband's whole business edifice came crashing down around their ears.

'Breakfast,' Linda repeated, egging herself on to enter the hotel dining room.

As she hesitated, a wave of uncertainty came over her. She hadn't planned out what she wanted to achieve by visiting the hotel; that was uncharacteristic. Even her husband was beginning to admire, unstated naturally, the detailed way that she organised whatever she did.

'Linda … Linda?'

There was a hesitancy first time, then a more confident

assertion of her name. Whoever was addressing her definitely knew her.

Linda stiffened and relaxed. It was not the voice of one of her trophy wife acquaintances who was quietly hailing her.

'Julie.'

They were hugging each other before Linda could even initiate any thought of the wisdom of such a public display of recognition and affection.

They disengaged.

It was clear that Julie had already been seated by the head waiter. She steered Linda into the buffet queue, silently signifying that she should join her. Linda followed Julie's lead.

'This is Janice. It's probably best not to ask!'

Julie's introduction was greeted by a surprised but friendly nod and grin from Linda. Janice's handshake was more cautious. The tension between Janice and Linda was immediately obvious to Julie. Janice recognised the expensively turned-out young woman as one of the new breed of Chinese women like herself; the suspicion that she might be one of the imported high-value woman was quickly confirmed as a name to fit Linda's face flashed up in her mind.

'Linda Shen.'

'You know each other?'

Julie looked surprised and Linda looked momentarily anxious. But Janice's opportunistic mind was already exploring possibilities. The tension eased.

'I know who Linda is,' she said, 'but we've never met.'

Julie was starving. She hadn't slept properly for several nights and the nervous energy that she had been expending had increased her metabolic rate considerably, or at least so she told herself.

They all ate silently for a while.

It was down to her, Linda said to herself.

The tension eased some more; Janice didn't appear to be threatening in any way. She had to grasp the opportunity of

300

meeting Julie. She had known that she was in Shanghai but hadn't expected to meet her; she had been more interested in David Hutchinson, in any case; her husband had told her about him. How he knew about the journalist notwithstanding the media blackout was another thing Linda didn't want to know. The problem for her nonetheless was Janice; Linda didn't know who she was and why Julie and she were on such friendly terms. But although Linda was beginning to see Janice as an opportunity, much as Janice was now seeing her as one, she still needed to know who she was.

Enlightenment came quickly. A uniformed policeman approached the table and hovered. Janice got up to go and talk to him. It didn't then take Linda long to realise what Julie already knew; Janice was in an official capacity and in authority.

'Are you working with her?' Linda asked, quickly taking advantage of Janice's absence.

'Yes. She's one of the good guys. If we get the chance, I'll tell you what's going on.'

Janice re-joined the two other women. If Julie was working with this woman, the risk in talking to her, Linda reasoned, had to be minimal. From everything she knew about her from the past, Linda trusted Julie's judgement. In any case, having eavesdropped on some of her husband's conversations, and listened to his convoluted justifications of his devious planned actions, she actually had an increasingly clear picture of what might be going on.

The ill-formed plan of speaking to David Hutchinson faded in Linda's mind.

She made an instant decision.

'My husband has gone to see Mr Xu; you know who Mr Xu is? My husband is a backer of many of Mr Xu's schemes.'

Janice knew who Mr Xu was. It was an unexpected and valuable piece of information.

The timing was right; Janice knew that she had to act now.

She had yet to consider how Linda could be usefully involved in the action that was to follow. With her husband visiting Mr Xu, the most obviously important thing was to keep his wife with them to avoid any risk of he or Xu being alerted.

The idea that Linda might be prepared to act against her husband had yet to form in Janice's mind.

'This is madness!'

Linda Shen had been surprised when her husband had made the effort the evening before her decision to seek out David Hutchinson at the Shanghai Yu Garden Hotel, to talk to her. Following events at the abortive wedding, he was clearly more concerned about the current clamp-down by the authorities than he had been about any of the others in the past. His confidence and trust in his small body of bought officials and politicians had been all but destroyed. Action was needed both to distance himself from the more risky aspects of his past activities but also to preserve and protect those other projects that he depended on for his income flow and wealth creation.

It was a situation that Mr Shi had discussed with his associates, but obviously not Mr Xu, and he already had the tacit agreement of his closest allies to sacrificing their fixer. He wasn't one of the tight elite group that commanded total loyalty, and Mr Shi suspected that Xu would always act on his own self-interest, just as he would be doing. And for this increasingly depleted elite group, action was imperative and urgent.

Linda's immediate and more practical concern, however, was about the unstable relationships that had developed between her husband and his retained corrupt officials and politicians. In their desperate efforts to run for cover and prove themselves whiter than white, the real risk of betrayal was from the fickle self-seekers for whom no clemency would be available within the Communist system. His placemen were not going to sacrifice themselves for her husband, of that she was convinced. Such a high-profile end to his business activities would threaten her plans for a smooth takeover of his assets for her son at his death. That Linda thought his imminent death a very real possibility had coloured her actions ever since the fiasco at the Hus' non-wedding.

Her husband, for once, seemed to want her endorsement of his decision.

'It has to be done. Xu is a liability. We can either buy him off, get him to disappear somewhere, or ... eliminate him ourselves.'

'Killing him won't get the authorities off your back.'

Her husband's dark look told Linda that she was going too far. He wanted endorsement, not criticism. There were limits to how much she could manage him, and she knew that she had now reached them.

'Then be careful.'

It was almost a pointless admonition; Mr Shi was always careful.

It didn't take Mr Shi a long time to get to Mr Xu's apartment. Xu was not alone. He was accompanied by a young woman, a niece, apparently his personal assistant among other things, called to the flat after the death of his most recent chief of staff. It did, however, take Mr Shi a long time to argue through his plans with Xu. Buying Xu off was not going to be easy.

The debate was heated. Mr Xu's assistant, one of the new modern, self-confident young Chinese women that Mr Shi particularly disliked, joined the argument with more force and subtlety than he was used to from any woman other than his wife. And his wife, so he thought, knew her place and when not to resist him.

The argument was going nowhere; manners and traditional courtesy were breaking down but neither party seemed prepared to change their stance. What with time out for tea drinking and the other inconsequential accompaniments to the negotiations, they had been talking for over two hours. In the end, resolution came violently and unexpectedly.

Janice made her way out through the Pudong District in a police van that was masquerading as an upmarket catering supplier, to the tower block of Mr Xu's residence. Julie went with her. They parked at the service entrance in the secluded backyard out of sight from any the flats' windows. Linda Shen went in her limousine. She swept into the main entrance publicly and openly. Her driver/minder was used to obeying without question and then reporting back to Mr Shi.

As always, Linda had a plausible story for visiting the area where Mr Xu lived. Her reason for stopping at the particular block of flats would have been unconvincing but, since she saw no need to explain herself to her minder, it wasn't tested. Her reason for willingly joining Julie and Janice in their visit to Mr Xu didn't allow for the fact that she had in effect been arrested by Janice. And as far as the driver was concerned, it wasn't the first time that her limousine had been given a police escort.

A small group of plain-clothed police officers was already in position around the block of flats and in the service areas.

Janice had no reason to suppose that she was being watched, but, with Mr Shi's empire steadily unravelling, she was mindful that many of his placemen in the various Chinese ministries were rushing for cover and were seeking to protect themselves. That made them dangerous, and as someone known to be investigating Mr Xu's relations with people like Mr Shi she was taking precautions. Her orders were very clear and it was important that Xu got no warning.

Mr Xu was an old man. Janice rightly supposed that the post-lunch period would be the best time to visit him when his guard would be relaxed and he was unlikely to be conducting any business. Mr Shi had come to the same conclusion and

Linda's decision to join forces with Julie and Janice was therefore timely. With her small taskforce Janice couldn't afford any surprises.

But Janice was good at her job. Now knowing that she wasn't the only person to recognise this period as a good time to visit, she waited. It was mid-afternoon before they set out. The only uncertainty would be whether Mr Shi had left or not.

Linda was already talking to the security supervisor for the tower block in the reception area when they arrived. She was looking worried.

'My husband is still with Xu. His PA is with them; she's also his bodyguard and likely to be armed. There's extra security but this stupid gorilla won't tell me what.'

'We don't have time,' Janice said as the security supervisor was forced away from the reception desk at gunpoint and manhandled into one of the unmarked police cars that had now been carefully parked by the three entrances to the flats.

The air conditioning in the tower block was arctic cold, but it wasn't that that was making the terrified receptionist's teeth chatter as she went to join the supervisor. As far as they could tell, Mr Xu had not been alerted to their arrival.

'We'll take the first lift. Follow in five minutes.'

With their experience as trainees with the Border Agency, Julie and Linda were familiar with the process of raiding the premises of a suspect. They were happy to be in the follow-up team, however, since neither knew what role they were expected to play. One of the police teams sealed the building and stood guard in the reception area.

The express lift left Janice and the police officer accompanying her with very little time to prepare themselves. As the doors opened at the twenty-seventh floor, the bodyguard lounging beside the apartment door tensed and moved his hand to his gun holster. The geriatric wheezing of the lift doors closing masked the sharp coughing sound of the silenced shot that struck the man in the forehead.

'Oh shit,' Janice muttered. Her instructions were to be as discreet as possible; they didn't need a huge body count. The policeman would have argued that the man was reaching for his weapon.

The shot was positioned in exactly the same place as the one that had killed Alice. Something of Janice's reluctance died. But she didn't have time to understand the mix of feelings that were worrying themselves to the surface of her mind.

There were only two luxury apartments on each floor of the tower block. The entry doors were side by side, and Janice assumed that they were mirror images and that as they entered the one on the right the wall to their left would provide protection for their backs. Janice had no idea what the internal layout would be. They simply hadn't had time for that sort of preparation.

With the bodyguard on the outside, Janice also assumed that the apartment door would not be locked. It wasn't.

Sheltering behind the door, she pushed it open sufficiently for her to pass inside and then followed her gun into the vestibule. The policeman crept in behind her. She closed the door silently. Advancing, still without a sound, across the thick-piled carpet, she eased the door from the vestibule into the hall open and pushed it wide enough to give her full access to the exit when she needed it.

A pantomime of gestures ensured that the policeman would stand guard, but would also let his colleagues in when they arrived with Linda and Julie. It was clear that the policeman was not happy with Janice proceeding further on her own.

'This is for Alice,' Janice told herself.

The feeling that had emerged into her consciousness was a desire for justice for Alice, a justice that would make sense to her. And even if the courts were open to manipulation, Janice didn't trust the system to deal with Mr Xu and provide Alice with that justice.

The hall stretched out in front of her, opening into what she decided was a dining room. As far as she could see, the dining room had a minimum of furniture and wide spaces between it.

'Plenty of space for Mr Xu's wheelchair,' she told herself.

The shot that rang out was close. Janice froze. The policeman moved silently to her side, his machine pistol at the ready.

41

As the noise of the shot reverberated around the close confines of the apartment, Janice and the policeman waited nervously. A gabble of excited Mandarin eventually broke the silence. The harsh male voice was accusatory and the strident female voice defensive and truculent. They seemed to be very close to where Janice was hiding. Both listeners raised their weapons and directed then at the corner at the end of the hall.

The woman was obviously the PA and bodyguard, and, equally obviously, had fired the shot. But at whom, and who the surviving male was, it took Janice a moment or two to work out.

A short shriek bitten off into a groan rattled around the apartment as the arguing voices seemed to move away. Whoever had been shot was still alive and not being attended to.

Janice knew they couldn't wait. If they called for help, they would be in all manner of shit.

She waved the policeman back to guard the door. Something of the tone of the male voice and the fact that the man and woman had made no move to leave told Janice that it was Mr Shi, or someone else whom they didn't know about, who had been shot. Mr Xu was still alive and therefore the danger for Janice was still significant.

Apart from some valuable early Chinese paintings, the hall contained only what Janice assumed was a storage wardrobe for outdoor clothes. She was no connoisseur, so the beauty of the paintings and the contrast they formed with the unpleasant character of their owner were lost on her.

She moved forward.

Pausing at the end of the hall, masked from view by moving along the right-hand wall but giving herself the best angle of vision, Janice stopped to listen. Allowing her breathing to settle and her heart rate to slow, she strained to hear voices. She could hear only one male voice.

This was what she had been expecting after what Linda had told her and what they had also learned from the receptionist for the apartment building. Mr Shi, for whatever reason, had not taken his own bodyguards; he had clearly not been expecting any problems with Xu. But these were only the principles; the possibility of there being another, or more, of Mr Xu's bodyguards still had to be considered. In addition, while the snatches of conversation had told her that it was the woman who had done the shooting, Janice had no way of knowing whether Xu himself was armed.

She had to go on.

Somewhere around to the right and out of sight, and as she imagined in a further room, she could hear the staccato exchanges of a heated argument again. Mr Xu did not appear to be a happy man. The woman was being surprisingly assertive.

Janice cautioned herself not to assume that, because they were arguing so violently, they would be off their guard.

A telephone rang.

Janice froze again, not knowing whether the telephone was in the same room as Mr Xu and his PA, or in the dining room out of her sight. She even didn't know whether it was a mobile.

It was answered by the female voice. The conversation was brief and Janice could hear the measured tones of the woman's voice as she reported its content. The voices faded away into the distance again.

Holding her breath, Janice once again followed her gun

around the corner and into the dining room. The longer she hung around, the more chance there was of her being detected. As she took in the wall displays of exquisite, ancient and clearly valuable pottery, she admonished herself; she didn't have time for sightseeing.

Holy shit! (The idiom of her brief stay in Canada kept coming through at moments of stress!)

Propped against the wall next to the door to what she assumed was the kitchen and breathing raspingly and irregularly, a middle-aged Chinese man stared silently at her. Linda's husband, she assumed. She felt no sympathy for him. For Janice, he was as complicit in Alice's death as Xu.

She paused, her gun trained on the man.

Don't! she thought, willing the man to stay silent.

A glance through the kitchen door told her that it was empty. To get to the lounge with the least chance of being seen, she was going to have to hug the wall and step over the injured man. She kept the gun pointing at Mr Shi's head as she passed over him.

This is for Alice, she reminded herself again.

Clutching his stomach with blood seeping through his fingers, Mr Shi seemed to draw himself into himself. As she glanced back, his eyes flickered. She didn't have time to speculate on what might be going through his mind. He had neither moved nor made a sound throughout.

In front again was a wide opening into another sparsely furnished but luxurious lounge area. Janice relaxed a little. Neither of the two people she knew to be there were immediately in her vision. A warm draught, in contrast to the arctic feel of the rest of the rooms, attracted Janice's attention. As she was to discover, the glass doors on to the balcony were wide enough open for Mr Xu's wheelchair to pass easily to and fro.

The young woman's gasp as she stepped into Janice's line of fire was terminated by the same sharp cough of her weapon.

Shot through the heart, Janice didn't have time to watch the

310

woman collapse in an untidy heap in front of her. Sidestepping the body, she bounded fully into the lounge area, tracking her weapon on to a man whom she instantly assumed to be a second but otherwise silent bodyguard. She fired as she steadied herself.

The man's shriek and then strangled groan told Janice that she hadn't killed him. Staggering back towards the doorway that she subsequently found provided access to the more private parts of the apartment, he pulled sharply at his own weapon. Her second shot at close range was devastatingly successful in ending his resistance. The Glock pistol that he had almost succeeded in aiming at her pitched from his grasp and slithered along the carpet to come to rest against the wheel of Mr Xu's chair.

For the first time, Janice was aware of Mr Xu.

What Janice was not aware of were the movements and noises both from the hallway and from the back stairs that opened into the apartment, as Julie and Linda and the police reinforcements arrived.

Much to Janice's surprise, the expression on Mr Xu's face was a mixture of distaste for her and irritation that his disability wouldn't allow him to reach down and retrieve the bodyguard's weapon. Janice had no doubt that he would have used it had he been able to.

As the sounds of gunfire reverberated away, the quiet hiss of the air conditioning resumed its place as the dominant sound.

Janice surveyed the scene quickly. Out of her sight and hearing, the arriving police captain assessed the situation. From the hall he could see no more than Janice had been able to. Concerned not to exacerbate any situation, he restrained his men. A groan from Mr Shi concentrated attention. The policeman who had accompanied Janice gave his officer a whispered briefing.

The captain cautiously peered around the end of the hall wall and saw the blood-covered Mr Shi. Joined by Linda, he was in time to witness the harsh, retching last breaths of the businessman.

Mr Xu's wheelchair was a lightweight model imported from Britain. As she continued to check out the apartment, the elderly Chinese man slowly but purposefully moved his chair across in front of the balcony entrance, but, as she quickly realised, also towards the opening into the dining room and entrance hall.

'You're a cool customer,' Janice said in as pleasant and as neutral a voice she could manage. She knew that Xu would understand English.

But she was worried that her calm wasn't going to last. Surrounded by the signs of such luxury, something that she would never ever have the opportunity to enjoy, her anger at the brutally pointless death of Alice began to boil up inside her.

She moved to confront Mr Xu standing over him with her back to the very area that he had clearly been heading for.

'You killed Alice Hou,' she said.

It was a cold statement.

Xu didn't quibble. The look of amused contempt that suffused his face was too much for Janice. Despite his vulnerability, Xu's arrogant disdain overrode any other feelings.

His eyes darted from Janice to behind her. He'd seen something else. But Janice was too focused on her sense of injustice to notice the change in Mr Xu's expression. All she saw, and thought she sensed, was the contempt for Alice, or at least for people like Alice. As she recognised later, Alice was little more than a photograph to Xu.

Still unnoticed by Janice, Xu looked behind her again and the smugness of his expression increased. He was clearly expecting the arriving police to protect him.

It was Xu's attempt to move forward again that finally forced Janice to concentrate all her attention on him. Then she realised what was in his mind.

'Shitty little bastard!'

Janice's anger welled up, heightened by the recognition of the pathetic inadequacy of her Anglo-Canadian invective and by the total lack of reaction from Xu.

'Janice!'

It was a command that she didn't hear.

In one swift movement she grasped the wheelchair, swung it round and propelled it out on to the balcony.

The startled grunt that the old man emitted sounded like the beginnings of the death throes of the family pig, a memory that instantly surged up from Janice's childhood.

'Stop!'

It was another command that Janice didn't hear. The strident order in Chinese from the police captain and in English from Julie Li simply didn't penetrate Janice's consciousness.

Quickly drawing herself back, she propelled the wheelchair at the balcony railing with all the force she could muster. Mr Xu pitched forward but was trapped by the wrought ironwork until Janice could reposition her hold and force the flimsy chair up and over the rail. Overbalanced by Mr Xu's weight which was now being unsupported in space, the wheelchair was torn from Janice's grasp.

The only noise at first was the collective gasp as Mr Xu ceased to be visible, then a babble of unintelligible questions, accusations and remonstrations took over.

Two hours later, in the office of her superior, Janice was contrite but not regretful. And to her astonishment she was neither discharged nor demoted nor even reprimanded.

Untroubled by grief at the loss of her husband, and planning her return to the UK with her son, Linda Shen could have told Janice that somewhere lost in the tortuous minds of the top echelons of the Communist system the fact that Mr Xu was dead was appreciated as a problem that no longer had to be solved. With the command of the media, with ranks closed around the remaining officials and politicians, irrespective of innocence or hidden guilt, the only public admissions that followed from the events surrounding the Hu Hengsen wedding and its aftermath, were of the existence of modest corruption and of the total success in suppressing it.

Janice Liang, Julie Li and Linda Shen were each in their different ways incredulous but each set about picking up the threads of their lives.

People's National Daily
Shanghai English-language Edition –
Friday, 19 November 2010
END OF PEOPLE TRAFFICKING INTO CHINA

The Chief of Shanghai Police announced the deaths of Xu Xichen and Shi Xiulu, two successful prominent local businessmen who had betrayed the ideals and honest endeavours of the Chinese People. The Chief of Police gave no details of how the two men met their deaths.

Following the arrest of several other prominent local Shanghai businessmen and the mayhem at the intended wedding of Hu Hengsen, the police are satisfied that the illegal trafficking of young women into China to provide trophy wives for these greedy parasites has been ended. It is believed that no more than twelve of these young women were introduced into China and married to corrupt businessmen with the intention of using their dual nationality to allow them to circumvent the PRC's regulations on the export of private capital.

Cooperation with the British City of London Police has determined that sums of money running into many millions of US dollars have been spirited out of the PRC and hidden in offshore accounts in various parts of the world. The Head of Major Fraud at the Ministry of Finance has been removed from his post for failing to adequately police the activities of these corrupt businessmen. The police in Beijing and Hong Kong continue to seek out and arrest corrupt officials and politicians.

The People's National understands that a number of the trophy wives have been arrested and will be deported to their countries of origin. These deportations are being confused by the fact that several of these wives have had children while resident in China who are Chinese citizens and who are being claimed by the families of the fathers. In several cases, the country of origin of these women is unclear as the women were trafficked twice to get them into China.

The Foreign Ministry has expressed its appreciation to a Western journalist who was witness to many of the events involved in the closing-down of the trafficking activity. The People's National *understands that a report by this journalist will be submitted to the United Nations Committee on Human Trafficking.*

42

'What the shit was that all about?'

Back in Canberra, back in the same motel room, back in the same hot tub, David Hutchinson's frustration, irritation and intense feeling of having been cynically and ruthlessly used boiled over. He was relaxed for the first time since leaving the UK and free to give rein to his more private thoughts and feelings.

'David, it's over. You did the job. You got paid. Now we're going home.'

Susie Peveral was just glad that they had got out of China unscathed, which in her case meant that her reputation and career were untarnished, if not actually enhanced.

'Shit, Susie – people died!'

'And people died when you were in Iraq, Afghanistan, Zimbabwe and Christ knows where else.'

It was true.

Running her hand over David's weather-beaten face, she tried to soothe his outrage. Having missed his presence, she was for once determined not to be sidetracked until her more basic appetites had been appeased.

The effect that her caresses had on both of them was slow to mature. Being more tired than he would have admitted to, David had spent some of the idle time while he awaited the outcome of the Chinese Security Service raid on Mr Xu's apartment wondering why he still did what he did. These last two jobs had had none of the satisfaction that most of his other

317

work had had. The reports that he had written were most unlikely to see the full light of day. He, at the time, had no idea that the Chinese Foreign Ministry was planning to pat itself on the back by sending his second report to the UN. What appeared to be lack of a tangible output from his work depressed him.

And a persistent niggle kept pushing into his consciousness that he had been set up, and not just by the Chinese but by the British – that is, by Susie – as well. He still wasn't sure why it had all happened; but his estimation of his journalism, and more particularly his integrity, was different from that of the Chinese authorities.

But Susie was now ready and she pushed herself physically on to him hungrily and urgently. All other thoughts and feelings relegated for the time being, they made love gently but intensely, the warm bubbling water around them adding to the pleasurable sensations. With the familiarity of practice, they both came together, and then again, and then subsided into the depths of the hot tub and just held each other, all hunger satisfied.

For David, they were the moments of almost stress-free tenderness that Susie was capable of when the mood took her. However, even relaxed and replete as he was, he knew her all too well.

'There were upsides …'

Susie's public-service jargon as always pervaded even her most intimate moments. David waited for the gem of retrospection that he knew would follow.

But soothed in her turn by David's lazy trawling fingers ambling across her breasts, Susie lost the thread of her thoughts.

The gurgling of the hot tub dominated for a timeless period during which neither thought, only felt. Then a different niggle that David knew had been buried for some time in his deepest brain pushed to the surface.

There's no future in this, he thought. *The sex is unbelievable and exciting, and what I've just been through could never have happened without her. But it's not a lifestyle. She's all order and process; I'm more about chaos and uncertainty. It wouldn't work! And she did set me up for this Chinese thing; the illegal immigrant nonsense in Britain was just to get me hooked.*

'So what about this Linda Shen then?'

Susie was back into her Foreign Office persona again. Linda fascinated her.

All David knew about Linda was what Julie had told him.

'She's one of the earlier "China Wives",' David said. 'Kidnapped in Canada while on a business trip, shipped to Australia and then to China. Apparently, she was one of only three out of the twelve women Julie knew about who was not from South America.'

'It was that simple.'

'Susie, I only know what Julie told me and what she knows is what the Australian Security Service told her when she was set up as a member of the trafficking gang.'

'Julie was set up by the Border Agency; Janice Liang was set up by the Chinese Security Service – so was Linda set up, too?'

'She and Julie were colleagues at the Border Agency until she disappeared, Susie. I'm sure you know more than I do about what went on with that lot.'

'Linda married this Shi guy, had his child. She helped him with his activities. Very successfully, it would seem. But she also signposted what she was doing in the UK, and in a way that those with detailed knowledge of Chinese criminal gangs and trafficking would recognise. Why did she do that, David?'

'Hell, Susie, I don't care. Your lot at the Foreign Office must know – ask them.'

'I was only making the point that Linda Shen isn't all that she seems.'

'Well, she's presumably on her way back to the UK with her

son. According to Julie, the Chinese authorities made no objections and stamped on the Shi family when they demanded the child.'

'As if that wasn't suspicious.'

'Susie!'

Epilogue

Linda Shen?'

It was a smile of recognition! The immigration official had been alerted by the airline manifest as to when Linda would be landing at Heathrow and arrangements had been made to welcome her. It was a week after the other participants in the action had returned and faded back into normality; she had had some complex affairs in Shanghai to arrange. It wasn't going to be quite the welcome that Linda would have preferred, but as a former UK Border Agency official herself she was well aware of the way that the Immigration Service went about its business.

With her passport firmly in the hands of the immigration official and accompanied by a petite but tough-looking police-woman, Linda was led away to an office in the underbelly of Terminal 4. Oblivious to everything around him, her son slept peacefully in his buggy.

'Linda.'

Being confronted by a grinning Julie Kershawe, who had now reverted to her proper role, was the last thing that Linda had expected. She was pleased, wary and reassured all at once.

The tall Afro-Caribbean woman standing next to Julie moved forward to take the baby from Linda. A look of fear followed by a look of anguish said that this was not something that she had expected to happen either.

'Social Services,' said Julie.

As the social worker left the room and the policewoman

took up a position by the door, Julie and the immigration official sat down, indicating that Linda should too.

Linda knew that it was interrogation time. This *was* something that she had expected to happen.

'David!'

'Julie?'

'I had no idea that you were likely to be in Aberdeen!'

'Nor me, Julie, but a dramatic helicopter ditching in the sea … well, it's a bit more like my normal fare.'

'I just spent time in London being debriefed, for what that was worth, then I got sent straight up here.'

'And you're living in this hotel in luxury at taxpayers' expense – not a bad life to come back to!'

'I guess we won't go there. How's Susie, David? I didn't really get to know her very well in Canberra.'

'She's back in China, Beijing. She got herself promoted to the overseas diplomatic staff. Her feet didn't touch the ground before they were shunting her back out there. I guess they think that she's a China expert after what happened, or, keeping her under the Chinese noses to reassure them, more like.'

'Cynical bastard.'

'So how is it with you?'

'Got the promotion I was in line for earlier before my lords and masters connived at my transfer to the Australian Security Service. Big apology; if *you're* cynical, you should try my departmental head.'

'So what happened about Linda, Julie?'

'Put her through the wringer the moment she got off the plane, like my lot do. Now she's on leave to sort herself and her son out pending joining me here. Everybody's trying to act as if nothing had happened.'

The interrogation hadn't lasted long. Fully briefed on Linda's

322

marriage and on her activities on behalf of her late husband and herself, Julie had been sympathetic to the idea of letting her return to the UK and restart her life. She had quickly recommended this to her bosses.

Much of the interview conversation had been about confirming what the various UK and European authorities already knew about the export of private capital from China and the methods by which it was achieved. When it came down to it there was no evidence that Linda had broken any UK or European laws, whatever she might have done in China.

The Chinese authorities demanded the return of the money. The subsequent intervention of Susie Peveral and the efforts of some Treasury whiz-kid in separating the accrued interest from the capital, and quietly funnelling this money into an account in the Isle of Man, at least meant that Linda would have a modest but useful nest egg as a legacy from her marriage and her experiences in China. There was again no evidence in the UK that the money that she had been working with wasn't Mr Shi's, and then hers on his death, despite the clamour from the Chinese Finance Ministry.

The formalities complete, Linda and Julie re-established their former friendly relationship.

'I never believed you did what the papers said you did.'

'And I never believed that you went to China as willingly as we supposed,' said Julie.

'The bastard was great in bed,' Linda responded with a grin, 'but a shit!'

'And you shouldn't sleep with shits.'

A fleeting vision of Tariq al Hussaini failed to establish itself in Julie's mind.

Acknowledgements

My thanks to Yang Xiaoxia and her husband, Mr David Smith, for their help with the Chinese names and insights into their usage. Any mistakes in the application of this knowledge are entirely down to me.